Here's :

 MW00477823

x!

The Bay Area Butcher

A Quint Adler Novel
(Book 2)
by
Brian O'Sullivan

BIG B PUBLISHING

B

Novels by Brian O'Sullivan

The Puppeteer
The Patsy
The Bartender
Revenge at Sea (Quint Adler, Book 1)

Short Stories

My Meeting With Trump

Acknowledgements:

To all my family and friends who read my early drafts and give me constructive criticism. To my mother, Judy O'Sullivan. My aunt, Maureen Kammer. And friends, Lorraine Evanoff, LuAnn Paddock, Jim Kostoryz, Nicholas Cueno, Bling Morley, Tomi Eto, Aaron Pewtherer, Stacey McDonald, and Marisa Wrobleski. Thank you all!

To Hamar, who designed the cover. And to Liam DiCosimo who will be doing the Audible version.

Finally, to my superlative editor, Therese Arkenberg, who dealt with me trying to edit this novel in a few short weeks while bombarding her with ten emails a day. She's the best!

This novel is dedicated to you –yeah, you—the reader! Without guys and gals like you, this wouldn't be possible. Thanks so much for all of your support!

This is a work of fiction. Names, characters, places, and incidents either are the product of the author's imagination or are used in a fictitious manner. Any resemblance to actual persons, living or dead, events, or locales is merely coincidental.

PROLOGUE:
THE KILLER TO BE

I began penning my first letter.

And with it, a spot in permanent infamy. There was no question about that.

I shook my head, barely believing it had finally come to this. I couldn't decide if my transformation into a monster was a million to one chance or had been written in stone from the beginning. To me, there could be no in between.

But it wasn't something I enjoyed thinking about. I'd resolved to become a killer, so self-reflection wasn't going to end well.

I decided to stop pondering what had brought me to this point.

It didn't matter anyway.

Serial killers would never get any sympathy. Especially one like myself.

You see, I wasn't bullied every day of my life. Or beaten by my father. I didn't have some sob story of broken homes and broken bones.

I just happened to be a horrible human being. I enjoyed seeing suffering. From an early age, I rooted for the bad guys in movies. And no, I'm not talking about the "shades of gray" villains. I'm talking the serial killers. The abusive boyfriends. The narcissists. I rooted for them all.

I was "evil personified," according to many people I'd met. And that was before I'd begun hatching my ungodly plan. Imagine what they'd say now.

Not that I cared.

Nothing anyone could say would stop me.

There were actions that might prevent my crimes from occurring, but words were no longer sufficient.

I was now committed.

I'd set up a heinous, vicious, hateful plan of murder and mayhem. I delighted in its simplicity.

Five horrendous bursts of crime and then I'd walk off into the sunset.

At least, that was the plan.

Obviously, I'd entertained the possibility I could be caught during one of the murders. Or before. But I didn't think either of those scenarios were likely.

I'd thought long and hard about what lay ahead. I'd read, listened, watched, and most importantly, absorbed, everything I could on serial killers.

How the feeble ones got caught.

How the extraordinary ones went on killing for long periods.

How the police departments generally conducted themselves and mistakes they made.

I felt I was the most prepared human in history to become a serial killer. No, that didn't mean I'd automatically complete my five crimes. There were too many variables. And it was very contingent on luck. A random jogger here. A nosy neighbor there.

It certainly wasn't an exact science, but I'd done all I could. If I was to be caught, it wouldn't be due to a lack of preparedness.

I constructed the first line of my first letter.

A mere four days before what was to be my first set of murders.

And with it, my first steps to immortality.

A week of firsts, you might say!

1.
Quint

If I could choose a minor superpower, it would be the ability to bottle the good times. Have some handy when the bad times come knocking at your door. Which they inevitably do.

The last eight months had definitely qualified as the aforementioned good times. Some of the best of my life.

After concluding my nightmare at sea, I'd become a bit of a local celebrity and was in high demand amongst the media in the Bay Area. I'd even given a few national interviews. I wrestled with the morality of getting paid for them, but I'd lost my job and been through a tremendous ordeal. So I took the money.

Quint Adler, professional interview giver. Certainly didn't see that coming.

But the media attention was not what made the time so rewarding. I'd never been closer to Cara, my on-and-off-and-back-on girlfriend of eight years. We'd always had an active sex life, but now we were taking walks, cooking for each other, and doing all the small but important things that successful couples do.

Cara was still as beautiful as ever, and I was lucky to have her. She'd allowed her usually shoulder-length brown hair to grow out, and it was now halfway down her back. I thought it looked great. Then again, Cara could even make a shaved head look great.

And how do I know that? Because the crazy kid gave herself a buzz cut a month into the coronavirus. And she was still a knockout. That being said, I was happy when she started growing it back out.

Her legs remained perfection. Long, athletic, and permanently tanned.

But more than her looks and her legs, it was her intellect. She was smart and she was quick. She kept me on my toes and called me out for my bullshit. I always appreciated that. She was more than my match. She was my superior.

I'd never been more in love with her.

They say that people who survive a life-altering event gain a new outlook on said life. I'd certainly qualify, and maybe that provided more stability in my relationship with Cara.

Whatever the reason, we were both extremely happy with each other.

My mother seemed to be in a good place as well. She soaked in all the attention that her only child was getting. I'd discovered that my father had been murdered, but he died a hero, trying to protect one of his students, so it almost served as a blessing. It became easier for her to grieve at that point.

And she decided to focus on the positive, thoroughly enjoying the calls and texts congratulating her on my actions. If I was featured in the newspaper or had an interview with a local news station, you could be sure my mother would post it on Facebook. My interview with *Good Morning America* provided her with days of social media attention.

It got to the point where I asked her to stop tagging me in all of the stories and videos. I told her to enjoy them with her friends, but that I was out. She understood.

She still lived in San Ramon, just twenty minutes from my place in Walnut Creek, and I'd go see her at least once a week. I loved my mother dearly, and the only time she raised my ire was when she'd ask if I was going to propose to Cara.

"You'll be forty-one years old before you know it," she'd say, and then add: "At least she's still in her early thirties."

The reference to her still being in prime childbearing age was implicit.

My stance was that if everything was going well, why rock the boat?

Of course, I'd probably be outvoted 2-1. Cara had, with almost zero subtlety, insinuated that she'd like kids as well.

I was taking a wait and see approach.

As for me, after about my fifteenth interview, I noticed that I was being recognized every time I went out in public. People would approach me and want to talk about taking down the villain Charles Zane. I had grown tired of it.

Much to my mother's dismay, I decided to put an end to the interviews.

How did famous people do it, getting mobbed every time they went out in public? Picking up a meal at the grocery store and getting approached by every fifth person? No thanks.

I decided to grab my anonymity back.

I'd moved back into my old apartment complex, Avalon Walnut Creek, located twenty-five miles east of San Francisco. The manager came and met me personally and pledged forgiveness for the way they'd handled my previous departure. That's what they called it. Even though we both know it was an eviction.

After being shot, no less.

I think they just wanted to have a local "celebrity" living at their complex. When they offered me the first two months free as a way of apologizing for giving me the boot, I let bygones be bygones.

They gave me a different apartment, but I was still on the fourth floor, and still had a balcony, something I used daily. I'd sit out with my cup of coffee and ponder the world. It was my form of meditation.

I'd penned a tell-all story that was published in the *New Yorker*. The generous commission, along with money from my various interviews, gave me some time to decide on my next gig. Tom and Krissy Butler, my bosses at the *Walnut Creek Times*, had asked me to come back and work full time, but I turned them down.

As much as I'd loved my co-workers, my reporting job had been writing in its most primitive form. I wanted more. So I asked Tom and Krissy if they'd mind if I wrote a couple of longform articles a month and got paid on scale. They quickly agreed, knowing any time my name was above the fold, they'd sell a lot more papers. So my new celebrity had some perks.

Detective Ray Kintner remained a good friend. We'd grab a bite to eat now and then and I even went bowling with him and a few buddies. I'd yet to meet his wife. Hey, some people liked to keep their private life just that. Private.

At fifty-four, he was still the old man of the Oakland Police Department, but his star had risen after my case. He'd arrested several people subsequent to Charles Zane's death and really spearheaded the entire investigation into Zane's criminal enterprise.

I was happy for him. He deserved it. After all, he'd saved my life out on the unrelenting Pacific.

I met Ray on a surprisingly cold day in May.

He'd picked a restaurant named Homeroom, located in northern Oakland. The place was packed, always a good sign. I'd heard positive things about the food, but this was my maiden visit.

The red awning outside made it stand out, and I told the maître d' I'd prefer to sit at one of the outdoor tables. I was ready to enjoy the brisk air while I could, with summer right around the corner.

It was a lunch meeting, so I assumed Ray was working. I was proved correct when he approached with his Oakland Police Department blues on, a few minutes later than I'd expected.

I gave him a friendly pat on the shoulder. Ray had put on a few pounds over the course of the last year. But it was almost like a badge of honor with him, one of the oldest active cops. The extra pounds actually looked right on him. Like he'd earned them.

He joined me at the table. The street was bustling and safe to say, I liked Homeroom before I'd even tried a bite of their food.

Ray must have been a regular. When he saw the waitress, a diminutive woman named Shelby, he asked for his usual. I ordered the Gilroy garlic bacon mac and cheese. With a gut bomb like that, an extra jog definitely lay in the cards.

"I'm lucky you were punctual when I was stranded at sea," I said, making fun of his tardiness.

"There are times I wish I was late then too."

I laughed.

Our friendship had been a longshot from the beginning. He'd been one of the officers who, suspecting me of murder, had arrested me. Usually that would be unforgivable, but when your life is saved by that same man, you willingly make exceptions.

"How's work?" I asked.

"How's Cara and your mother?" he responded. He inquired about the two women in my life every time I saw him.

"I think Cara wants to move in. She's over all the time."

"You're like a fungus. You just grow on people."

"I'll take it as a compliment," I said.

"When it comes to landing Cara, it is."

"I'll tell her you question her judgement."

Ray smiled. "And your mom?"

"She continues to love my newfound celebrity. Apparently her friends don't grow tired of hearing about what I went through. And she loves to tell the story."

"Your mother is a very nice woman."

"Thanks! She'll enjoy your summation more than Cara."

"You're too much, Quint."

"My mother said if my story ever gets made into a movie, she wants to be in the background for one shot."

"I didn't know she was a ham for the camera."

"Me neither," I said. "Going to have to tell dear old Mom she's getting too big for her britches."

"It's cute."

"She says the movie should be called *Revenge at Sea.*"

"Sounds cheesy," Ray said.

"Right? I was going to go with *Quint.*"

"That would never sell! You have to get 'Revenge' or 'Murder' or 'Thrilling' in the title. That's what sells these days."

I shook my head.

"You're probably right."

"Plus, it would never get greenlit. It's not a comic book or a sequel."

"Maybe for the best," I said.

"What do you mean?"

"Sometimes celebrity isn't all it's cracked up to be," I said. "And listen, I know I'm the Frank Stallone of flash-in-the-pan local celebrities, but every time I go to the store, someone wants to come up and talk. Imagine if they made a movie out of my story. It would only get worse."

Ray looked at me with probing eyes. I realized he wanted to tell me something.

"You're not completely innocent in this. You did do *a couple* of local interviews." He accentuated 'a couple' to underline it was a lot more than that.

"I'd been fired from my job. I didn't have much choice."

"And the interview with *Good Morning America?"*

I laughed. "They paid well. But listen, I haven't been on T.V. in several months. I've decided celebrity is not for me."

"That's the problem with celebrity. You're never really out of the public eye. Even when you think you are."

"That's cryptic."

"Listen, Quint. There's a reason I invited you here."

The waitress came over and filled our glasses of water. We paused our conversation and thanked her.

"This meeting seemed more official than usual," I said as she walked away.

"There's so many wackos out there who think they know these celebrities. Even if it's just the Frank Stallone types."

"You're beating around the bush, Ray. Is there something you want to say?"

He fiddled with his napkin. Whatever it was, he was having a tough time getting it out.

"It appears you've come to the attention of one of those wackos," he finally said.

"What do you mean?" I asked.

"We received a letter addressed to the OPD yesterday. It was a little jarring, to say the least."

Ray took out a xeroxed piece of paper from his back pocket. "Before I let you read this, let me say something. There's a million crazies out there and hardly any of them ever act on their rage. It's almost pointless to worry about them. They're just barking at the moon, trying to get attention. Probably pissed off at their own pathetic lives."

"It's a nice filibuster, Ray, but can I just read the letter?"

He handed it over. The original letter had been typed on a computer, so handwriting experts couldn't get a crack at it. That was my initial disappointment. It got worse.

This is a monumental moment in history!

It may seem trite as you first read this, but people are going to write books about these letters. Make movies. Produce documentaries. Mark my word.

To the police departments of the Bay Area: You will be busy this summer!

Sorry, no taking your fat asses to the beach and reading Michael Connelly novels.

Instead, you'll be peeling bodies off the streets of your cities.

San Francisco. Walnut Creek. Oakland. San Jose. Tiburon.

And now, for a plot twist: There will be only five sets of murders total.

Once I have finished the coup de grace, I will walk off into the sunset. Maybe to return somewhere in the future, but it will not be in the Bay Area. You have this summer to catch me.

A warning: Be prepared for some savagery.

I'm going to make Ted Bundy look like an angel. Jeffrey Dahmer a saint. And the Zodiac a Girl Scout.

But in the vein of the Zodiac, I will converse with you.

Mock you. Ridicule you. Rub your noses in the murders.

I'll even keep you in the game. Give you guys a fighting chance.

So I will periodically give you hints.

And here are the first two:

One, I've been mentioned in an article by Quint Adler, that annoying fuck who can't get enough of the camera.

Second, the first murder will occur this Friday, May 12th.

And yes, there are hints within the letters themselves.

But those you will have to figure out on your own.

By the time your police departments receive this letter, you'll have about three days.

Use them wisely.

The game is on.

Should be an exciting summer.

Happy Hunting!

The unusually cool May air grew colder and colder as goosebumps lifted on my skin. I had finished reading the letter a second time when the waitress arrived with my Gilroy garlic bacon mac and cheese.

I pushed it aside.

I was no longer hungry.

2.

Several minutes and only a few bites later, Ray and I left the restaurant. It felt like everything had changed. Sure, the clouds still hovered above us. And the wind remained brisk.

But intuition told me that my eight-month vacation was over. The man (and I was sure it was a male) could have been some crackpot we'd never hear from again, but I didn't think so. Something about the intensity of his letter told me this wasn't something to be taken lightly.

Maybe we'd get lucky. Maybe the police would catch him in the next few days before his purported first murder. Maybe I'd save the day and make my way back out on the interview scene.

But maybe not.

"Quint, why don't you come back to the precinct with me?"

"Your bosses going to like that?" I asked.

"Probably not. But you're mentioned in the letter and we're going to need your help looking through old articles. So they'll allow it."

I followed Ray back to the Oakland Police Department's headquarters on 7th Street. It was much sleeker than the multiple other locations I'd been to, with a huge blue and gray OPD shield blazoned above the front door.

It was technically their headquarters and Ray's base. However, he'd been with the force so long, he could walk into any precinct of the OPD and be met with smiling faces.

Which, ironically, I didn't see many of as I followed him past the officers guarding the front entrance.

"He's okay," Ray said, allowing me to bypass the huge metal detector.

We walked by the humorless officers and made our way to the elevator.

I believed there was a little jealousy when it came to yours truly. I'd gone out on my own and helped take down one of the most dangerous men in the Bay Area, one who'd ordered countless murders over the last few decades. And to top it off, I'd become a media darling. I'd praised the Oakland Police Department, and Ray specifically, every chance I got, but I guess that wasn't enough for them. Hopefully upper management felt a little more gracious than the officers stuck watching the door.

"What the hell is he doing here?"

I guess not.

The question came from a bear of a man right as we walked off the elevator onto the third floor.

"He's mentioned in the letter, Captain."

Even the captain didn't like me. Great.

"And we're going to have to work with him to go through all of his articles," Ray continued.

"Fine," the captain said, although it was a different four-letter F-word that his voice conveyed.

I peeked at his badge. Miles Lockett. Captain Lockett was probably 6'5", definitely yoked, and seemed a no-nonsense type of guy. At least toward me. He looked to be in his mid-forties with salt and pepper hair. For the moment, pepper was winning, but we all lose that battle in the end.

Ray opened a door and led me into a rather large conference room. Approximately ten chairs surrounded a long, charmless gray table. But we wouldn't be filling them all.

There were myself, Ray, Captain Lockett, and three other OPD officers who likely sided with Lockett on their opinions of me. Although I did get a slight nod from one of the younger ones.

Hey, I'd take what I could get.

We all took a seat except for Captain Lockett, who remained standing. He looked out at the rest of us.

"So," the captain began. "We've now all read this crazy fucker's letter. Because we're going to be needing Quint Adler's help, Officer Kintner decided to include him in this meeting. Welcome."

It was a start.

"Thank you," I said. "I'm here to help in any way you need. And call me Quint."

The officers nodded at me, and I seemed to have put a small dent in their impenetrable wall.

"Okay, Quint. And I hope you don't take offense, but I think we'll only include you for the part of the conversation that involves your articles. Let's leave the investigative work to the professionals."

"I'm fine with that," I said.

Despite my reputation for rocking the boat, I was on my best behavior. For the moment.

"Detective Kintner, do you want to say a few words?"

"Sure. Thank you, Captain Lockett."

Ray rose from his seat and positioned himself at the head of the expansive table. Lockett sat down.

"So, time is of the essence, gentlemen. The wannabe killer has said that he will commit his first murder on May 12th, which is just two days away. Our only other lead is that his name was mentioned in one of Quint's articles. Quint, do you have any sort of rough estimate as to how many articles you've written over the years?"

I cleared my throat. "I worked full time at the *Walnut Creek Times* for nine years. And I probably averaged an article a day or so. So there's probably a few thousand."

An audible groan came from one of the officers.

I continued, "There's good news, though. A lot of what I wrote were generic articles, talking about bike thefts or crime in general, without mentioning names. If we're just looking for articles in which I mentioned someone's name, we're looking at something more in the hundreds. A few hundred, if I had to guess."

Ray gave me a slight smile. Having become a good friend, he'd been hoping I'd pass my first test in front of his fellow officers. His reaction confirmed I'd done just that.

"You no longer work there, though, correct?" Lockett asked.

"Not full time. But I still write the occasional article and I'm allowed in the building."

Lockett nodded, confirming I'd answered his real question—whether we'd have access.

"Tom and Krissy Butler will help us out?" Ray asked.

He knew the answer was yes, being friendly with the owners of the *Walnut Creek Times* himself. The question was for the other officers' benefit.

"Yeah, I have no doubt they will. We've got a great database where you can pull up any article in seconds. We might be able to narrow it down to articles in which I've mentioned someone by name."

"That would be very helpful," Lockett said. It wasn't exactly cordial, but it wasn't gruff either. We were trending in the right direction.

"Captain, since time is of the essence, I think someone should head back with Quint to his office and start looking at these articles."

"Since you are friendly with him, you'll go. And take Detective Fields with you as well."

"Yes, sir."

A younger Black man, who I assumed must be Detective Fields, nodded in the captain's direction.

Lockett stood back up. "Quint, why don't you head back to Walnut Creek and get prepped for my officers? We'll be done here in thirty minutes, and then I'll send them over."

He was subtly telling me it was time for the big boys to talk amongst themselves.

I'd checked myself for long enough. I had something to say. "Of course. Before I go, could I give you my initial impression of the letter?"

Lockett's disgust returned. He was offended that I thought I could add anything to their investigation. But they needed me. So I was extended an olive branch.

"Alright, give us what you got."

I felt all the eyes in the room turn to me.

"He's a male and he's in good shape," I said.

Ray chimed in. "We assumed he was a male, but what makes you say he's in good shape?"

"Because he said 'fat asses'. Someone who is fat likely wouldn't call other people fat asses."

Lockett looked on. He didn't appear all that impressed. "Anything else?"

"The guy is young," I said.

"How would you know that?"

"Can I see his letter, Detective Kintner?" I tried not to call him Ray too often in front of his fellow officers.

He removed the copy from his pocket and handed it to me. I walked over to where Lockett was standing and set the piece of paper down.

The other officers' eyes made their way toward me. Surely they thought I'd gone crazy, trying to upstage their captain.

"Look at the breaks between sentences. What do you see?" I asked.

"I see spaces! What the hell am I supposed to see?"

His tone was combative.

I saw a one-sheet memo pinned to a wall. I walked over and looked at it, making sure it was what I expected.

I removed it from the wall and set it next to the other sheet.

"Do you see a difference between the sentence breaks?" I asked.

He held up the paper I'd grabbed from the wall and compared the two.

"There's a larger space at the end of sentences on this memo. But what the hell does that mean?"

I took the other memo and pinned it back to the wall, then returned to the table. I had their attention.

"Since the beginning of typewriters, and on to word processors and then computers, we were always taught to use two spaces at the end of sentences. I'm forty years old and my generation was certainly raised on two spaces. But things changed about ten years ago, and they started teaching the next generation to only use one space. I'm guessing our guy is young. Could be thirty-two or he could be twenty-two. Or anywhere in between. But I highly doubt this is some fifty-two-year-old guy using single spaces between sentences."

Lockett looked up at me in admiration, bordering on awe. If I was doing a stand-up routine, this is where I'd drop the mic.

"Pretty impressive work," Lockett said and shook his head. "That could be some valuable information. Thank you, Quint."

"Just here to support you guys," I said, deciding to downplay my help. "It's something you would notice as a writer."

Lockett looked me over and I half expected to be invited to stay for the rest of the meeting. It wasn't in the cards, however.

"Thanks for your help. And I'll soon be sending Detectives Kintner and Fields to the *Walnut Creek Times*. I'm sure you'll have to talk to your bosses, but don't let anyone else know what we're doing there. I don't want this getting out. Is that understood?"

"Yes. I'll only talk to Tom and Krissy."

"Thanks. And Quint, if you have any more nuggets, be sure to let us know. As you may have realized, I'm not the biggest fan of reporters." He smiled and then continued. "But I hate the idea of a potential serial killer much, much more. I'll do anything to catch this bastard. So don't be afraid to share your opinion."

"I won't," I said. "Thanks, Captain."

I turned to go.

As I left the office, I heard Lockett mutter to the other officers, "I hate to say it, but he's a really smart guy."

Who was I to argue?

3.

I drove back to Walnut Creek with a smile on my face. There was the looming dread of what might be to come, but in the moment I enjoyed what I'd accomplished in the OPD conference room.

I'd turned a hostile crowd in my favor. And gave them a possible clue on the wannabe killer. The likelihood he was young wasn't going to solve the case, but a bunch of small factors could contribute to a better profile.

My smile began to fade when I remembered the killer knew about my articles, and felt inclined to mention me in the letter.

Why had he chosen me? Was it just because he was mentioned in one of the articles? I hoped that's all it was. But the fact that he'd called me "that annoying fuck who can't get enough of the camera" made it more personal.

For now, I vowed not to focus on it.

I parked my car a block from the office. They only had a select amount of parking spaces, and being that I was no longer a full-time employee, I could park on the street. I grabbed my navy blue backpack, which held my trusty laptop. I took it everywhere.

I approached the red stucco building that had been my work home for almost a decade. It was funny. Despite only being there a few days a month, I was now by far the most famous writer at the *Walnut Creek Times.*

Downtown Walnut Creek bustled with restaurants, bars, and high-end shopping. Our bright red building had always stood out, and according to our neighbors, not in the best way.

Walking in the front door, I loved seeing the familiar faces. Staff writers Trent Buckley, Greg Alm, and Crystal Howell had set up a memorable happy hour last year. Weirdly, that party now felt like five years ago. I said hi to them individually.

Our editor, Jan, walked down from the upstairs of the two-tiered office. She was followed by the owners of the paper, the husband and wife team of Tom and Krissy Butler. They were around sixty years old, but must have discovered the fountain of youth at some point. Both looked great.

"What are you doing here, stranger?" Tom asked. "You have a deadline I forgot about?"

"I'd like to go on T.V. shows and only have one deadline a month," Greg said.

A few people laughed.

"Newsroom humor certainly hasn't improved," I said.

Everyone smiled. It had been a great place to work and nothing had changed. I still considered all of them my friends.

"Actually, Tom, I'm here to talk to you and Krissy. Can we do it upstairs?"

"Quint is now too cool for his fellow reporters."

I couldn't give anything away, so I had to remain mum. "Nothing personal, guys. I'll come back down and shoot the shit before I go."

That got them off my back.

I followed Tom and Krissy up the stairs. We had an elevator in office, but my forty-year-old knees weren't shot just yet.

Krissy, usually the most outgoing member of the paper, hadn't said a word.

"Krissy, you're quiet," I said.

"Just soaking in seeing you, Quint. The office isn't the same when you aren't here."

"I appreciate it, but everyone seems to be their old selves."

"We miss your ugly mug."

Tom laughed. His wife always joked around with me. Some might see it as playful flirting, but that wasn't the case. Tom and Krissy had been married for decades and were one of the happiest couples I knew.

"You mispronounced handsome," I said.

She shook her head, but wouldn't commit to a smile.

We arrived upstairs and walked directly into the conference room, my second one in less than an hour.

"So, what is it?" Tom asked, getting right to the point.

"Is our database of articles still a finely oiled machine?"

"It sure is. Want to dive into some of your greatest hits?"

"Yeah, but not for the reason you think," I said.

Krissy could tell from my tone of voice that it was something serious. "What is it, Quint?" she asked.

"I was just at the Oakland Police Department. They received a letter from some nutcase, threatening to kill a bunch of people this summer."

"That's terrible. Not to be insensitive, but what's that have to do with us?" Tom asked.

"He said he was mentioned in one of my articles."

Tom and Krissy became deathly serious.

"Like, you had reported on one of his crimes?"

"I don't know," I said. "He wasn't exactly specific." I tried to remember the exact wording. "It was something like, '*I've been featured in one of Quint Adler articles*' and then he called me an annoying fuck."

"Jeez," Tom said. "Why get personal with you?"

"I don't know. But the OPD now want to go through all of my old articles."

"Understandable. Why aren't they here with you?"

"They're coming soon. I was sent beforehand to set everything up."

"Is Ray coming?" Krissy asked.

"He is," I said.

Tom and Krissy had a lot of connections in the Bay Area and many of them were law enforcement. They'd known Ray Kintner for years and had sent me in his direction when the Charles Zane case started a year earlier.

"The officers can work in here. I'll email you the link to the database, and they can use the printer if they want specific articles printed out. You remember how the database works, right?"

"It's been awhile, but I should be fine."

"You can search by author, date, keyword. It's pretty easy. Did you bring your laptop?"

I patted my backpack. "What's that American Express ad? Don't leave home without it!"

"You're too young to remember that commercial," Krissy said.

"Forty is the new fifty," I replied.

She laughed. "Yeah, I don't think that's how the saying goes."

"I hate doing this, but the OPD wants you to keep this between yourselves. I know everyone else will see the officers here, but you can't tell them what I told you. At least not yet. If they release a statement, then obviously it's fair game."

"Our lips are sealed, Quint," Tom said. "We rely on a lot of connections and have learned how to keep our mouths shut."

"Makes me wonder what's been kept from me over the years," I said.

"I'll never tell," Tom said.

I smiled. "I'm going back down to wait for Ray. He's bringing another detective as well. And then we'll come back up here to the privacy of this conference room."

"I'll send the link to the database right now. If you have any questions, let me know."

"Thanks, guys."

I headed back downstairs.

The two detectives arrived fifteen minutes later and I led them up. My co-workers stared after us, but no one said a word.

Ray greeted Tom and Krissy and introduced Detective Fields, whose first name was Freddie. Freddie Fields, hard to forget.

He was handsome, possibly still in his twenties, and seemed both affable and a tough guy at the same time.

The three of us entered the conference room. I took out my laptop, went to my email, and clicked on the link that Tom had sent. I checked to make sure I was connected to the *Walnut Creek Times* printer, which I was.

"So here's the database. It has a rather boring home page with several different categories. 'Writer' is separated into all of the staff members' last names. 'Adler' comes first on the drop-down menu. And that's not a judgement of best writers. Just alphabetical." They chuckled weakly at the attempt at humor. "Under subject you have *crime, obituary, personal interest, sports, weather, other.* A lot of my articles were crime related, but I've written every one of these types of articles at one time or another. The third category is year and I've been here since the beginning, so you can't skim there. Finally, there's the search feature, where you can enter a keyword. Here's an example."

I typed "murder" in to the search bar and pressed enter. A total of 246 options popped up.

"That can't be right," Ray said.

"Looks more like Oakland's database," Fields responded.

We all laughed in spite of ourselves.

"Obviously we haven't had that many murders in Walnut Creek. The database merely pulls up any article in which the word 'murder' has been used. If an article mentioned 'a murder of crows' it would pop up here. Plus, there could be ten articles written on the same murder."

"Understood. Thanks for setting this up, Quint."

"You're welcome. Do you guys need any help from me?"

"For now, we can handle this. But when we're done, I'm sure there will be some names I'd like to ask you about."

"Of course. Although, honestly, it's not like I've followed up on my subjects over the years."

"We get it. But maybe there's something that will ring a bell."

"I really have no idea what we are looking for."

"Neither do we, Quint," Fields said. "But this psycho mentioned you and your articles, so we have to do our due diligence. Maybe, by some miracle, something will jump out."

"Of course, Detective Fields. I'll stay around the office in case you guys need me."

"You call him Ray. You can call me Freddie."

"I will. Thanks, Freddie."

Ray spoke next. "Today is the 10th, Quint. Sorry to break the bad news, but you are at our beck and call for the next forty-eight hours."

I halfheartedly smiled, knowing I didn't have much choice. After letting them know my laptop was connected to the printer so they could print out any and all articles they wanted, I said my goodbyes and walked out. I was spending half my day walking in and out of conference rooms.

Two hours later, Ray came downstairs and asked me to follow him back up.

We discussed around thirty articles that had caught his and Detective Fields's attention. I answered the questions as truthfully as I could, but there wasn't much to add. I certainly didn't know what happened to some guy who committed a robbery six years ago.

And as hard as I racked my brain, no one story stuck out. How the hell was I supposed to know which article I'd mentioned the maniac in?

We were looking for the proverbial needle in the haystack.

4.

"Why the hell did he pick you of all people?" Cara asked.

When I told her that some potential killer mentioned me in an article, it was her eyes that turned murderous.

She'd been sitting on my couch watching the news, but joined me in the kitchen soon after I mentioned the letter. I had a six-hundred-square-foot apartment, so it's not like she had to venture far.

I had some chicken baking in the oven and was making a sauce with wine, butter, cream, capers, and lemon in a separate pan.

I'd decided to bring the news up to Cara that night while cooking. I assumed it would seem more casual that way.

"Because he was featured in one of my articles," I finally answered. I used a rubber spatula to move the sauce around.

"So? Is that any reason to bring you into it?"

She was wearing jeans and a beige sweatshirt with her hair back in a ponytail. As always, she looked gorgeous, but it certainly wasn't the time to tell her so. Although the way she crossed her arms made the sweatshirt fit her even better.

"This guy is talking about killing people. I don't think who he brings into it gives him any pause."

"And now you're working with the Oakland Police Department?"

"I wrote these articles. In case a name or a crime stands out, they need me."

Cara looked at me and started to calm down. She even mustered a smile.

"I remember when dating a writer/reporter was a bit boring," she said.

I couldn't help but laugh. "Yeah, me too. This is going to be nothing like last summer. I promise."

I leaned into kiss her. She let me.

"How's Ray?" she asked.

It was her way of somewhat changing the conversation. I stirred the sauce a little more. It was thickening up and looked delicious.

"He's doing well, but I'm sure this case is front and center on his mind. The killer said he's going to strike in two days, on the 12th."

"Well, I hope they catch him beforehand, obviously. For selfish reasons as well. We had plans for June. Remember?"

The school year where Cara taught would end in late May. We'd planned a trip to Austin, Texas for a few days in late June. Have drinks and watch some bands on Sixth Street.

Plus, the real reason we were going. Cara's sister Charlotte lived there. With her husband and four children.

Which, when mentioned, would usually lead to a conversation like this:

Cara: "We should have a child."

Me: "We're not even married or engaged."

Cara: "That doesn't make your age stand still. You're not getting any younger."

I often felt guilty being an only child and not having given my mother any grandkids. Not that you owed it to your parents, but I knew it would mean the world to her.

And my father, if he was looking down on me. I'm not a religious guy, so I have to say *if.*

I'd given the possibility more consideration lately. The problem was that although I'd saved up some money from my media appearances and the *New Yorker* article, I didn't currently have a nine-to-five, and wasn't sure it was the best time.

I knew it would come to the forefront when we went to Austin.

"Of course I remember," I said. "It's only May 10th. This thing will be a distant memory by late June. We'll be going, I promise you. I can't wait to see your nine nieces and nephews."

"Very funny, mister. Charlotte has four kids."

"Can't you just pretend one of them is yours?"

"Nope. Have to go through the whole process."

"I'll remind you of that when you're throwing up from morning sickness."

"I'll take that as a small victory," Cara said. "At least you're acknowledging what we'd go through."

"You really want to have a kid out of wedlock?" I joked.

"We could change that too. Unless you think a semi-out-of-work writer could do better than this." She sexily shook her hips, and I immediately reverted back to the first time I met her. I was smitten all over again.

"Probably not," I admitted.

She continued moving her hips, doing her best Shakira impersonation. "Probably?" she said.

I leaned in and kissed her. She moved her hands to my face and kissed me back. Our hands started sliding up and down each other's bodies.

"One second," I said.

I went over and turned the electric burner off, sliding the saucepan off the heat. I removed the chicken from the oven as well.

"Good thinking. Let's burn the bed down, not the apartment," Cara said.

"You should have been the writer," I said.

I picked her up and took her from the kitchen to the bed, where we spent the next twenty minutes. And the twenty after that. And the twenty...okay, you get the point.

We emerged from the bedroom over an hour later, and having worked off a lot of calories, ate the chicken piccata with no regrets.

Having enjoyed the carnal and culinary aspects of our relationship, we both spent the next few hours working. Cara sat on one end of the couch, finalizing a lesson plan for her students. I was at the other end, reading some old articles of mine, hoping something would jump out. Nothing did.

I pulled out my phone, where I'd screenshot the psychopath's letter. I read it again.

But nothing clicked.

Cara stayed over and we went to sleep around midnight. Well, she did. With May 12th right around the corner, I found it tougher to close my eyes. Eventually, around 1:30, I succeeded.

5.

Thursday, May 11th came and went.

Ray and I kept in contact throughout the day, but I never went to any precinct. He told me they were deep in police work and I'd be persona non grata. I was fine with that.

He'd asked me about a few names from my articles. I told him what I could.

"You've written about hundreds of names," he said. "We have one day until this asshole says he's going to kill. We could hypothetically knock on two hundred doors. But then what? 'Hey, are you the guy who sent the letter threatening to kill people?'"

I understood his frustration. At least after a murder, you have forensics, possible motive, etc.

Before a crime was committed, we truly had nothing.

He told me they were analyzing the envelope for any DNA. Also trying to find out where it was sent from. And once they found that, they'd look to see if there were any cameras in the area. Potentially find the guy on film.

Other Bay Area police departments had also turned to analysis and camera searches, since letters had been mailed to several of them.

It sounded like they were doing a lot on their end.

Cara had gone back to her apartment and I slept alone that night. I had as much difficulty time falling asleep as on the previous night.

I woke up on Friday the 12th at six a.m. It didn't matter how late I fell asleep, my internal alarm clock always woke me at the crack of dawn.

I went downstairs to my local Starbucks, but instead of hanging out, I took my coffee back to my apartment.

It was too early to call Ray, so I went to my computer and devoured more of my articles. Nothing left an impression, just as I'd suspected.

The search came up empty. Again and again.

I'd read the prospective killer's letter at least ten times. Something remained just a little off about it. But I couldn't decide exactly what it was.

I read it again. Something clicked.

He'd mentioned five cities in the Bay Area. San Francisco, Oakland, and San Jose were the three most populous, so they all made sense. The *Walnut Creek Times* was obviously located in Walnut Creek so that belonged.

The fifth mentioned was Tiburon, a small, wealthy city just north of the Golden Gate Bridge. It seemed an unlikely choice.

So why mention it?

He could have been a spoiled rich kid living in his parents' elaborate basement in Tiburon. That was possible.

But would you mention the city in which you lived?

I didn't know. There was so much that I, and the OPD, were in the dark about.

Hopefully, it wouldn't take a murder to bring us into the light.

Like on the day before, I talked sporadically to Ray. They were making the rounds and he said they had extra OPD officers patrolling the city. The same went for the SFPD and other Bay Area police forces.

I told Ray that I thought Tiburon stuck out like a sore thumb, compared to the obvious choices of the other four cities.

"I'll tell Captain Lockett," he said.

"Might be better if you take credit," I responded.

Just before midnight, I got a call from Ray.

"This can't be good," I said.

"No, it's not."

"The guy killed someone?"

"Three people. I'll wait and give you the details, but they are ghastly. Captain Lockett wants you to come by the precinct tomorrow morning at eight."

"Sure. Did you find a connection to one of my articles?" I asked.

"No."

"Then why does he want me?"

"Because the murders took place in Tiburon."

6.
THE KILLER

I chose my first victims as they crossed the street.

Something as random as that.

At least, that's what I hoped the Porky Pig Police would think.

In reality, I'd long ago chosen the three people I intently watched.

It had been a long time since I'd seen them. So I didn't think they'd recognize me. But I certainly wasn't going to get close enough to find out. So I watched from afar.

The daughter had become an extraordinarily beautiful young woman. When I'd last seen her, she was probably thirteen or fourteen, and even then I knew she was going to be gorgeous. But she was now off the charts. I was going to have fun with her.

But probably with gloves and while holding something. Using my own appendages would only leave DNA and land me in jail. And I had more people to kill, so as pleasurable as the daughter would have been, there would be no sex. At least not using my dick. Maybe a different instrument lying around the house. Hahaha.

My connection to them did bring the potential their murders might lead back to me. But I found those odds to be miniscule.

No, I didn't think they'd tie me to the Langleys' murders. And part of that was my own doing.

I'd written my letter as if I was unhinged, creating the notion that a psycho was on the loose.

Which, while partially true, would have the authorities looking for an undisciplined, crazy man. They'd assume I was just killing to kill. It's unlikely they would think I'd carefully selected my victims.

I wouldn't get any credit for meticulously planning all this. At least, not yet. Eventually, it would all come out. And I'd be praised as a diabolical mastermind.

For now, they'd just think I was crazy. Which is how I wanted it.

I looked back in the direction of the daughter. Innocent. Supple, but firm. Perfectly tanned skin. She was wearing some Daisy Dukes and the Dark Side of the Moon shirt with the prism. I wasn't the only man looking.

Her parents were dressed immaculately, him in a tan suit and her in a light green dress that almost made her pass as her daughter's older sister. She was quite beautiful as well. Just as she had been when I'd last seen her.

They walked down the street and I continued following them from a distance. They stopped at a few shops, but didn't stay long.

Tiburon was a small town, and eventually they'd finished walking the downtown area. I felt no need to follow them anymore. I knew they were heading home.

And I'd be joining them that night.

7.

"Try to be on your best behavior. A lot of these guys haven't slept," Ray said, greeting me outside of the 7th Street headquarters, the shield staring down at us as we entered.

"I'll try," I said.

He once again whisked me through security. "And they aren't going to let you sit in on the meeting. The chief is here and this is very official business. But Lockett wants to hear why you were suspicious of Tiburon."

"I told you why."

"He wants to hear it from the horse's mouth."

We approached the elevator and waited.

"What happened in Tiburon?" I asked.

"You'll see it on the news."

"I want to hear it from the horse's mouth."

"C'mon, Quint."

Ray didn't like his words being used against him. But I was pissed.

"You dragged me out here. That's the least you can do," I said.

The elevator opened. We were the only two to enter.

"When these doors open back up, I'm done talking about it," he said.

"Okay. Go."

"A family of three. Murdered. Tortured. Made to suffer. A couple in their fifties and a teenage daughter. She suffered the most."

I shook my head, trying not to let any visuals pop into it. We were arriving on the third floor.

"What else?"

"It was an extremely expensive house with views of the Bay."

Ray looked at me and I could tell he had something else to say, something very painful. I knew it.

The doors opened.

"What else?"

"The motherfucker painted '*1 down, 4 to go*' on the wall. In the victims' blood."

I didn't have time to react as we stepped out of the elevator. It was nothing like a few days previous when only a few officers were there. The floor was packed with Oakland's finest.

I recognized Alfred Ronson, the Chief of Police. He was on the news from time to time. Though he was approaching seventy years old, he had slicked-back black hair that was the most obvious dye job in human history. Ronson's wrinkles made Ray look like a newbie. Of course, Ronson wasn't out in the field looking for the bad guys. Age didn't matter in his position.

He eyeballed me as Ray and I made our entrance. Captain Lockett was by his side. They approached.

"Hello again, Mr. Adler."

"Nice to see you, Captain Lockett."

"This is Alfred Ronson, our Chief of Police."

I extended my hand and was greeted with an overly ambitious handshake. I thought he was trying to tear my hand off. He may have been seventy, but I wouldn't want to fuck with him.

"Detective Kintner told me you suspected Tiburon. Why?"

Officers milled around, but only the four of us were privy to this conversation.

"I read the killer's letter many times. I couldn't understand why Tiburon was included in the cities mentioned. San Francisco, Oakland, and San Jose are the biggest and most famous in the Bay Area. They made sense. Similarly, Walnut Creek fit because he'd mentioned my articles in the *Walnut Creek Times.* Tiburon stood out. That being said, I was still shocked when I heard the murders occurred there. It was a total guess on my part."

The chief eyed me suspiciously. "Have you ever reported on a story from Tiburon? Or remember any articles pertaining to Tiburon?"

I'd considered that on the drive over. "Nothing that rings a bell. We almost exclusively cover Walnut Creek."

"Those murders you got yourself involved in last year took place in Oakland," Chief Ronson said. Not in an ironic way. More accusatory.

"The first guy murdered was from Walnut Creek. So I followed the story."

"I've heard you like to follow the story."

Captain Lockett looked at me with some compassion. Who would have thought I'd come to see him as an ally?

"I guess so," I said.

"You're not trying to get your face back in the news, are you?"

"I'm not sure what you're saying," I said.

"Just seems peculiar that murder seems to follow you around."

That incensed me. I didn't care that he was the Chief of Police. "If you're suggesting I had anything to do with these murders, you're even older than I thought. Better get that melon tested. Might be some early onset."

The slightest of smirks crossed Ray's face. I continued.

"Detective Kintner told me about the letter about three days ago. That was the first I heard about it. I helped the OPD with my articles and then texted him my suspicions about Tiburon. That's it!"

"Calm down, Mr. Adler. I'm not saying you are the *actual* killer."

Although that's exactly how it sounded.

I astonished myself with what I said next.

"Listen, you old asshole, the OPD already falsely arrested me for murder last year. And now you're trying to insinuate it again. Maybe I should sue your damn department."

I'd been framed for murder partially using an old coffee cup that I'd left in the Starbucks trash. A few of the baristas had come to my defense, and thus vaulted themselves into a well-publicized Bay Area case.

I was still a regular, and they told me that they'd get questions about it every few days. They seemed to enjoy the attention and after what they'd done for me, I was all for it.

After looking at my watch and seeing thirty minutes had passed since Ray's call, I took the elevator down and walked through the parking garage that led to my favorite coffee shop.

Sarah and Fatima, two of the baristas who'd helped me out, were behind the counter.

"Your usual?" Sarah asked.

"Yeah. And let me get a Venti Pike as well," I said, ordering for Ray Kintner.

"Better make that two," a voice said from behind me.

It was Captain Lockett. He and Ray had sneaked up right behind me without me noticing. Another reason they were the cops and I wasn't.

"That's on my card too," I said.

The two women waved at Ray, having been interviewed by him when they came to my defense.

I turned to the officers in uniform.

"Let's sit outside," I said. "Give us a little more privacy."

The drinks were made and I handed the two coffees over. They followed me outside and we found a table facing Treat Boulevard. A small bridge crossed over Treat and a paved trail wound only feet away, so there was never a lack of people-watching to do.

It was one of the things I liked about it.

We each took a seat.

"Alright, guys, what's up?"

Captain Lockett grabbed something from his pocket. He unfolded the piece of paper, and I knew what it was before he handed it over. A second letter from the killer.

I'd been shocked by what he wrote the first time, but this one hit even closer to home. I couldn't believe what I was reading:

Hello San Francisco, Walnut Creek, Oakland, and San Jose. Both police and media alike. I'm sure everyone will be reading my letters now!

One down and four to go! Exciting, isn't it?

Hope you had a nice time squeegeeing the brains of Paul Longley and his family. I consider myself an elevated type of serial killer, but sometimes you have to get your hands dirty. And If I'm going to stake my claim as the greatest serial killer of all time, I have to master all disciplines. You can think of me as a jack-of-all-trades killer.

But in all honesty, I'm not sure hand-to-hand killing will be my forte going forward. I'm not sure it's all that necessary. After all, it's not like Hitler was on the front lines of Auschwitz. And, as great as Ted Bundy or John Wayne Gacy was, Timothy McVeigh killed many, many more.

So don't expect any more home invasion murders. And are you kidding me this fucking nickname I've been hearing? The Bay Area Butcher? C'mon, you can do better than that.

I've given you another hint, by the way. I've excluded Tiburon in the introductory sentence. For good reason. There will be no more killings there. But the other four are battling each other for what city is next.

Once again, I will give you the date of the upcoming murder. Another Friday. May 19th. Not that far away. And the date is unlikely to help. I have already proven my brilliance and Bay Area cops are lagging far behind. It's hundreds of officers vs. the lone me. And I'm winning. You guys are fucking pathetic.

And one last thing, although I'm sure you've noticed by now. The ends of my sentences are accompanied with a 2-space break. Maybe I'm older than you think, huh Quint?

And one last hint on the Quint front.

As I said, I was mentioned in exactly one of his articles.

But my first name is in every article that Quint has ever written. But only Quint will be able to find that one. It's an inside joke that I can't share just yet.

I think that's enough hints. Even a blind squirrel gets a nut and if I give any more, you might just stumble on to me.

I promise to make my second set of murders even more elaborate than my first. And by elaborate, I mean brutal!!

Happy Hunting.

I took a deep breath and laid the paper back down on the table. I'd realized early on in the letter that he was using two spaces between each sentence. But it still hit me like a ton of bricks when he mentioned it. And me by name.

"This copy is for you," Lockett said. "Obviously, you are to share it with no one."

I folded it up and put in my pocket.

Ray spoke next. "What the hell, Quint? How many people did you tell about your suspicion on the spacing?"

"I only mentioned it at the meeting. No one else."

"Not Tom or Krissy or anyone at the paper?"

"No."

"Not Cara?"

"No."

"Not your mother?"

"No."

"Then how the hell did the killer know?"

I racked my brain and could only come up with one answer. They weren't going to like it.

"It had to be someone else in the meeting. One of your other officers."

"Here's the thing, Quint," Lockett said. "We considered that and contacted every one of them. They all swear down the line they didn't tell another living soul about our meeting. And I believe them. Just like I know Ray or I didn't break protocol."

He looked at me and it felt similar to when the Chief of Police had been accusatory.

"I didn't tell a soul. I'll swear on a stack of a hundred Bibles if you'd like."

"You don't strike me as the religious type."

"I'm not. My Dad was the least religious guy I've ever met. My mother was Irish Catholic and tried to raise me under Catholicism, but that didn't last much past puberty. Too restrictive."

Ray mustered a smile.

"Listen," I continued. "I'll swear on my unborn children if you'd prefer. Just know that I didn't tell anyone!"

They looked like they wanted to believe me. But if they did, that meant one of their own officers had lied to them. That was worse.

"I'm in a predicament here, Quint," Lockett said. "I have to side with my fellow officers, which means you'd be lying."

"What do you think? I'm talking to this deranged killer? Or I accidentally told Cara, who relayed it to one of her students, who then told their father, who just happens to be the killer? This is insane! I didn't tell a fucking soul."

I wasn't prone to excessive swearing, but calling the chief an asshole before and saying the F-word at this point both seemed apropos. These accusations had to stop.

"Well then, how do you explain it?" Ray asked. He was trying to take my side, but he was in a tough spot.

I tried to think, which wasn't easy considering I had a detective and a captain of the OPD staring at me.

"Give me a second," I said. I took a sip of my coffee, hoping the jolt of caffeine might make my mind a little sharper.

I don't know if the coffee deserves any of the credit, but something immediately came to mind.

"This is a longshot," I started. "But if everyone is telling the truth, then we've got to think outside the box. Ray, do you remember when Dennis McCarthy and Paddy Roark helped me listen in on Charles Zane?"

"Of course. You think the killer planted a listening device in the conference room?"

Captain Lockett adjusted his chair and moved closer to the table. This had gotten his attention.

I looked around just to make sure no one was within earshot. "That's possible. But unless he's a cop, finding his way into the police station, and that conference room specifically, would be a huge risk. There's another possibility."

They looked at me intently. I continued.

"Recording devices can be made extremely small these days. The killer could have slipped one onto the clothes of one of your officers. Subtly bumped into them and attached it to a shirt or a jacket."

"Or to you," Ray said.

He was right. It made perfect sense.

"Shit, I'd probably be the most likely suspect. He'd know you guys would contact me since he mentioned me in the letter."

"We met with you on Wednesday, two days before the killing in Tiburon. Do you remember what you were wearing?"

"I can probably narrow it down to one or two outfits. I haven't done laundry since."

"I'll tell the officers at the meeting to do the same. And if you happen to see a recording device, try not to handle the clothes too much. Might be some DNA or fingerprints to get off of it," Captain Lockett said.

It was good advice. I took another sip of my coffee.

"This is freaking crazy."

"And if the killer's new letter is true, it's about to get worse."

We all sat in silence for a few moments.

"I'll call you once I go through my clothes."

"Thanks, Quint," they said in unison. Which, along with their intent gazes on me, felt kind of creepy. But then so was the rest of this case.

I tossed my empty coffee cup in the garbage and made my way back up to my apartment. My anxiety levels were off the charts.

If he'd somehow planted a listening device, I sincerely hoped it hadn't been on me. *Please let it be on one of the detectives.* The idea that the killer had come close enough to touch me scared me to no end.

I took the elevator up to the fourth floor and walked the long hallway to my apartment. Luckily, my new place was on the opposite side of the complex. I didn't have to retrace the steps of where I'd been shot a year previous.

But the hopeless feeling I'd had back then was returning. And somehow, it grew worse.

Arriving back at my place, I tried to rack my brain to remember last Wednesday. Six days ago. I couldn't think of what I'd been wearing, so I tried to envision the day. Ray called me and we met at the restaurant called Homeroom. I visualized us sitting outside along the bustling sidewalk. Him in his police uniform and me in…

I remembered! I had worn a long-sleeved black hoodie and some cream-colored pants.

I started going through my laundry basket. I made sure to be deliberate, not wanting to knock any instrument off. Unlikely as it were. I slowly picked up the more recent clothes and set them on the floor next to me. I was near the bottom of the basket when I saw the pants.

Careful to only grab them in one spot, I moved them around but saw nothing that shouldn't be there. I laid them on the pile.

Next, I saw the black hoodie and picked it up. As with the shorts, I kept my grip on one part of it, not wanting to move my fingers all over and hinder any potential evidence.

I flipped it over and that's when I saw it. A small, silver, disc-like shape on the back of my sweatshirt. It was less than an inch long, but with technology these days, it was certainly big enough to record a conversation.

This ruthless killer had attached a listening device to my hoodie. Without me noticing.

Had he done it at Starbucks? At Homeroom? Out on the street? Was he on the elevator with me at Avalon Walnut Creek?

I shuddered at any and all of the possibilities.

Had he continued listening when I got home? Heard me talking to Cara? To my mother?

I felt sick.

9.

The Oakland Police Department confirmed it was a recording device. No useful fingerprints were found, and they weren't confident any DNA would be either.

This was all relayed over the phone. They discouraged me from coming to see them. Despite my friendship with Ray and my improving relationship with Captain Lockett, it appeared the OPD was giving me the stiff arm, Heisman style.

The dinner with Cara and my mother turned out to be a disaster. My mind had been on the letter I'd read that morning and they could tell my thoughts were elsewhere. Mom even told me to be more present the next time we had dinner. That hurt. Cara turned down an invitation back to my apartment.

I wasn't going to tell my mother a single thing about the new case. I'd prefer that she was in the dark as opposed to worrying about me again. She'd done enough of that last time.

The media, to this point, had avoided mentioning that the killer had dropped my name. They talked about the threats to the Bay Area, but didn't get more specific than that. I doubted that would last much longer, however. And when they finally mentioned me, I'd be having a long talk with my mother. But I was going to wait.

As the letter had referenced, I'd heard a few media outlets dub him The Bay Area Butcher. But it hadn't completely caught on. And yet, I somehow knew it would.

Was I walking right back into the middle of another horror movie? It sure seemed headed in that direction.

In my defense, I hadn't chosen it this time. I'd been blindsided by the first letter, and how it mentioned me and my articles. Which got me thinking about the most recent letter.

I took out the copy that Captain Lockett had given me and read it again.

He said his first name was used in every article I'd ever written. And that only I would be able to find it. What did he mean?

I tried to think of words I'd use in any article.

I'd certainly used words like "The" or "And" in every article, but surely no one was named anything like that.

Could his name be Quint?

I'd texted Ray to check for people named Quint or Adler in the Bay Area, saying there couldn't have been many.

He replied: *If only we had thought of that*. His terse response showed me that this case was getting to everyone.

The murders of the Langley family had been the lead story on the local news for four days now. The information seeped out slowly, so there was something new every day. The gruesomeness of the killings had finally become public, and the dual murder weapons of a knife and cleaver were brought to light. I'm sure that brought some unwanted visuals to anyone hearing it. And surely had been the reason for his nickname.

The fact the killer had written a letter to local police departments fascinated the general public, bringing many comparisons to the Zodiac Killer. Which only added to the intrigue.

Being shunned by the OPD forced me to go in my own direction. Which was generally when I worked best.

I started researching Micronomy, the company that Paul Langley had worked for. I found employees that had worked there, using their website, LinkedIn, and Google to make as comprehensive a list as I could muster.

At the same time, I started listing all the people who had made an appearance in at least one of my articles.

I then cross-referenced the lists, but couldn't find a match. For a moment, I thought I had one. I'd mentioned a bank robber named Josh Davie in one article and a Josh Davies worked for Micronomy. I celebrated a second too long before I realized the last names were a letter off.

The unlikelihood of a bank robber being employed by a big dot-com company hadn't entered my mind. It was just a knee-jerk reaction of excitement that I'd found something.

And though it didn't amount to anything, I'd built two lists of names of possible connections. Which might be useful down the road.

The chances were extremely high that the killer never worked for Micronomy. Most serial killers chose people at random, so I wasn't confident the killer knew Langley, much less worked for him. But I had to start somewhere. And the viciousness of the murder made it seem personal.

I wanted to make a list of people who lived in Tiburon and cross-reference them with people who'd been mentioned in my articles. Tiburon was a small city and its population was listed at only 9,000. Sure, it was still going to be a lot of work, but at least it wasn't Oakland, with its population of 429,000. That would be impossible.

But I quickly realized that I didn't have something as simple as the yellow pages. It didn't appear you could just go online and get a list of people who live in a specific city.

So instead, I'd google every name mentioned in my articles, adding 'Tiburon' to the search, hoping one of them had lived there or worked there. It was tedious work.

I didn't know if I was going to strike gold or strike out, but I was working hard. There was something to be said for that.

After several hours, I'd come up with four names of people who'd been mentioned in my articles and had some affiliation with Tiburon. One lived there, one got in a fight and was arrested there, and two people appeared to both work for Sam's Harbor Cafe, a famous restaurant that sat right on the Bay.

I texted Ray the list, knowing they could do more with the names than I could. Regardless of whether it led to anything, I had done great work. I knew that. I wasn't a police officer, but the work I'd done was police-officer worthy. I felt proud.

My work was done and I was mentally exhausted, so I sprawled out on my couch. I called my mother, apologizing for my behavior at dinner the previous night. I asked if she wanted to have lunch in two days and she quickly agreed. I looked at my phone. The lunch would be on May 19th, the same day the killer was set to strike again.

10.

Exercise had long been my refuge when I was stressed out. While some people turned to yoga or Pilates, I found that a good run refreshed my mind like nothing else. So, on the morning of May 19th, I went for a three-mile run, sweating profusely the entire time. It was like each bead of sweat represented a small level of anxiety, and when they flew off my body, I became a little bit calmer with each stride.

I'd run along the Iron Horse Trail, which went almost thirty miles through the East Bay—Concord, Pleasant Hill, Walnut Creek, and even as far west as San Ramon and Danville. You could make your own personal marathon out of it if you so chose. But three miles was plenty for me.

I felt reinvigorated when I went to lunch with my mother. She'd chosen a restaurant called Fat Maddie's Grille, only a few miles from her home.

I loved the name of the place and I immediately knew why "Fat" had been used. They offered grilled cheese, fried chicken, pork chops, clam chowder, and other gut-expanding dishes. Given my run that morning, I ordered the fried chicken guilt-free. My mother chose the Cobb salad, probably the healthiest thing on the menu. And with bacon, blue cheese, and fat-filled dressing, it wasn't exactly a dietician's dream.

In the small, cramped dining room, every seat was taken. It was nice to see that restaurants were making a recovery after the horrific toll the coronavirus took on the industry.

"Would you be mad if I started dating again?"

So much for an innocent, carefree lunch with my mother.

"Of course not, Mom."

"It's been almost two years since your dad died. Trust me, he will always be the love of my life. We were together for over forty years. No one can replace that. But I do get lonely from time to time."

While it was a bit odd to think of your seventy-year-old mother dating again, the most important thing was her happiness.

"Then I think you should go for it. In fact, I bet Dad would be in favor of it. He'd want you to be happy."

"Don't think I'm not joyful, Quint. I am. I love you. I love Cara. I've got some great friends. It would just be nice to have a man that I could go see a movie with. Or the opera."

"I'm all for it. Just don't give me any details."

My mother started laughing and almost spit up her water. "I'm looking for companionship. Not a roll in the hay."

It was my turn to laugh. "Not that you need my permission to date, but you have it. Now, can we change the subject?"

"Maybe we'll double date with you and Cara."

"Stop, Mom," I said, although my smile belied me.

"I will. Just wanted you to know that no one will ever replace your father. That's impossible."

"Thanks. I know how much you loved each other."

"I've told you a million times, but he'd be so proud of what you did last summer."

"You're right. You have told me a million times."

She laughed again. "And he'd be even prouder if you took the plunge with Cara. Are you guys still going to Austin?"

The current situation had put the trip in doubt, but I couldn't tell her that. The press still hadn't mentioned my name. Although I knew that could change at any moment. My guess was the police departments had told local media there were some things they couldn't announce.

"Yeah, we are still going."

"Are you going to hang out with her sister?"

"That's the main reason we're going."

"What's her name again?"

"Charlotte."

"That's right. I knew it started with a C. Do you like her?"

"A lot. She's very similar to Cara. Upbeat with a good outlook on life. Makes her fun to be around."

"I'd love to meet her someday."

"You will. Although I can't guarantee it will be at Cara's and my wedding."

"You read me like a book, Quint."

"Yeah, I guess I do."

As a child, I often knew what my parents were going to say before they said it. It was a blessing and a curse.

A few minutes later, the Cobb salad and fried chicken arrived and we each took a bite.

"How's your chicken?" she asked.

This meant the more serious side of our conversation had ended.

"It's delicious."

"Do you remember that time your father tried to make fried chicken and it was so underdone, it's like the bird was still alive?"

"Someone had the good idea to cut into it first." I laughed.

"That was me. As much as I loved your father, I never quite trusted him in the kitchen."

"Whenever he broiled anything, he'd forget about it until it started smoking."

"So true. He always put it on the top level like two inches from the broiler. Be smoking in seconds."

We smiled at each other, soaking up the good memories of my father.

"He could make some good banana pancakes, though," I said.

"They were delicious. It was his one saving grace in the kitchen."

"I miss those."

"Do you know what his secret ingredient was?"

"I don't," I admitted.

"He always threw about a quarter cup of rum in the batter."

"You guys were boozing me up as a kid?"

"He'd say the rum would burn off when the pancakes cooked. I had my doubts."

"Next time I have you over, I'm making those things. Extra rum."

My mother nodded, laughing. "I'm in. I haven't been over in awhile."

"Hey, we had dinner three nights ago and lunch today. You're getting enough time with me."

"I know, Quint. You're a great son."

"And you're a great mom. Now, enough of the mutual admiration society."

We went back to eating. I was much more present than I'd been at the dinner and was happy I'd set it up.

After finishing our meal, I dropped her off at home, promises of rum pancakes to come.

My life for the last week had fluctuated between lighthearted moments and brutal news about the deranged killer. So when I returned to my apartment and turned on the news, I expected to hear there'd been another awful murder. But it was just local news, sports, and weather. Boring, but I'd take that any time.

Afternoon turned into evening, and I decided to go for another run. I couldn't just sit around waiting for the bad news sure to come. It was driving me crazy.

I ran, arrived back home, showered, and turned on the T.V. Still nothing. I sent a text to Ray, who responded with *Nothing yet.*

Was it possible the guy had decided to stop killing? Been caught? I wasn't confident of either, but that doesn't mean I wasn't holding out hope.

But my hope proved unwarranted. At eleven p.m., I got the text I'd been dreading.

11.

San Jose is one of the most overlooked big cities in the United States. It's the most populous in the Bay Area. While being overshadowed by San Francisco, Oakland, and even Berkeley, San Jose has over a million residents and lies within the heart of Silicon Valley.

It should be more famous than it is.

It's also the third most populous city in California and tenth in the United States. But for some reason, San Jose isn't considered sexy. People don't come from Paris, France (or Paris, Texas) to visit San Jose. If they are coming to the Bay Area, it's for San Francisco.

Even their professional sports teams, the Sharks of the NHL and the Earthquakes of the MLS, pail in comparison to the 49ers, the Giants, and the Warriors. It's almost treated like a second-class city even though it's anything but.

I was guilty of that as well. While San Francisco and San Jose were about equidistant from my apartment in Walnut Creek, I'd choose San Francisco any day of the week.

Sadly, on this day, San Jose had been chosen for me.

Ray's text sent me to the Willow Glen section of the city. I'd been there before and it was very charming, with tree-lined streets and lots of shopping.

But there would be none of that on this night.

The address was actually just two cross streets, Cherry Avenue and Willow Street. Cherry and Willow. Peaceful and tranquil-sounding names.

They didn't fit the occasion, that's for sure.

I parked my car about two hundred yards away and started walking in the direction of Cherry and Willow. I had wondered why Ray didn't give me a specific address. As I made my way closer, I realized why.

Much to my dismay, San Jose police officers were coming in and out of several homes at once.

Had the madman killed several people at different addresses? What the hell was I walking into? This case was getting worse by the minute. A pit opened in the bottom of my stomach. I was genuinely scared to find out what had happened.

As I approached the perimeter of the crime scenes, I saw Ray standing next to Captain Lockett. Luckily, the Chief of Police was nowhere to be seen. In fact, Ray and the captain appeared to be the only two officers representing the OPD.

Obviously, jurisdiction went to the SJPD, but with these crimes targeting the entire Bay Area, I imagined officers from every big local city had arrived at the scene.

Several different houses had yellow tape around them as I looked down the block. I couldn't see where the series of crime scenes ended.

Ray and the captain stood just outside the tape, looking inward. People milled around in every direction, but they were standing by themselves.

"Thanks for coming," Ray said.

It looked like he may have been crying.

Captain Lockett nodded in my direction.

"What the hell happened?" I asked.

"It's unfathomable," Ray said.

I looked out at the multiple crime scenes and my imagination ran wild.

Ray continued. "Around twenty people have been poisoned by this fucking psycho."

I was taken aback. With all the terrible things I'd imagined, I never could have expected something so extreme.

"My God, how horrible," I said.

"Approximately fifteen homes in this area were delivered cookies between 9:00 and 9:30 tonight. They were all accompanied with this note."

Ray took out his phone and showed me a screenshot. It was an orange leaflet, probably around three inches by four inches. Black block letters read:

You have been the greatest neighbors since we moved in. I love Willow Glen. This is a token of our appreciation and we really hope you enjoy the cookies! Love, Maxine and Bill.

A shiver went up my spine. He'd pretended to be a grateful couple to poison a neighborhood.

The MO was so far off from his original murders. For a brief moment, I wondered if it was the same killer. But I knew it had to be. This was the night of his next murders, after all.

I was scared. For myself, but most of all, for the people of the Bay Area. Most serial killers killed in one specific way. This was new. And downright petrifying.

I hated asking the next question, but I had to. "How many have died? Tell me they're all just a little sick."

Captain Lockett shook his head and I knew we weren't going to be that lucky. Ray's moist eyes should have given it away as well.

"Three have already died," he said. "And ten more are in the hospital. Including several teenagers and a few young kids."

I turned away from the two men in front of me, about to cry myself.

Teenagers and kids? I wanted to rip the heart out of the killer. Be left alone in a room with him and see what happens.

"What type of poison did he use?" I asked.

"They don't know yet, but one officer told me they think it might be fentanyl. He headed to the hospital to talk to some doctors. I'm sure they will know shortly if they don't already."

"And Maxine and Bill are just some random neighbors?"

"It looks that way. The SJPD has been interviewing them. My guess is they've moved in recently and the killer knew that. And a neighbor said they are just the nicest couple, so people would likely feel compelled to try their cookies."

"He certainly knows his crime scenes beforehand," I said. "Just like Tiburon."

"My guess is he scopes out the area for a few days. Probably found out who the new neighbors were."

There was a brief silence in which none of us knew what to say.

"This is…catastrophic," I said, searching for a word that fit. None could.

"And it will likely get worse. This is a very fluid situation, obviously. Who knows how many could be dead before the night is over?"

I shook my head. "I've never been more disgusted in my life.".

Captain Lockett nodded. "I've been around a long time, and I can safely say the same thing. What a horrific act."

It was as if we were trying to one-up each other with terrible-sounding adjectives, although we all knew none would suffice.

"There must be cameras around here, right?" It was a half question, half statement on my part.

"Not many. There's no businesses. All residential. Two neighbors have cameras, but he didn't drop off cookies to them. I'm sure that was no coincidence. But a few of the neighbors did see the man setting the cookies down. He didn't knock or ring the doorbells for obvious reasons. If there's any sort of silver lining, it's that several families never tried the cookies. Some weren't at home and others never saw them sitting on their doorstep since he didn't ring the doorbell."

"How did they describe the guy?"

"I heard this from my SJPD friend also, so it's secondhand. A neighbor told him he had a hat pulled tight around his head. Plus a hoodie. Average height and weight and probably in his twenties or thirties."

"Did any of these neighbors see him up close?"

"No. It appears he only left the cookies at about every third or fourth house. Trying to avoid being seen by every neighbor, who would have realized it wasn't Bill. Or obviously, Maxine."

"So how far down does this crime scene go?" I asked.

"We haven't been to the end, but it stretches a few blocks for sure."

"Just terrible."

"And I don't have much confidence we'll get a good ID. The sun had set. This guy is nothing if not meticulous. Nightfall, a hat, a hoodie. It's going to be next to impossible."

"Maybe the fentanyl can lead us to the guy," I said.

"Do you really think that?"

"No," I admitted. "Like you said, he's meticulous. It seems unlikely he'd allow himself to be caught that easily. And sadly, fentanyl probably isn't that hard to get these days. Probably more a reflection on our country than anything else."

"You ever write about any cases of poisoning?" Lockett asked.

I thought about it. "I seem to remember a husband trying to poison his wife. But certainly nothing like this."

"I'd like to see that article, regardless."

"Of course," I said, although we all knew it would amount to nothing.

Hearing some loud noises, we turned around and saw a white van entering past the yellow tape.

"Can't be the coroner, can it?" I asked.

"No. They got everyone to the hospital after the first few people started getting sick and they discovered the cookies."

"Sadly, it wasn't quick enough for some of them," Captain Lockett said, stating the obvious.

"Probably more fingerprint experts," Ray said. "Although I'm sure he was wearing gloves."

No one said anything for a minute.

"Why was I invited out here, Ray?"

"The chief ordered it. He may not like you personally, but he said the reference to your articles is one of the few things we have to go on."

"He's right," I said. "But I'm really no help out here."

"I know, Quint. But I have to follow protocol. And maybe, just maybe something might have jumped out."

"I guess," I said.

More noises sounded behind us as a few cop cars exited the perimeter. With the exception of fingerprints and talking to neighbors, most of the police work would be at the hospitals now.

I hated imagining people fighting for their lives at that exact moment. For eating a fucking cookie.

"This is going to be national news tomorrow," Captain Lockett said. "After the first murders, we had the chance to keep it local. But it's too late for that now. We're going to be infested with media tomorrow. And probably the FBI as well."

"Great," Ray said sarcastically.

"We'll keep in touch, Quint, but if the feds truly take over, you'll probably be seeing less of us."

"I'm not going anywhere. If you need me, I'm here. If not, I understand," I said.

We heard Ray's name yelled by one of the SJPD officers.

"I'll be right back," he said.

Tears still showed in his eye.

It had the odd affect of becoming contagious, similar to a yawn, because as I looked back at the houses, a tear appeared in mine as well.

I hung around for another thirty minutes, even though my being there was unnecessary. It's almost like I wanted to postpone the inevitable. I knew that tomorrow morning the shit would really hit the fan.

The local serial killer was going to go national.

12.

"Nice to have you back! Looks like it's been almost eight years," the older, bespectacled woman—a really stereotypical librarian—said to me.

"Let's blame Amazon," I said. "It's become too easy."

When the death toll hit six that morning, I had to get out of my apartment. Imagining people choking to death, or vomiting, twisting in agony, or collapsing, or however they went, was driving me crazy.

Like Captain Lockett and Ray feared, it had gone national. It was the lead story on every national news outlet I saw.

America, and for that matter, the world, always had an infatuation with serial killers.

And here was one who had butchered a family of three to death and then killed six more through poisoning. He was getting his fifteen minutes, but worse, I expected he was going to get a lot more than that. I didn't see an end in sight.

Early reports were that fentanyl was used. Just like Ray had told me.

After a local news station posted pictures of someone who had died, I turned the T.V. off.

And decided to do something that might help me understand this killer better.

I drove to the Contra Costa County Library-Walnut Creek, a mouthful of a name. I decided I needed to read some books on serial killers. And I didn't want to wait a day or two to get them from Amazon.

The stereotypical librarian had been very polite, but as I set the macabre books on the counter, I wondered if she might change her tune.

Zodiac: The Shocking True Story of the Nation's Most Bizarre Mass Murderer. The Bundy Murders: A Comprehensive History. The Big Book of Serial Killers.

"Not the usual books we get checked out on a Saturday morning."

"Well, I'm not a usual guy," I said, quickly realizing it sounded creepy considering the books I'd checked out.

"But I'm not a serial killer either. Just research," I added.

The librarian smiled. "I know who you are! Quint, right?"

The name was on my library card, so there was no use in lying.

"Yup, that's me."

"I followed the Charles Zane case very closely. You're a hero in my eyes."

"I appreciate it," I said.

"And I read somewhere that you were named after Robert Shaw's character in *Jaws*. Is that true?"

Not sure what I'd done to earn the talkative librarian, but I wasn't too happy about it.

"It is. My parents saw that movie on their first date."

"I would have dated Robert Shaw," she said and started to blush.

This wasn't the "naughty librarian" I'd dreamt about as a younger man.

"He was quite an actor," I said, hoping to expedite the check-out process.

She started scanning the three books.

"Wait, you're not working on the new serial killer case, are you? I saw all about the second set of murders this morning. Dastardly stuff."

Any other time and I would have found the phrase "dastardly stuff" humorous, but I'd lost the ability to laugh at the moment.

"Just doing some personal research," I answered generically.

"You brought down the bad guy last time. Not the police."

But she pronounced it *po-lice*.

"The police saved my life. And did all the behind-the-scene things to get the bad guys off the streets. I just got the credit."

"If you say so," the librarian said, but I could tell she enjoyed imagining me as the hero.

If I had to guess, she had a little crush on Robert Shaw's namesake as well.

She put the three books in a little bag and handed them back to me.

"I hope you'll be back, Quint!" she said. "And good luck going after the Bay Area Butcher."

Great. Everyone was calling him that now. "It's a terrible name."

"You'll catch him though, won't you, Quint?"

I was tired of this conversation.

"The police will," I said and turned to go.

"Hope to see you again," she said.

Doubtful. I'd be returning these books through the mail slot.

The trip up to my apartment was no less awkward. Evelyn, an older woman around the librarian's age, and Tad, a younger guy from the complex, were waiting at the parking garage elevator.

Several hundred people occupied four different buildings, so it was impossible to know everyone. But I knew these two. Tad lived on my floor and Evelyn was constantly complaining on the Avalon Walnut Creek Facebook page.

As I entered the elevator, I accidentally bumped into the wall and my books fell out of the library bag, sprawling around our feet.

"Oh my," I heard Evelyn say.

The three serial killer books lay on the ground directly in front of her, with Ted Bundy staring straight up from the elevator floor. I scrambled to pick them up as quickly as I could, returning them to the bag.

"It's nothing," I said.

It was more than nothing to Evelyn, that much became obvious. She moved flush against the corner of the elevator, getting as far away from me as possible.

I looked at Tad for some relief and he smiled at me.

I wouldn't be getting the same from Evelyn, who briskly exited when we arrived on the second floor.

"Scaring old ladies your thing?" Tad asked after the doors had shut.

I laughed. "I don't think Evelyn has ever liked me."

"Wow, you know her name?"

"She's always complaining on Avalon's Facebook page. Someone was up too late. A pigeon crapped on her balcony. Rap music was playing."

"That's her? Didn't realize."

"Management says she's a handful. Somehow, I'm not surprised."

"Not too friendly either," Tad said. "But in old Evelyn's defense, those are some jarring book titles."

"Some light reading material," I said.

He laughed. "I'd be afraid to see the hard stuff."

I smiled, still a bit embarrassed from the look I'd received from Evelyn.

We arrived at the fourth floor.

"Have a nice day, Tad."

"You too, Quint."

And we both went our separate ways off of the elevator.

I spent the day reading about the most gruesome serial killers of all time.

The Zodiac Killer had always been fascinating, though mostly because of the aura surrounding him. He didn't have the most victims. Far from it. But he did have some flair, writing letters and mocking the SFPD. Promising to shoot a school bus of children.

And maybe the most important reason of all.

He'd never been caught.

That had led to a few generations trying to find out who the real Zodiac was.

For a brief, brief moment, I considered if our new guy could have been a return of the notorious Zodiac, but then realized the guy was most likely dead, and if not, in his eighties or nineties. No, this wasn't the Zodiac.

Ted Bundy might be the most infamous of all American serial killers. His good looks and charisma certainly had a lot to do with that. And the fact that he escaped from jail two separate times just added to his myth. His murders were gruesome, including necrophilia.

Jeffrey Dahmer did the same and was probably the most well-known serial killer of my childhood. The things he did to people's bodies were unbelievable, including keeping body parts soaking in formaldehyde. I couldn't imagine what officers saw upon entering his Milwaukee apartment.

There were so many others. John Wayne Gacy, the clown killer. H.H. Holmes, the savage who killed during the Chicago World's Fair in the late 1800s. The Garden State Killer, who had finally been caught in his seventies. Dean Corll. Gary Ridgway. Richard Ramirez. The list could go on for days.

I had hoped to find similarities to our killer. Some *modus operandi* that fit and could maybe paint a generic description. Unfortunately, with the most recent set of murders, finding a consistent MO was going to be very difficult.

Two sets of murders. Two completely different sets of circumstances.

Finally, after hours of reading the most gruesome stories imaginable, I started to draw some bath water.

I was a shower guy 99.9% of the time, but I felt the need to fully cleanse my body from all I'd read.

Cara had bought me a candle that sat in my bathroom and I even lit that. Who the hell was I?

I sat in the bath for twenty minutes, trying to think what type of serial killer our guy was. Young and debonair like Bundy? A raving maniac like Gacy? Cool and calculated like Dahmer?

I wasn't an FBI profiler, but I started to draw my own conclusions.

I'd go with: White, twenties or early thirties, in shape, intelligent.

I felt relatively sure of those four.

There were other characteristics that I believed to be true, but couldn't be positive on: Bay Area native, heterosexual, owned a car.

The character trait I wrestled with most was whether he was outgoing and charming or more of a recluse. I could see him as either.

The majority of serial killers would be categorized as introverts, but there were several exceptions, Bundy being the obvious one. Gacy as well.

With so much information to digest, I decided to focus on the only thing that was concrete. The letters. The killer had said clues lurked in the messages themselves. And I hoped to find them.

I decided to chat with the best puzzle solver I knew.

My girlfriend.

13.

"I notice a few things right away," Cara said.

We met at the Lafayette Reservoir. Lafayette was a fun little town, contiguous to Walnut Creek, and we'd often walk or run the three-mile circumference of the reservoir. It became very steep at parts and you definitely got your money's worth.

Today was different. We weren't there to get a workout in. Instead, I'd packed a huge blanket plus a few BLTs, and we sat on the grass that overlooked the water, eating our sandwiches. It was peaceful and tranquil. A nice respite from this crazy world.

Which had become even crazier after the arrival of the Bay Area Butcher, now being adopted by every news agency. Anything referencing cookies just seemed too weird, so his first set of murders won out by default. The nickname of the Bay Area Butcher was here to stay.

The murders continued to dominate the airwaves and I tried to avoid listening when I could. It was all too much.

"Let's hear it," I said to Cara, trying to focus on the matter at hand.

"They're probably obvious things that you or the police have already noticed."

"That's fine, just tell me everything you observed."

We had the two letters spread out on the blanket in front of us. She grabbed the first one.

"He called the cops 'fat asses.' Would a heavyset man use that word? I doubt it."

"I said the exact same thing the first day I read it."

"There's also the mentions of the cities. San Francisco. Walnut Creek. Oakland. San Jose. And Tiburon."

"Yeah, Tiburon stuck out like a sore thumb from the beginning."

"That's not what I'm getting at, Quint."

I looked over the cities one more time. She could see that I was struggling to understand.

"Look at the order," she said.

And then it hit me!

"Oh my God," I said.

"Yeah! The murders are going in reverse order of how they are listed. Tiburon was listed last. San Jose second to last."

"That would mean Oakland would be the next murder, if this wasn't just random."

"I did the math," Cara said. "If it was random, there's a one in five chance Tiburon would be the first city and then a one in four chance San Jose would be next. Multiply them together, and there's only a one in twenty chance that this was random. More than likely he's knocking off these cities in reverse order."

I literally had never been prouder to call Cara my girlfriend. Sure, when people noticed her beauty, I took pride in that. But this was something more powerful. She was an extremely intelligent and insightful woman.

Not that any of this surprised me. I'd known for a long time. But this moment stood out, because of just how important the circumstances were.

"I'm going to call Ray right now," I said.

I stood up on the bright green grass and looked at the reservoir below us. A huge lighthouse sat near the front of the water. It was the defining characteristic of the Lafayette Reservoir. I admired it as I waited for Ray to answer.

At last, I heard his familiar voice. "Hello?"

"Hey, Ray. I was talking to Cara and she brought up something that I think you might find important."

"I'd chastise you for talking to people about this investigation, but it's Cara, so I won't. Let's hear it."

"She noticed that the cities mentioned in the letter were being eliminated in reverse order. He'd listed Tiburon last and San Jose second to last. And as we know, the first murders occurred in Tiburon and then San Jose."

I heard a groan from the other side.

"And Oakland falls next on the list," Ray said.

"Yup," I said, confirming the obvious.

"It could just be a coincidence, you know."

"Cara did the math. It's one in twenty that's how the cities would shake out."

"Have I told you you've got a keeper?"

"Only every time you see me," I said.

"Listen, Quint, as you've probably gathered, I rarely like to mix my home life with my social life. However, my wife said she's heard so much about you and Cara that she wants to put faces to the names. Would you guys like to come over for dinner tomorrow night?"

"I'll run it by her, but I'm sure she'll say yes."

"Great. I'll text you our address and a time."

"See you tomorrow."

"Yes, you will. Now I've got to get back to work. I'm sure Captain Lockett and Chief Ronson will be delighted to know that the investigative team of Quint and Cara are a step ahead of us again."

I laughed. "If it saves you some grief, feel free to say you came up with it."

"Sorry, I've got to play it by the book."

"Do you have to tell them Cara is involved?"

"That I can probably fudge a little bit. I'll say it was you."

"That's fine. Rather not have there be any mention of her in any of this."

"I understand. See you tomorrow."

"Bye, Ray."

I hung up the phone and looked down at Cara.

"You letting Ray take the credit for me?" she asked.

I smiled. "He's going to say it was me. But only because I don't want anyone to hear your name."

"I'm all for that. And what were you going to run by me?"

"Ray and his wife want to have us over for dinner tomorrow night."

"I'm not even sure I knew he was married."

"He's very quiet about his private life. He must really like us if we're being invited over."

"What's not to like?"

I leaned in and hugged her.

We stayed another thirty minutes on the grass, looking out at the water and lighthouse below us.

The next twenty-four hours solidified the terror around the Bay Area. Sure, the case had gone national (and likely international), but the fear resided locally. We were the people in harm's way, after all.

No new letter appeared and that made it worse. No clues to the killer's thought process. Without any word, it's like a psycho walked invisibly amongst us. Which one did.

The nickname "Bay Area Butcher" had become ubiquitous, even monotonous. Every newscast used it several times. It was a predictable and disgusting name, but sadly, catchy as well. The media probably loved it.

Everyone had an opinion. Rinky-dink blogs were alleging they'd seen the killer. With zero evidence. And zero pictures. The police established a website for leads and every crackpot in the Bay Area was probably blaming it on a neighbor they didn't like.

The funerals for Paul, Nadia, and Mia Langley had taken place in San Francisco with a reception in Tiburon. The service had been reported on by all the local media. It had truly become a frenzy.

It affected everyone. I was on edge. In fact, I had more reason to worry than most people. He had repeatedly mentioned me, and more than that, he'd attached a listening device on my back. He'd been close to me.

And with no idea what he looked like, he could get close to me again.

I tried to not think about it, but it was nearly impossible.

The killer was definitely living rent-free in the minds of people in the Bay Area.

Including my own.

That night, the victims of the cookie killings were announced. Roger and Celia Tiller, both aged 55. Harry Shaw, aged 62. Emily Atwater, aged 14. Bruce Pocklington, aged 39. And Ariana Pocklington, aged 15.

They flashed pictures of each victim on the screen. Each face delivered a gut punch, but especially the pictures of the two young girls. They had names, Ava and Ariana. They no longer had a future.

It left me both heartbroken and disgusted.

I found it hard to even view the killer as a human any longer. Who randomly killed like this? And putting people who had just started their lives in harm's way...

I cried that night as I watched the T.V.

14.
THE KILLER

I was so tempted to let everyone in on the secret to come.

I knew that Quint would be shocked. In the best way possible. From my point of view at least.

I watched from afar as he talked to Cara at the Lafayette Reservoir. I didn't linger for long, but my blood boiled as I watched him enjoying his time with her.

It was the same feeling I'd had when I watched the Langleys walk across the street in Tiburon.

Rage. Fury. Madness.

Quint didn't deserve to be with a woman of her beauty.

I wondered if maybe I should have left him and Cara some cookies as well. It would have been so easy.

No, I enjoyed the game more with Quint around.

I preferred to kill him by a thousand paper cuts. I'd allow Quint to stay alive. For now.

I decided it was time to start writing another letter. All while planning my most personal murder to date.

Well, not personal to me, but to Quint. Which, in turn, made it personal to me.

15.

"Welcome! I'm Glenda Kintner. I've heard so much about you two."

Her red hair matched her bright red lipstick. Her smile was wide. She wore jeans and a lightweight pink sweater. She was probably in her fifties and still an attractive woman. The nice aura surrounding her stood out to me immediately.

"It's great to meet you." I extended my hand.

"You must be Cara," she said, and we all laughed.

Safe to say, we liked Ray's wife from the start.

"Come here, the real Cara," she said and gave my girlfriend a huge bear hug.

They lived in Rockridge, a residential neighborhood in Oakland. It was most famous for having a BART station and lots of cafes and restaurants lining its streets. A quiet area, it ran in slow motion compared to the rest of Oakland. I'm sure it was a nice change of pace for Ray.

The house itself was small and quaint. It had been painted gray, but every perimeter, be it windows or the front door, stood outlined in white. It was a clean, attractive home.

Ray and I shook hands and followed the women inside.

In the dining room, adjacent to the kitchen, we were seated by Ray.

"Dinner will be ready in about fifteen minutes," Glenda said. "Can I get you some wine to start with?"

"We'd love some," Cara said.

"We've got sauvignon blanc or a cab."

"Whatever you think pairs well with dinner."

"Cabernet it is."

I looked at the slats of the dining room table and could tell they'd shrunk it to make it more cozy for the four of us. The room itself was bright and inviting, with some artwork adorning the walls that I'm sure Glenda had picked out.

Ray was a great guy, but art enthusiasm was unlikely to be one of his hobbies.

"I really like your home," Cara said.

"Thanks, Cara! Sorry it's taken so long to have you over."

Glenda emerged from the kitchen with a bottle of wine. "This is a 1957 Rroja Reserva from a small village in Spain."

Cara and I looked at each other. And then Glenda started laughing.

"I'm kidding! It's some twenty-dollar bottle that I bought from Trader Joe's."

Glenda was a character. No doubt about that.

"Thanks, dear. And you guys are great company. I'd like to do this again soon."

"Let us host you guys."

"Okay. We could use a nice dinner away from home."

"Is that okay, Quint?" Cara asked.

"Of course," I said. "I've got this great hamburger surprise recipe I've been wanting to test out."

Glenda laughed.

Ray grabbed a few more plates and headed back toward the kitchen.

The night was winding down.

A few minutes later, we started to say our goodbyes.

"We'll have you over soon," I said.

"Thanks, Quint."

"No, thank you, Glenda. We had a spectacular time."

"I'm glad to hear it."

I gave Ray a hug as the women continued to talk in the corner.

"We'd be here all night if it was Cara's choice," I said.

"Glenda too."

"Thanks, Ray, we had a blast."

"You got it. I'll call you tomorrow."

I walked back over to the women.

"Alright, Cara, it's time we head back to Walnut Creek. Let's give Ray some time to do the dishes."

"See, he's learning already," Glenda said.

They hugged each other for a good ten seconds and we said our last goodbyes before stepping through the door.

It had been a splendid evening.

16

The third letter arrived the next day.

I got a screenshot from Ray, with a message that merely said *"Just received this."* There was no acknowledgement of our dinner the night before. I'm sure he was busy as hell.

It read:

Hello to the police, the media, and my friendly Bay Area neighbors.

Would you agree that artists get better over time?   Seems logical to me.   I promise to keep improving.   Sadly, I've been burdened with the moniker of the Bay Area Butcher.   I'm so much more than some savage with a knife (that was only one set of murders), but I guess I don't get to choose what name is bestowed upon me.   Time to move on I guess.

As you may have noticed, I didn't begin by mentioning cities.

I thought I might have given myself away, eliminating cities as we went.   That would be too obvious, even for the pathetic police departments of the Bay Area.

So now I'm putting everyone on watch.   Those hippies in Berkeley.   Concord. Los Gatos.   Fremont.   Burlingame.   Any of your cities may be next.

And as an artist becomes better, he branches out as well.   So my next killing will not be a home invasion.   Or a poisoning.   I'm thinking a drive-by.   Or in honor of the Zodiac, a school bus of children.

I can smell the fear now.

I'd like to thank the media for making me the most famous killer in the world at the moment. It's truly an honor. Just wait until they see what happens next.

Although it won't help catch me, I will stick to my edict of giving you the date.

And that date is…drumroll please…June 4th!

Happy Hunting!

The first thing I'd noticed was the excessive spacing between each sentence. This was the first letter in which he'd failed to mention me by name. But he'd given me the big middle finger by having five to six spaces at the conclusion of each sentence. I knew he intended that not-so-subtle dog whistle for me.

Second, his decision not to mention the original cities. Could he have listened to our conversation at the Lafayette Reservoir? Had he gotten close enough to attach another recording device on me?

I checked the clothes I'd worn at the reservoir. I found no recording device on them.

I called Cara and had her check. An excruciating few minutes passed as I waited for her to get back to me. I could handle a lot, but if he'd attached something to my girlfriend, that would have been too much.

To my relief, she spotted nothing on her clothes from that day.

I tried to focus on the letter. I couldn't let my mind wander. These first impressions mattered.

It was disgusting to mention a drive by shooting. And a school bus of children.

He likely meant to scare the already petrified Bay Area just a little more. And there was no doubt his comments would succeed at that. People's psyches were already frazzled. This would only make everything worse.

I hoped against hope the letter could be kept under wraps, but I knew that was next to impossible. Especially since the killer had been sending them to the evening news channels and the newspapers as well. His letter was bound to get out.

And it did. I sat alone in my apartment that night and watched the letter appear as the lead for the five o'clock local news. And I could just feel the tension ratcheting up, not to mention see it filling the faces of the local reporters.

It led the national news as well. The Bay Area had already become the focal point of the nation, and with another letter to "fawn" over, the media frenzy was only going to increase.

I, for one, did not look forward to it.

17.

The enemy of my enemy is my friend. So goes the saying. But what if that shared enemy is dead? Are they still your friend?

I decided to find out.

I showed up at Boyle's, a San Francisco grocery store, that next morning Paddy Roark was the reason.

Paddy had been integral in helping me find out the movements of Charles Zane. Which led to everything that followed.

It may not have been out of the goodness of his heart, since his boss Dennis McCarthy was a rival of Zane's, but they'd still come through for me.

And we'd established a bit of a bond. Dennis was the biggest bookie in the Bay Area, and Paddy his right-hand man. They likely resorted to some untoward collection practices from time to time, but I saw them as honorable people. They'd been nothing but candid with me.

But now that Zane was dead, I wanted to find out if they were still my friends.

I spotted Roark walking down one of the aisles. Boyle's was very Irish themed, with green and orange everywhere. Roark stopped in the corned beef section. As always, his intensity was off the charts. His eyes could melt steel. Easily one of the tougher-looking guys I'd ever come across.

"Quint. What do we owe this surprise to?" he said.

I was happy I'd become friendly with him. It made the intensity a little less intimidating.

"Hello, Paddy. It's been a long time."

"It sure has."

"I never got to properly thank you," I said.

He leaned in and whispered his response. "The fact that the police never came knocking was thanks enough."

"They'd have just thanked you for helping them out."

"Somehow, I think they'd have had more to say. But alas, they didn't show."

"Can we talk?" I asked.

"Of course," he said, knowing that the type of talking I referred to required some privacy.

The store was pretty quiet, but the last thing we needed was some nosy customer listening in on our conversation.

"Follow me," Paddy said. And I did.

We headed toward the back of the store like I'd done many times during the Charles Zane case. Roark led me through the revolving door past which customers were no longer permitted. We entered his office. Dennis McCarthy was sitting behind the computer. He looked splendid with his orange Vineyard Vines vest and a long-sleeved white T-shirt beneath it.

If I was meeting with the Beauty and the Beast of bookies, McCarthy was definitely the former.

"Quint, how are you?"

"Hello, Mr. McCarthy. I didn't know you were going to be here."

"I told you way back when to call me Dennis. That still stands."

"I'm sorry, Dennis."

"Don't worry about it. It's nice to see you, Quint. You became a stranger after we helped you."

"I thought that's what you'd prefer," I said.

Dennis finally stood up and shook my hand. "You're a smart lad. That was probably for the best."

"Thanks. And you're welcome."

"So what brings you here today?"

"Should we sit?" I asked.

"No, let's stand," Dennis McCarthy said.

While I'd become friendly with the two men before me, these tough dudes liked to show their dominant side. There was no valid reason to remain standing, but Dennis wanted it known that he'd make the suggestions, not me.

"Fair enough," I said. "This likely won't surprise you guys, but I've found myself in the middle of a pickle again."

"Yeah, we know," Paddy Roark said.

The surprise must have shown on my face.

"C'mon, Quint," Dennis said. "I hope you remember who you're talking to. You don't think we've seen the letters that went to the police?"

The media never read the letters verbatim and mercifully had kept my name off the news, so I hadn't expected anyone to know. But these guys...

"I should have guessed," I said.

"Yes, you should have," Dennis said, putting me in my place. "Always remember, our eyes and ears are everywhere."

"Do they happen to have seen or heard anything about the killer?" I asked.

"Is that why you're here?"

"Yes. We're at a dead end and the next murder is coming up quick."

"First off, we didn't give the killer the recording device he used on you."

We all had a short-lived laugh. The irony that a recording device had helped me take down Charles Zane, but now another had been used on me by the Butcher, was not lost on any of us.

"Wish you had. That would make this easy."

"We only give recording devices to people named after shark hunters from the movie *Jaws*."

"I'm touched."

"This killer is a stain on this great area. And we'd love to help the police catch him. But as for what you want us to do, I'm at a loss."

"I don't know exactly. I'm trying to help, but besides Detective Kintner, I can't get much from the police. You guys are powerful and know people. Just thought I'd ask."

"If we knew anything, we'd go straight to the police. This is a serial killer, after all. Not some deadbeat gambler we can deal with ourselves," Paddy said.

Dennis was the boss, but Paddy was the furthest thing from a wilting flower. He didn't need permission to speak.

I told them, "I think the guy is in his twenties, in good shape, from the Bay, and as you must know, he's been mentioned in one of my articles."

"We know. As I said, we've read the letters, Quint."

I didn't like being treated like a kid, but they were right; they'd already made it clear they knew everything.

Dennis said bluntly, "Everyone is grasping at straws. Ourselves included. I think we're going to have to wait till this guy fucks up."

"I don't want to wait that long."

"You have no choice," he said, and I once again felt like a scolded child.

Paddy Roark decided to play mediator. I imagine that didn't happen very often.

"We'd love to help you, Quint. But we've got nothing. Nor do the cops, so it's not like we're in the minority. If we learn anything, we'll tell the cops and then tell you."

"Thanks," I said. "I'm not sure what I expected coming here."

"It was good seeing you, if that's any consolation."

"We did good work with Charles Zane, didn't we?"

"You did the work," Dennis said. "We just gave you a little push in the right direction."

While it was fun reminiscing, I knew the visit wasn't going to pay any dividends.

"Nice to see you guys again."

"You too, Quint. I don't think we've seen the worst of this psychopath, and he seems to have a hard-on for you. Be safe, you hear?"

I shook their hands and left with a worse feeling than I'd entered with.

18.

Before I knew it, June 4th had arrived. I'd gone by the *Walnut Creek Times* and looked through some more old articles. As usual, however, nothing jumped out.

I could have done it at home from my computer, but I'd hoped being at the paper itself might help jog my memory. It didn't.

I gave my mother a call. She was on pins and needles, knowing it was the day the killer was supposed to strike. The media had talked about the date since the letter came out, so everyone in the Bay Area had gone on high alert. With all of us as vigilant as possible, hopefully, this would lead to a citizen seeing something and alerting the police.

I invited Cara over, but she said she preferred to stay at her apartment. I think she actually wanted to see me, but was trying to prove that the Bay Area Butcher wasn't getting to her, even though the creep was getting to everyone. I appreciated her stubbornness. It's one of the traits of hers that I loved.

But I still wished she'd come over and stayed with me. I pleaded a second time, but she remained resolute.

Ray gave me a call around six p.m.

"Hello?"

"Staying safe, Quint?"

"I am."

"I'm always nervous on these days, obviously. But especially for you, since you seem to be the apple of this psycho's eye."

"I'm alone in my apartment. You don't have to worry about me."

"I figured you'd have Cara close."

"I tried. She's trying to show how tough she is."

Ray laughed. "We've both got great women."

"Didn't get to tell you how much fun we had the other night. Thanks so much!"

"You were plenty complimentary throughout dinner. But I appreciate it. Glenda loved you both dearly. I think she and Cara have a similar tough-girl streak."

"Your wife was delightful," I said.

"That's true," Ray agreed. "But that doesn't mean she doesn't have a tough streak."

"I can't argue with that."

"Listen, Quint. I was thinking."

"Congrats."

"Don't be a smart-ass."

"Sorry. What is it?"

"I think you should get your Private Investigator's license. You're good at this stuff. And while you may not admit it, I think you enjoy the chase. You'd never have a dull moment. And as good a writer as you are, I'm sure that can be a little boring at times."

"I can't argue with that either. You really think it's something I'd be good at?"

"There's no doubt. You took down the bastard Charles Zane almost singlehandedly, and you've had the best suspicions about the Bay Area Butcher. So the answer to your question is a resounding yes. You'd be very good."

"Is it time consuming to get your license?"

"Do you have a nine-to-five I don't know about?"

"Your point is taken."

"Start doing some of the little stuff each day. I bet you could get your license in six months if you put your mind to it."

"I appreciate your confidence in me, Ray."

"It's warranted."

"Thanks."

"Start tonight."

"I'll start tomorrow, if you don't mind. Hard for me to concentrate knowing this is supposed to be the night of a killing."

"I understand," he said ruefully. "But don't let a day become a week, then a month. Get on this soon. You won't regret it."

"Thanks for everything, Ray. If I have any questions, can I hit you up?"

"You already know the answer to that."

"I do. Cheers."

"I've got to run. As you may have guessed, we've got a long night ahead of us."

"Stay safe, Ray."

"You too, Quint. Take care."

"See you, buddy."

I called Cara a third time, but she was staying put. I respected her for it, even if I didn't like the decision.

I sent her a goodnight text at eleven p.m. and she quickly responded in kind. I went to bed that night with a certain peace. At least, as much peace as you could feel with a serial killer on the loose.

19.
THE KILLER

The degree of difficulty involved in the impending murder should be nothing after the first two sets of killings.

The home invasion of the Langleys brought many potential threats. A failure to contain the family. One of them breaking free. A neighbor walking by and hearing something. A family member with a weapon. A cell phone call to 9-1-1. And surely others I hadn't thought about.

The cookies were a different animal, but also very risky. Roaming that neighborhood, slowly and deliberately, setting the plates full of cookies on doorsteps. I had to make sure I wasn't seen up close. My hoodie, hat, and glasses helped in that regard. And obviously, I'd timed it for after sunset.

So killing a single individual should be easy in comparison. But that didn't mean I didn't have to be careful. I was infamous worldwide and I didn't want it to end. I wasn't going to be dethroned by a silly mistake. Especially in something as relatively simple as what was to come.

I looked down at my watch.

Soon.

20.

I woke up at six the next morning and received a phone call less than ten minutes later. It was from a 510 number that I didn't recognize. Usually I would just let it go to voicemail, but with all that was going on, and being that it was an Oakland phone number, I knew I had to answer.

"Hello?"

"Is this Quint?"

"Yeah. Who's this?"

"It's Captain Lockett from the OPD."

"Hi, Captain. Did the killer strike?"

I figured he'd call for that reason. I was somewhat surprised not to hear the news from Ray, but he'd probably had a long night. Maybe he was even still sleeping. It was just after six a.m., after all.

"He struck alright. Ray is dead. He was shot outside of his home last night. The psycho fucking killed one of my best friends. And yours."

I didn't say anything for several seconds. I wasn't in denial, I just couldn't come up with any words that could do the occasion justice.

Ray Kintner, my good friend, was dead. A man who had helped save my life.

I'd talked to him less than ten hours previous. I'd had dinner with him and his wife just a few days ago.

I was heartbroken. Devastated. Shocked. Grief-stricken.

And fifty other words that still wouldn't do his loss justice.

I bowed my head, although I wanted to throw it back and yell at the top of my lungs. But I knew I had to control my emotions or I wouldn't be able to get through the phone call.

"What happened?" I finally asked.

"He got off a little after eleven p.m. after a long day investigating. He drove straight home. Ray was supposed to be off at eight, but knowing the killer was out there, he wanted to stay on as late as he could. Finally, by eleven, he was exhausted, so he was told to go home. And he was ambushed when he got there. His wife Glenda heard the shots and called 9-1-1."

"Can I go see her?" I asked.

I'd only met Glenda the one memorable time, but I knew that Ray would have wanted someone to look after her.

"She's at the precinct, surrounded by scores of Ray's fellow officers. This wouldn't be the right time."

"I understand."

out concrete information, you can call us, but you will not be included in our investigation any longer."

I looked for any defenders in the room, but nobody stepped forward. I couldn't tell if they believed in what the chief said or were just afraid to stand up to him. Regardless, I was now persona non grata within the Oakland Police Department. I could live with that, and almost understood it, but not being invited to Ray's funeral delivered a punch to the stomach.

"Is there anything else?" I said.

"No, you can go now," Chief Ronson said.

I looked over at Captain Lockett, who gave me a slight nod of his head. It told me two things: One, he didn't feel the same as the chief. And two, he wasn't going to let those feelings be known.

I was on my own.

And seemingly expelled from having anything to do with the OPD.

21.

The next several days were spent grieving. Alone.

The funeral for Ray took place on June 7th, three days after his murder.

I hadn't been able to make my peace with not being invited. In fact, it incensed me. I was willing to bet I'd been friendlier with Ray than 95% of his fellow officers. How many of them had been invited over for dinner recently? Probably none.

But the last thing I wanted to do was create a commotion at his funeral. What if I was escorted from the proceedings as the cameras rolled? Thoughts like these kept me from showing up unannounced. Instead, I watched the ceremony live on T.V. like everyone else in the Bay Area.

Just when I thought my eyes couldn't cry anymore, they started bawling as I saw Glenda, dressed in all black, sitting in the first row. The tears continued to flow as the speakers shared their memories of what a great man Ray was. And finally, when the twenty-one-gun salute resounded for their fallen comrade, I lost it one final time.

Glenda did not speak herself, although both of their children did.

I decided that I needed to call her soon. I'd heeded the OPD's wishes and avoided the funeral. But I knew if Ray was looking down on me, he'd want me to reach out to his wife.

So I would.

The day after the funeral, I finally got the courage up.

"Kintner residence."

Courage or not, I almost lost it right there.

"Glenda, this is Quint."

A slight pause followed, and I wondered if she was pissed at me for waiting so long to contact her. Or for contacting her at all. Maybe my disinvitation from Ray's funeral hadn't only been the OPD's idea, although I hated to think that.

"Why didn't you come to the funeral, Quint? Over the last year, he was as close to you as anyone."

"Trust me, I wanted to. But the OPD made it clear they didn't want me there."

"Because you'd be a distraction?"

"Partly. But mainly because they don't see me as one of them. I'm the outsider and they are tired of me always crashing their party."

I immediately regretted the term I'd used.

"Ray would have said fuck the guys who didn't want you there."

"Yes, he would have. Maybe I should have just shown up unannounced," I said, leaving out the party-crashing metaphor this time.

And I heard Glenda Kintner's laugh. I can't imagine there had been many of those recently and it made me feel good.

"Ray would have liked that. Sure, he was a proud member of the police department, but he didn't believe in all that 'You're not one of us' bullshit. He liked everyone. Especially you."

"And everyone liked him. Especially me," I said.

"Thanks, Quint."

"Look, Glenda, the OPD is going to make sure that I'm no longer part of this investigation. And I'll respect their wishes, but that doesn't mean I want to lose contact with you. Can Cara and I take you out to dinner sometime soon?"

"Of course. It's going to be pretty lonely around here."

And that's when I thought of something. I'd bring my mother to that dinner. For all the wrong reasons, she had a lot in common with Glenda Kintner. Widowed, and widowed in the worst way possible. I didn't know if Glenda would want to open up about her grief, but my mother could certainly listen and sympathize.

"I'd like to bring my mom as well, if that's okay?" I asked.

"That would be fine."

"I'll call you soon and set up a time."

"Thanks, Quint."

"And I'd just like to let you know that Ray was a phenomenal man. I loved him dearly. He not only saved my life, but became a great friend. I'll miss him every day."

"So will I."

The tears were about to come once again, so I decided to get off the phone.

"Take care, Glenda. I'll see you soon."

"Thanks for calling, Quint."

I tried to spend the next few days remembering the great friendship I had with Ray. While at the same time trying to ignore the madness overtaking our beautiful section of Northern California.

The Bay Area Butcher ruled the first fifteen minutes of any half-hour local news program. He seemed to consume everything. And they'd inevitably show pictures of Ray, so I tried to avoid the news whenever possible.

And no new letter had been posted from the Butcher, so the news was just rehashing events I didn't want to rehash.

Instead, I remembered the good times we'd had. How Ray had saved my life. How he'd accepted me when most of his fellow officers in the OPD had not. How he'd invited Cara and me into his home, the nicest gesture of all.

I was on my third level of grief. First, you're shocked. Then you grieve and feel terrible for the friend you have lost. And finally, that gives way to a form of acceptance. And when that occurs, you can go back and relish the great times you shared.

That's what I tried to concentrate on now. Which doesn't mean I wasn't still livid and eager to rip the heart of the Bay Area Butcher. But I was trying to focus on the nice times I'd had with Ray.

I remembered first meeting him outside of the house in Oakland where Griff Bauer had been murdered. How, at first, I thought he was just some old, washed-up police officer. How he started to grow on me and how we developed a nice back-and-forth. How our friendship seemingly ended when he arrested me for a murder I didn't commit. How he redeemed himself (and then some), by saving my life out at sea.

And how all of that had led to a great friendship over the last year or so. Which had culminated in finally meeting his wife, someone it seems he rarely introduced anyone to.

I grieved for Glenda more than I did for myself. I'd been friends with Ray for a year. They'd been married for close to three decades and had raised two children together. It must have been unimaginably tough on her. Just as it had been on my own mother.

After Ray's funeral, I tried to spend some time smelling the flowers. Watching the birds. Enjoying the sunrise. And just taking in the finer things in life that we so often take for granted. Life is short, and I'd been reminded of that, so I tried to soak in everything around me.

And I have to say, somewhere in the sadness, those were a peaceful, tranquil few days.

That tranquility proved short lived, vanishing when I approached my apartment one day.

A letter fluttered, pinned to my front door. I'd already paid rent for June, so this shouldn't be some sort of reminder of that. Maybe it reported a maintenance issue for the complex. With four buildings and hundreds of tenants, that happened quite often.

I removed the red tack holding it up and grabbed the letter. I opened my apartment door and threw the tack in the garbage.

I opened the letter and my heart froze.

At the top, written by hand, was the following:

I didn't see you at the funeral, Quint. My guess is the OPD is pushing you away. So, I decided to hand-deliver a letter myself. This will be sent to the usual suspects as well. And I'm sorry about Ray...but he had to go.

My hands started shaking so badly that I dropped the letter. I picked it back up and, trying to hold myself steady, I read the printed section below his personal note.

Three down, two to go. It was a nice little funeral you guys threw, but where was Quint? Ray enjoyed his company more than all of you fellow shitty cops. And I do mean that. What kind of cop lets a stranger kill him outside of his house? Especially with all that's going on. Just pathetic. Maybe Ray didn't deserve to live.

I think all of you are catastrophically inept at your jobs. Which is good for me. It could even mean I'll go on killing forever. But I've only got two more for this summer. And then I'm going to vanish for awhile.

Not forever, mind you. I'll return at some point and start a new killing spree. You see, I'm the smartest serial killer there has ever been. I know that if you just go on killing and killing, you will eventually be caught. So after my next two sets of murders, I'll be going underground for a while.

And you'll never find me. But when I do pop back up, everyone will say just how pathetic the Bay Area police forces are. You'll be laughingstocks to the entire world. If you aren't already!

Just a final reminder before I go: The death of Ray may cut deep, but it's going to be a picnic compared to the final two sets of murders. No more killing of a lone cop. Time to step up my game. There will be lots of victims. And I do mean lots.

Happy Hunting!

I set the letter down, careful not to touch anything but the corners. I grabbed a paper towel and used it to fish in the garbage for the tack, which I set on top of the letter.

My mind rocketed and ricocheted in a million different directions.

I'd only been gone a half hour, drinking a coffee at the Starbucks downstairs. A few of the baristas had become friendly with Ray and we'd spent a few minutes reminiscing about him.

So the killer had been outside my apartment very recently. That scared me, there's no way around it.

There were two things I had to do.

I dialed a number.

"Oakland Police Department."

"I need to talk to Captain Lockett."

"May I please ask who's calling?"

"Quint Adler. It's extremely important."

Thirty seconds later, Lockett came on the phone. "Quint, I thought we made it clear we'd call you if needed."

There was no point getting into that right now. "The Butcher was just at my apartment."

"What?"

"He thumbtacked a letter to my door. I saved the letter and the tack."

"Have you called the local police?"

"Not yet. No offense to the Walnut Creek police, but I thought of calling you first."

"I'll call them right now and coordinate something. Stay at your complex We'll be there soon. What number are you?"

"481."

"We'll see you soon."

Now to the other thing I had to do. I walked down the hallway carefully, not to say nervously, and took the elevator to the first floor.

Usually, four or five employees of Avalon would be working at the front desk, but I only saw Kayla when I approached. That was fine. The fewer people, the better.

And I knew I had to watch what I said. No reason to let them know what had happened. That could wait until the police arrived.

"Hey, Quint," she said, looking up at me.

"Hi, Kayla. I know this is going to be a weird question, but do we have cameras outside Avalon?"

"No, we don't. Can I ask why?"

I tried to keep a causal tone as I lied, "Just saw a guy who looked like a troublemaker roaming the fourth floor. Wanted to see if he had left the building."

She frowned. "I'm sorry, Quint. We don't have cameras. But if you want to file a report with the police, they could be on the lookout for him."

"Alright. Thanks, Kayla."

That had amounted to absolutely nothing.

I headed back toward my apartment, knowing it was going to be treated like a crime scene shortly.

Soon members of the Walnut Creek police started arriving, followed by the OPD ten minutes later. A few local sheriffs came as well.

I realized this could take awhile.

I called Cara and asked her if she wanted to come over. I didn't tell her why.

Ten minutes later, she was walking down my hallway. I'd planted myself outside of my apartment and headed in her direction, meeting her halfway between my door and the elevators.

"What the hell happened?" she asked.

"The killer left a note on my apartment door."

Cara looked at me and her expression said it all.

But she also spoke, making a good point: "Can we take a cruise around the world and just get the hell out of the Bay Area? We're in the line of fire. The letters mention you. Ray's been murdered. And now the creep who killed him comes by your apartment?"

I really had no comeback. She was right.

I was in harm's way. And maybe she was too. And maybe my mother. I shuddered at the thought.

"We'll talk about it, but let me see if they need anything else first."

I approached the officers. Two of them stood at the front door, using a device to dust for fingerprints. Six other officers wandered around in my apartment, but I'm not sure exactly what they were doing since the killer had never set foot inside.

Freddie Fields approached me. He was the only one I recognized. He led me to the corner of my living room. Cara was within earshot, but she didn't follow us.

"How long did you say you were gone for?"

"About thirty minutes," I said.

I'd answered these questions when the Walnut Creek PD arrived first, but I'd liked Freddie and didn't mind talking to him.

"And where did you go?"

"The Starbucks downstairs. Some of the baristas had gotten to know Ray and we started talking about him."

Freddie nodded. "I know how much he meant to you, Quint. And he was a friend to me as well." I believed him on both counts. Ray had liked him and I'm sure he was crushed. His sympathy also seemed genuine.

"I know, Freddie. It's all so terrible. You and Ray coming by the *Walnut Creek Times* seems like it happened a lifetime ago."

"It certainly does. Now, where would you exit when you left the apartment complex?"

"I got off the elevator at the first floor and walked through the parking garage to the Starbucks."

"So if someone was parked down there, they would have seen you walk out."

"Yes. Is that what you're thinking?"

"I doubt the killer would risk leaving that note unless he knew you were gone. What if you had been inside and heard him putting the tack in your door? Way too risky for a guy who has been so diligent to this point."

"Yeah, you're right."

"How about getting into the complex? Would he need a key?"

"You need a fob to get into the complex. Hypothetically."

"Hypothetically?"

"There's always people going in and out. And no one says anything if you just follow someone in. If he saw me leave, it would be fairly easy to wait a minute or two and follow the next person in. My girlfriend just got up here without a fob," I said, motioning to Cara.

"And you didn't see anyone suspicious when you left the complex or when you returned?"

"No. A few people were on the elevator, but I recognized them as tenants. And I didn't see anyone suspicious walking inside or outside the complex."

That was the truth, despite what I'd told Kayla earlier.

"Alright. We're going to need another hour here."

"I'm going to go for a walk with my girlfriend," I said.

"Stay close, just in case we need you. In fact, give me your number, Quint." I did, said goodbye, and then went to Cara.

"Where are we going?" she asked.

"I need some fresh air. Let's go for a walk."

We headed out of the apartment and took the elevator downstairs.

Across the street from Avalon was the Iron Horse Trail, which I often ran along. I took Cara's hand and led her in that direction.

While my initial plan was to go for a walk, a lot of people were currently using the trail, strolling or jogging, and I didn't need anyone hearing what was going to say.

A few vacant park benches sat about twenty feet from the trail itself. "Let's go sit down," I said.

Cara followed me there, but I could tell she was tense. She never kept this quiet.

We sat down and watched a few people run by.

"I wish I could be like them right now," I said. "Not a worry in the world."

"What are you going to do, Quint? I remember you said this wasn't going to be like last year, but it's exactly like last year. You have this monster's attention."

I put my head in my hands, propped up, barely, by my elbows on the park bench.

"What can I do?" I asked.

"I'm on summer break now, so we really could travel around the world until this ends."

"I don't exactly have a travel-the-world budget."

"We won't be gone that long. The guy has said he's committing five sets of murders. That's only two more. We can return when he finishes."

"We're going to believe what some psycho says? And worse than that, we're going to have our lives dictated by him?"

By Cara's expression I knew she agreed with me on the last point. We couldn't change our lives just because of this asshole.

"Okay, fine, I'll grant you that. But what? We can't just keep things as is. He knows where you live."

Just then, a group of five bikers sailed by along the path. I'd never liked the idea of bikers and runners doing their respective endeavors on the same narrow strip of pavement. It was a recipe for disaster. Bikers should have stayed on the streets and let runners and walkers have the trail. I reined in my wandering mind and looked back at Cara.

"He won't come back to my place. He'll assume we have the apartment videotaped from now on."

"Seems like he took a pretty big risk to me. How could he know you guys didn't have cameras?"

"He wouldn't know. But he may have seen all the people who walk out every few minutes and figured he'd blend in. Maybe he was wearing a hoodie, I don't know. And I guarantee you one thing. He was wearing gloves. The officers won't find anything useful at my apartment."

"How do you know?"

"Because this guy is ultra careful. He's not going to get caught doing something like this. It's not going to be that easy for us."

"God, I hope you're wrong."

"So do I. But I'm not. We're either going to have to do great detective work to catch him or get lucky. It won't be a fuck-up by him. And certainly not something as small as forgetting to wear gloves."

Cara looked on pensively.

"Then why don't we do it?" she asked.

"Do what?"

"Become quote-unquote 'detectives' and pour everything we have into catching him."

A smile, both excited and incredulous, stretched across my face. "You're serious?" I asked.

"I am."

My smile vanished, although the excitement remained inside me. "We're not going to get much help from the local police departments. I can promise you that."

"It will just be us."

Against all better judgement, I was intrigued.

"Did I tell you the last thing Ray ever said to me?"

"No."

"He told me I should become a private detective. He said I loved the action and there'd never be a dull day."

"Was he right? About the action, I mean."

"I think so," I said.

"Then let's do it. I hate to sound so pragmatic at a time like this, but I've got the whole summer off. This maniac's murders will surely end before I have to go back to teaching. Especially if we step in to stop him. We could do this."

"You're right. You are being way too pragmatic."

She smiled.

"You didn't say no," she said.

"We're both crazy, you know that? We are going to be investigating the worst serial killer this area has seen since the Zodiac."

"If we're going by body count, he's already much worse."

"You're always a step ahead."

"Then let's be a step ahead of this asshole!" Cara said vehemently.

I couldn't argue with that and didn't want to.

"Alright, I'm in," I said.

"Where do we start?" Cara said.

"Once the police leave, we'll make my apartment our investigative headquarters. I'll make a storyboard, just like I did with Zane."

"Sounds good."

"There's one disclaimer, however."

"Anything," Cara said.

"You have to move in with me. At least until this is over. I can't trust that you'd be safe out there on your own. He's found me, he could find you. At least if you're at my apartment, I can try and protect you. And as I said earlier, I don't think he'll be coming back to Avalon."

"You know I've always wanted to move in together. I can safely say this wasn't how I thought I'd finally finagle it, though."

We laughed together.

"You know what," she said, "I do want to take that walk. Let's go."

I grabbed her hand and we stood up from the park bench. The police were going to be in my apartment a while longer. I'd spend that time walking the Iron Horse Trail with my new roommate.

22.

The police left soon after we got back from our walk. Before they did, I asked Freddie if they had found anything useful, and despite saying he couldn't discuss it with me, he gave me a slight shake of the head. Which told me all I needed to know. And what I'd expected, anyway. The Bay Area Butcher was way too smart to get caught that easily.

Once they left, Cara got started.

We spent the evening decorating my bedroom wall. And by decorating, I meant putting up letters, timeframes, and murder locations of this killer.

I knew it was going to cause me some sleepless nights. But I did it anyway. For Ray. For the Langleys. For the victims in San Jose. Which still was hard to fathom. Dead because you ate some laced cookies. Just horrible.

And most of all, for the chance that we wouldn't have to add another family of victims to the collage.

Its location, directly in my line of sight if I sat up in bed, wasn't very subtle. Which is how I wanted it.

If Cara and I were truly going to do everything we could to stop the next murders, it should be on our minds at all times. Not hidden in some corner of my apartment. And so there it was, taking up an entire wall of my bedroom.

"Should I hang the map of the Bay Area above all the evidence?" Cara asked.

"Actually, let's put it below. I like having the evidence right at eye level," I said.

Cara approached this the right way. She wasn't excited or pretending this was some great adventure we were going on. She knew the risks. And there would likely be some more heartbreak to come, although nothing could be as bad as losing Ray. At least, I hoped not.

We added a picture of Ray in the corner of the collage, along with the other victims. They served both an extremely sad reminder and a message to keep pushing. To prevent the next Ray.

"How about some of the headlines from the newspapers?" Cara asked.

We'd gone to the library, asked to look at the old newspapers, and made photocopies of them. My favorite elderly librarian had been nowhere to be seen. Luckily.

"We can include them, but they don't add much, so put them out on the edges."

"Alright. And how about putting up individual maps of Walnut Creek and San Francisco? Since those are the last two cites of the five he originally mentioned."

"Yeah, I like that idea. He's now mentioned other cities, but I've got a sneaking suspicion that SF and Walnut Creek are still his preferred targets."

"I'll print them out," she said.

My printer was getting more usage than it had in months.

"It's really starting to take shape," I said.

Cara came and put her arms on my shoulders as I looked over the collage. My eyes instinctively kept going to the picture of Ray, and I think she could sense this.

"He would be proud of you," Cara said.

I thought about our last conversation. "I'm going to start taking those steps to becoming a private investigator."

"Good. I'm not sure how long the process takes, but maybe we'll earn some advantages."

"I almost definitely won't become certified before this thing plays out, but it can only help us if I'm taking classes or in the process of legally becoming one."

Cara swiveled me around and I knew she had something important to say.

"After our walk today, I called my sister."

"And?"

"And I told her I was going to cancel our trip to Austin."

"There's always a chance the guy is caught before then. It's June 10th, we've still got two weeks."

"Do you think we are going to be good company after looking at this collage every day? Diving deep into the mind of the most famous serial killer in the world?"

"Okay, I get your point."

"We can reschedule for later this summer if we want to."

I paused, making sure that part of the conversation was over. Once I felt sure it was, I shifted to a new topic, asking, "Cara, from what we know, do you think this guy is a recluse or an outgoing, normal guy? Obviously, he could be something in between, but if he was one of those extremes, which one would it be?"

She pondered the question for a good thirty seconds, her eyes flickering over the collage and past it.

"Normal," she said at last. "In the sense of outgoing. Maybe even more outgoing than normal. The way he writes the letters, with seemingly no fear of the police or the public, makes me think he's got a high opinion of himself. He doesn't strike me as a virgin living in his parents' basement."

I nodded.

"Does that mean you agree?" she asked.

"I do. I've thought about it a great deal, but I think you're right. This guy likes a show. I almost think he wants to be found out. Not caught, but have his name up in lights. He's a showman, and that's much more characteristic of an outgoing guy than a recluse."

"I'm glad we agree. But how does that help us?"

"I'm not sure yet. But every little tidbit helps us form an overall view of the guy."

Cara approached the collage. It was sure to get bigger, but it already stretched about eight feet wide and four feet tall.

She moved closer to the copies of killer's letters, which we'd enlarged before printing out.

"The secret lies in these messages. They read almost like a puzzle. And he mentioned in the first letter that he would leave clues in each of them. I'm not talking about the obvious ones like leaving the date. Or mentioning he's in one of your articles."

"You're right. But I've read each of them so many times. Maybe, as we gain more information, something will jump out."

I leaned in next to Cara and started reading the letters one more time. Nothing took.

"What should we do with all of your articles? Obviously, there's way too many to pin all of them to the wall."

"Let's build a little drop basket and we can put my articles in there. So we can have them close and read through them whenever we want to."

"Sounds good. That should be easy enough," Cara said.

She walked to the front of my apartment and returned a minute later with a basket.

"Sorry, you're going to have to find another place to store your mail. This thing is going up on the wall."

"This is fun," I said. "Not a fun subject, obviously, but I'm enjoying doing this with you."

Cara hugged me with one arm, still holding the basket in the other. "So am I. We're doing this for Ray."

I looked at the picture of him on my wall. He was a good man gone way too soon.

"We're going to avenge your death, Ray," I promised out loud. "We're coming for this asshole."

23.
THE KILLER

Ali had Frazier. Palmer had Nicklaus. Evert had Navratilova.
Where was my rival?
I felt like Michael Jordan in a world of Karl Malones.
Quint certainly wasn't shaping up as one. He hadn't done a single
thing to prove he was on my level.
Of course, I was an exceptionally talented rival. One who'd prepared
for this for years. Maybe I asked too much in hoping he could rise to
meet me. Or at least something approaching my level.
Maybe Cara would be my rival. I watched her entering Avalon Walnut
Creek with some pads, papers, and printouts. Was she trying to join the
investigation and help Quint out? Boy, how I hoped that was true.
Ray had been the only murder I'd planned to personally affect Quint.
And with only two sets of murders left until I vanished for a while, I
couldn't be sure killing the beautiful Cara would fit in the cards.
But fuck, I sure would love to.
Maybe I could make a few alterations to my final murder. The coup
de grâce that would have the world talking.
Not the Bay Area. Not California. Not the United States. The world!
Of course, I was still in final planning stages for the second to last
murder. And that wasn't going to be anything to wince at.
It would be a Picasso in its own right.

24.

Not all investigative work was sexy. Both in the journalistic field and now, in my prospective new field as a private investigator.

I'd gotten the really boring stuff out of the way early in the day, when I went online and researched getting my license. It seemed like it would be a laborious process, and I most certainly wouldn't obtain it while the Bay Area Butcher remained at large.

But there would be more cases down the line, and I had to lay the groundwork by doing the paperwork. Oh, fun.

The start of our investigation into the Bay Area Butcher didn't prove much more exciting.

We started looking at every single person I'd ever mentioned in print while working for the *Walnut Creek Times*. We would do follow-ups and try to find either the person themself or a relative to verify that they weren't out massacring people.

We started at the beginning. While my articles had never been uniformly fascinating reads, the early articles were particularly boring.

My first two articles reported on a set of T.V.s stolen from a parked flatbed truck and a recap of a junior varsity basketball game.

"Yeah, but the way you described that game-winning free throw was spectacular."

I was happy to have Cara with me, even with her sly comments.

"It's the sign of a talented writer," I said. "They teach you in journalism classes that if you can make a free throw exciting, you can do anything."

"Even a JV free throw?"

"Low blow," I said, but her snicker turned out to be contagious. I hadn't expected that we'd enjoy ourselves this much.

"And this stolen T.V.s piece. They should have rewarded you a lifetime Pulitzer if there's such a thing."

"Yeah, laugh it up. Wait till we get to my stolen bike articles. Those were my forte."

"You'd be the Hemingway of stolen bike free throw shooters."

I couldn't help but laugh some more.

"I'm sorry. I had to," Cara said.

"I'm a big man. I can take it."

"You mention the man who makes the winning free throw by name. Are we going to follow up with him?"

"Yes," I said. "He never said the article had to be about him committing a crime. The guy was in high school nine years ago and probably still has local ties. He should be easy to find. What's his name again?"

Cara looked down at the article.

"Mason Weatherly."

"Alright, let's start making a list. Write down the person's name, what he was mentioned for, and the date the article was published. This can build a master list over the next few days. Then we'll search the internet or make some phone calls and try to find out what's happened to these people."

"I think we should do it a little differently," Cara said.

"Alright, what do you got?"

"Time is of the essence with this killer. No, we don't know when he's going to strike again, but we know he's out there, probably doing prep work for his next set of murders. Why wait until we finish a master list to start finding out what happened to these people?"

"Point taken. How do you propose we do it?"

"You can start amassing the names, dates, etc. And I'll start doing research and find their phone numbers, and as soon as I find one, I'll call it"

"Smart," I said. "In fact, it's probably better we have you calling anyway. People would rather give up some information to your sweet voice than mine."

"Your gravelly voice?"

"My voice is not gravelly."

"Okay, Quint. It's a pristine configuration of perfect harmonies."

"You should have been the writer."

"I don't do free throws."

I started laughing some more. Considering all that was going on, it was a welcome if unexpected reaction.

For our lunch break, we went down to a local bar/restaurant called Hops and Scotch. With a name like that, you'd think it was all booze, but they had some above-average bar food.

The little outdoor patio was perfect when the weather was nice. And in Walnut Creek, that was almost always the case. Especially in mid-June.

We waited to be seated and the waiter showed us to our table of two. I ordered for both of us, having eaten at Hops and Scotch fifty times: first, a Burrata plate that had sun-dried tomatoes, arugula, and a rosemary sourdough baguette. We'd follow up with a chicken quesadilla that had become my go-to dish.

After I ordered, I told Cara I had to make a phone call. I walked out on the sidewalk running parallel to Treat Boulevard. Cars went sailing by me as I dialed and listened to the ring tone.

"Oakland Police Department."

"Yes, this is Quint Adler. I've called three times for Captain Lockett."

"I'm sorry, the captain isn't in right now."

"Alright. Will you please have him call me?"

"Sure. But I can't guarantee when. He's busy trying to catch the man who killed Ray."

I hung up the phone before I said something I'd regret. The officer who answered had obviously added his last line to twist the knife in me. Fury killed my appetite, but I walked back into Hops and Scotch, where they'd just set the burrata plate down in front of Cara.

"What's wrong?" she asked at the look on my face.

"The OPD is still giving me the cold shoulder."

"We'll have to bring something to them that they can't ignore."

"I'd rather do it myself," I said, still pissed.

"They can do a lot of things we can't, Quint. Arrests. Warrants. Need I mention them all?"

"No," I said succinctly.

"I know you were a one man tour de force when it came to taking down Charles Zane. But let's be honest, we're probably going to need the OPD or if not them, any other Bay Area PD to take down the Butcher."

I looked around. Luckily we had enough space between us and the closest group of people. This wasn't a conversation I wanted others to be privy to.

"I've got no problem with that, Cara. But it's hard to work with them if they keep ignoring my calls."

"I understand. So let's find something concrete on this psycho. Then they'll have to take our calls."

"You're very convinced that we're going to. I just feel like we're trying to find the proverbial needle in a haystack. If we get ahold of Free Throw Guy's parents, are they going to tell us they have suspicions that their twenty-something son is actually the most famous killer in the world right now?"

"We'll never know unless we follow up on each case."

I looked across the table at Cara and realized she was being much more professional then me.

"As usual, you're right. Sorry for being a stick in the mud."

"Don't worry about it. When I'm down, make sure you prop me up."

"Of course. How's the burrata?"

"Delicious. Like every other cheese in the world."

"Amen to that. Never met one I didn't like."

"Put a sun-dried tomato on top and then put it on the baguette. Delicious."

"Oh, is that how this is supposed to work? I thought we ate them all separately."

She laughed at my joke and my anger with the OPD evaporated. Kind of like the burrata plate, which was finished in seconds.

The quesadilla arrived next and we started going to town on that.

"We can order in next time," I said.

"No, I like this," Cara said. "If we're going to be shacked up for awhile, i would be nice to get out and enjoy some fresh air. Let's eat outside wher possible."

"I'm fine with that."

And I grabbed a slice of the quesadilla, for a moment thinking of nothing but how delicious the chicken and melted cheese would be in my mouth.

I finally got a return call from Captain Lockett later that afternoon.

"Hello?"

"Quint, this is Captain Lockett. You called."

He sounded gruff, but I wasn't sure if it was because of me or everything else going on.

"I feel like the OPD is pushing me away. I called three times."

"It's because they are, Quint. You heard the chief last time you were a headquarters. He doesn't want anything to do with you."

"Even after the Butcher left a letter on my door?"

"We dusted for fingerprints. Looked for DNA. We did all we could."

"So you're telling me nothing came of it?"

"You can draw your own conclusions."

"Can I get updates on any evidence you might find?"

"You're not a cop, Quint. That's not going to happen."

"Is that your opinion or the chief's?"

"I could lose my job if he knew I kept interacting with you. I can't risk it."

I felt for Lockett and knew he was in a tough spot. It made me a little less frustrated with him in particular, whatever my feelings about the entire situation.

"I thought we got along pretty well while Ray was alive. I wouldn't want to lose that."

"My hands are tied, Quint. I like you, but unless you come with something concrete on the killer, it's probably best if we don't talk anymore."

It would be useless to continue pleading my case. Lockett had made his mind up. He'd had to.

"I'm sorry to hear that."

"Take care of yourself, Quint."

And with that, he hung up the phone.

25.

"I'm going to be honest, Quint, I was expecting you sooner."

Tom Butler had the look of a disappointed father.

I'd walked into *The Walnut Creek Times* a week after Ray's death.

"I should have come earlier," I said. "But I was pissed off I wasn't invited to Ray's funeral. And I went into a cocoon for a few days."

"That's no excuse. Krissy and I had known Ray for over ten years and we weren't invited. We didn't go hibernate."

Everything he said was true. But it didn't mean I had to like hearing it.

"I'm sorry, Tom. I don't know what else to say."

"You're forgiven, Quint. Now let's hug it out and talk about Ray."

I'd cried myself out in the days immediately following Ray's death, but I still felt emotional giving Tom a hug. He was the one who had introduced me to Ray in a roundabout way, having him approach me at a crime scene.

Ray had often mentioned how much he liked the Butlers, and I know the feeling was mutual. The police must have really limited the funeral to mostly cops.

"Where's Krissy?"

I'd walked up to the second floor, where I saw Tom and the paper's editor, Jan. But no Krissy.

"She's having lunch with Ray's wife."

"That's nice," I said. "I called Glenda a few days ago. Cara and I are going to take her out too."

"The less downtime she has, the better. Being left alone with her feelings right now is probably not the best idea."

"That was my thinking as well."

"So, I have to ask," Tom said. "How involved are you on this case? You know I'll give you any manpower you need. Any and all of the reporters downstairs are at your disposal if you think they'd help."

"The OPD has cut all ties with me. So officially, I'm not helping at all. But unofficially, Cara and I have made it our pet project."

I didn't like calling it that, even though the term had quickly jumped to mind. It was too cute sounding. And didn't do Ray's death, or any of the other victims', enough justice.

"I kind of figured that might be so. Without a nine to five and no deadline due here, I was imagining you mired in this case."

"Well, you were right. And 'mired' is certainly the word for it. It's disturbing investigating a serial killer. It's making me miss some of the fluff articles wrote here."

Tom laughed. He knew our paper wasn't *The New Yorker*. He embraced that, and we did as good a job as possible for a small, local newspaper.

At the same time, neither of us had fluff on the mind as he asked earnestly "What can we do? Give me anything. I'll have each reporter spend fifteen o thirty minutes a day on it. Maybe we'll find something."

"I guess you could look back over my articles. See if one stands out. I've read them fifty times each, but some new eyes couldn't hurt. Thanks."

"Of course. I'm doing it for Ray. And the rest of the Bay Area."

"I'm afraid his next murders are going to be even more horrific."

"Well, your gut instincts have been pretty damn good over the years, so I'm not going to doubt you. Wish I could. Let's hope we can find out who he is first."

"Amen to that. Thanks for your help, Tom."

"You're welcome, Quint. Listen, I've got something I'm working on, but stop by here more often. And I'll be in touch if any of the staff find anything."

"Thanks for your help, Tom."

"You're welcome. Be safe."

It was the way people said goodbye to me these days.

I learned about the killer's fourth letter that afternoon, but it didn't come from the police.

Instead, it was a screenshot sent from my favorite bookie's strongman Paddy Roark.

As had become standard, I read it several times.

Hello, everyone!

I feel like we're all old friends now. I realize this letter is a quick follow-up to the last one, but it's necessary.

This is the last letter you'll receive before I commit my fourth set of murders Although Ray Kintner was technically just a single murder, I guess. Oh well it felt like more since it cut so deep for those close to him. Here's looking a you, Quint.

These last two sets of killings are going to be so over the top, so majestic that I'm going to need some time.

But I am a man of my word, so I will give you the date. And since Fridays have been so successful, I feel no need to change it up.

On Friday, June 18th, the world will be shocked. Aghast. Speechless.

And because you're so far behind, and have basically zero chance of catching me, I'm going to leave you with a little riddle.

It will help answer the question of how my name is mentioned in every article. But Quint, I'm afraid only you will be able to get this one. The entirety of the Bay Area is waiting on you. If not, there will be more carnage.

So, here goes:

If queen, king, ace, two, three was a straight in poker, then maybe you'd see my name...

And that's it. Talk to you guys again soon.

Happy Hunting!

I had played my share of poker in my life, but I had no idea what he meant. And the stakes were higher than in any poker game I'd ever been involved in.

26

Peter Vitella was a legend in the Bay Area. For all the wrong reasons.

He was the Jerry Springer Show in print.

His weekly column in the *San Francisco Chronicle*, "The Vitella Vine" was full of rumors, innuendo, and every other thing journalists should avoid using. But Vitella didn't care.

Keeping his column interesting, and ahead of the curve, was all that mattered to Peter Vitella. He'd taken down many people during his thirty-plus years writing it. Politicians, VIPs, Silicon Valley tycoons, even beloved Bay Area athletes.

No one was immune.

One of the earliest examples had been the story of Maxfield Unger, a huge fundraiser around the Bay Area. He proved ubiquitous. If there was a mayor being sworn in, a huge skyscraper being christened, or the opening of a new ballpark, Maxfield Unger would be there.

He was a mysterious person, because you'd see him at every big-time event, but would never be quite sure how he got there. Most people assumed he supplied the money behind the money.

An angel investor, as it's called now. But before the internet, no one really used that term.

The rumor went that his family had made tens of millions in the oil business in the 1960s and Unger had inherited the money when his parents passed.

In 2020, this would have been easily verifiable, but in 1990, people were able to keep their private lives much more private.

So Maxfield Unger remained a riddle to the Bay Area. People were fascinated by him, but really didn't know all that much about him.

That is, until Peter Vitella struck.

His column usually contained a hodgepodge of anecdotes and rumors, a series of small stories. But he dedicated an entire column to Maxfield Unger. He titled it, "I'm Madder than Mad, Max."

In the article, Peter Vitella laid out the case that Maxfield Unger was a pedophile.

He talked to fifteen different boys and girls who'd said Unger had gotten way too touchy with them. No, Vitella didn't use their real names or verify them in any way. People understood. These were kids, after all.

Vitella also stated that members of the SFPD had found old video cassettes of child pornography. He was known to be close to many police officers, so people took this at face value.

The article was plastered with pictures of Unger alone with kids. Many of the pictures had been cropped to remove other people from them. It was shoddy journalism to say the least, but it was also a different time.

After the article, you couldn't find Maxfield Unger with the Hubble Space Telescope. He'd become a permanently uninvited guest to any of those grand openings that he'd become famous for.

Stories spread of him being cussed out the rare times he did appear in public. He bought a full-page ad in a rival newspaper in which he swore his innocence up and down. Some people may have believed him, but who is going to stand up for an alleged pedophile? It could ruin their own career, reputation, and personal life. So people stayed silent.

Oddly, no police charges were ever filed. Or not odd at all, if you believed that Peter Vitella worked in conjecture, unsubstantiated rumors, and lies.

But those could still be enough to wreck someone.

And they wrecked Maxfield Unger. Six months after the article was published, he walked out on the Golden Gate Bridge on a beautiful Saturday morning. On this summer day, many people were walking the bridge connecting Marin County and San Francisco.

Unger walked over the railing, and looked out over the water below. He sat there for a minute.

A crowd developed. Some people had cameras of the bulky analog type used in those days and they snapped pictures. Others told him to step back over the railing.

Maxfield Unger said three things only. The first two would never be proved or disproved. But the third sentence he uttered has undoubtedly become true.

As people looked on in horror, Unger stood up on the railing and grabbed one of the world-famous bridge's bright red poles.

He looked down at the assembled crowd and said, "I never improperly touched any little kids. I'm not an animal. And this yellow journalism, especially Peter Vitella, is only going to get worse and wreck more lives."

With that, Maxfield Unger let go of the pole and jumped toward the Bay below. Several members of the crowd shrieked, and parents tried to cover their children's eyes.

An extremely high majority of people who jump from the Golden Gate Bridge end out dying, and Maxfield Unger was no different. They found his body a few days later.

Many people had wished it had been Peter Vitella who had jumped.

But over the last several decades, he'd proven to be a cockroach. Impossible to kill.

He'd go through many more Maxfield Ungers over the following decades. And his column flourished despite backlash and people calling for his job. He sold papers and that's what mattered most, apparently.

A brash thirty-year-old kid back in 1990, Peter Vitella was now sixty, but no less venomous.

And now he was coming after me.

I first heard about the article on the morning after receiving the Bay Area Butcher's new letter. Nothing could be worse than Ray's death, but it did really feel like I was being hit on all sides.

My mother called first.

"Quint, I need you to go read Peter Vitella's article this morning. And then call me back. We're going to need to have a long talk."

"Okay, Mom. I'll be in touch."

I could have read the article online, but I was old school and still preferred reading the actual newspaper. So I went down to my local Starbucks and grabbed the Style section where Vitella wrote his article.

Fatima, one of the baristas who'd kept me out of jail, worked behind the counter today.

"Can I take this one section?" I asked.

"Of course. We've got like five papers lying around."

I ordered a coffee as well.

With my purchases, I walked back to Avalon and got on the elevator. I saw Tad and the elderly Evelyn on the elevator together, just as I had a few weeks back.

Once Evelyn departed, I told Tad people were going to start thinking they were a couple if they kept appearing together.

"Don't quit your day job," Tad said, but he was laughing.

I exited on the fourth floor and headed to my apartment. With every step my stomach churned.

I'd long known Peter Vitella was bad news, and now I'd been caught in his crosshairs.

I proceeded to my couch, took a sip of my coffee, and started reading.

QUESTIONS FOR QUINT!
BY PETER VITELLA

Quint Adler, a previously unknown Bay Area writer, became a feel-good story last summer. He bypassed local law enforcement and recklessly took things in his own hands to go after the archvillain Charles Zane. He succeeded and took down one of the worst criminals in Bay Area history.

Good for him.

However, history is not repeating itself.

This time around, his maverick streak is not only undesirable, it's deadly. As we all know, his friend, Ray Kintner, was killed by the Bay Area Butcher.

And the killer himself called out Quint in his latest letter to the police, media, and anyone else reading it. Which happens to be the whole world at this point.

While I rooted for Quint last summer, this man has become a nuisance. Who does he think he is? Some self-avenger representing the Bay Area? Count me out if that's how it is. Leave this case to the SFPD, the OPD, and all the other experts in the field.

And maybe, just maybe, we won't have another officer killed while you're busy trying to be the hero.

That goes for your girlfriend, too. The beautiful Cara.

I've heard from a respected connection that Cara was seen taking some papers and diagrams into Quint's apartment complex in Walnut Creek. Looks like they might be working the case together.

My advice to Cara: Stay out of this.

People who hang out with Quint for too long seem to have a nasty habit of turning up dead.

But you do you, Cara.

Apparently, Quint was named after Robert Shaw's character in Jaws.

So I've got a quote for him.

We're going to need a bigger body bag count!

Stay out of it. Let the experts handle it before more people end up dead.

Sincerely,

Peter Vitella

The entire thing filled me with fury, but one line stood out.

"But you do you, Cara."

I wanted to rip the fucking heart out of Peter Vitella. Blaming me for Ray's death was bad enough, but going after my girlfriend lay beyond the pale.

If Vitella had arrived at my apartment at that exact moment, I might have thrown him off the balcony.

I wish I was joking.

"I didn't know you were so involved with the Bay Area Butcher case," my mother said.

I had to make the call even though I knew it wouldn't go over well.

"I was mentioned in his very first letter. I couldn't avoid it."

With the phone to my ear, I caught myself pacing back and forth in my apartment like a crazy man.

Only two days ago, the killer had left a note on my door. And then Car.
and I made the collage. And now I was staring at an article in the *Sai
Francisco Chronicle* that was going to change everything.

All while having to deal with a worried mother.

"Of course you can avoid it, Quint. It's just like Charles Zane. But yo
couldn't say no then, either. You had to move forward."

She was right.

"There's a murderer on the loose and I might be one of the few people wh
can identify him. It's impossible to just leave it alone."

My mother paused before responding, and I knew I'd struck a chord.

"I just wish it wasn't my son who was involved."

"Well then, you're going to hate this, Mom. I'm not only going to kee
investigating this case, but I'm looking to become a private detective."

I expected a tongue lashing, but none came.

Instead, she said, "You'd be pretty good at it."

"That's not the response I was expecting, Mom. I'm pleasantly surprised.

"Doesn't mean I like it."

"Then why the sudden change?"

"I just thought of your father for a moment. About him trying to protect tha
student even when it led to his death. Maybe you're just trying to protec
people."

"That's exactly what I'm doing, Mom. This guy is the worst killer this regio
has seen in decades. Maybe ever. And he's going to kill again and it's goin
to get worse. I can't just sit idly by."

"That's all true. But you're still my baby. And my only child."

"I'm going to take every precaution available. There were ten cops at m
place a few days back. I'm safe."

I realized my mistake immediately.

"What happened at your apartment to warrant ten cops being there?"

"The killer left a letter addressed to me," I admitted.

"Jeez Louise! We need to meet up, Quint. There's obviously a lot of thing
that you haven't been telling me."

"You're right, Mom. I haven't. But you have to know that it's from a plac
of love and I'm just trying not to worry you."

"Well, I'm worried now. So you don't have to keep any information fron
me anymore."

"Alright, I'll tell you everything."

"Tell me in person. I haven't seen you in awhile."

I tried to think. She was right, we should meet up again soon.

"How about this afternoon?"

"That will be fine. Do you want to get lunch?"

My mind went to the killer and how he seemed to be a step ahead of me
I couldn't risk him seeing my mother with me out in public. The last thing I'

ever want was for her to get wrapped up in the investigation. That Cara had become involved was bad enough.

"I don't have that much time," I said. "I'll just pick something up and we'll eat at your place."

We always ate out, but if she found it suspicious, she didn't say anything.

"Sounds good. What time?"

"I'll be there at two."

"See you then."

On my way to my mom's house, I found myself checking my rearview mirror way too many times.

Did I really think the Butcher was out there following me?

It certainly seemed possible. He'd proven to be a step ahead at all times.

I arrived at my mother's with a racing mind, but tried to calm down for our visit. I'd picked up a few sandwiches from a local deli named Morucci's and gave her first pick. She took the tempting-looking pastrami and I was "stuck" with a delicious turkey and avocado.

She had a million questions, but I tried to appease her as much as I could considering the circumstances. I told her ten times that I hadn't mentioned being called out by the Butcher himself because I didn't want to worry her.

Now that Vitella had gabbed about me in print, I was sure the local news would run with it as well. There was no use trying to hide it from her any more.

We parted on good terms after I told her for an eighth time how vigilant I would be.

I also told her Cara and I would love for her to join us when she had dinner with Glenda sometime soon. She seemed excited to meet her and, as I'd expected, empathized with her loss. It gave me hope that her meeting Glenda would be good for the both of them.

When I returned to my apartment, I made the mistake of looking at Peter Vitella's article online as well.

The comments were embarrassing. Mainly for the people who left them, but for me as well.

"Never liked that camera hog!"

"His articles were fluff personified."

"He got lucky with Charles Zane. He's a hack!"

"I kind of hope the Butcher goes after him next."

"The Butcher is infinitely smarter than Quint."

And that's when I stopped reading. I imagined they got worse.

As long as there was no mention of Cara, or God forbid, my mother, I could deal with it.

I looked back at the article. Currently 294 comments. Peter Vitella was a big deal, and I had a feeling I would regret having entered his sphere. Not that it had been by choice. Or that I didn't already regret it.

People who loved gossip and conspiracy theories, of which Vitella had many, weren't often the most rational people.

I could already imagine having some confrontation with some tinfoil-hatted jackass at my local Trader Joe's.

Knowing this wouldn't lead anywhere productive, I walked from my couch to my room and looked over the collage we had made.

I tried to focus on the real villain at hand. The Bay Area Butcher. Peter Vitella was a nuisance, but nothing more. I could deal with him.

Studying the collage, I focused in on the letters. I read them again, for what might have been the hundredth time. Nothing clicked.

Just then, my phone vibrated with a call coming in from Cara.

"Hey," I said.

"What are you up to?"

"Went and met with my mother. Where have you been?"

Cara and I trusted each other implicitly and I never worried about her being out on her own. Obviously, that could change the closer we got to the Butcher.

"I met up with Maddy and Melanie."

"Ahh, the M&M's."

I had patted myself on the back a little too hard when I'd come up with that. I think a five-year-old could have done the same.

"Yeah, they're still really impressed with your nickname."

I laughed. "How are they?"

"Still roommates. Still single. And still on the prowl. Got any single friends you want to introduce?"

"No, I like my single friends too much. Maddy and Melanie are the preying mantises of humans."

"Can't argue with that. They spit out men by the handfuls."

"I like ninety-eight percent of your friends," I said.

"And the M&M's are the two percent?"

"You're a step ahead of me. Hey, have you ever heard of Peter Vitella?"

"Everyone from the Bay Area has. Why?"

"We're mentioned in one of his articles."

"You are?" A pause as she assimilated what I'd said. "*I* am?"

"Yup. I'll tell you all about it. But the stakes just got raised again."

"I told you I signed up for it," she said bravely.

"You did. And I respect you so much. And by the way, I love you."

"I love you too," Cara said. "I'll be home in an hour."

"Want to fool around?"

"Oh yeah."

As we lay in bed that night, recovering from some great sex, or more like relishing the aftermath of it, we devised a plan going forward. To use a basketball analogy, we planned to use a full court press. To use a non-basketball analogy, we would leave no stone unturned.

Were we going to bring ourselves to the killer's attention? Very likely.

But I was already firmly on his radar, and Cara knew everything she was signing up for.

If I didn't have so much faith in her, I would have been more worried.

Maybe I should have been.

27.

When I was a full-time writer for *The Walnut Creek Times*, I did most of my heavy lifting in the morning. That was when my head was clearest and the early coffees were just kicking in. Obviously, there were many times when I'd write at the office later in the day, but I always thought I was at my best when the sun began rising.

So it was no surprise that I'd come up with what I viewed as a winning idea at six thirty a.m.

Halfway through my first coffee, it came to me: I should have someone tail me for a week.

The killer had gotten close enough to attach a listening device on me. He'd mentioned me in every letter, sans one, and was obviously way too interested in me. He'd even entered the Avalon Walnut Creek complex to hand-deliver a letter to my apartment.

The guy had come close to me several times. But more than that, I had a feeling he was always a step ahead of me. And the police.

Maybe, just maybe, he remained out there, occasionally following me.

The OPD had made it clear I was no longer part of their investigation, so they certainly weren't going to help me.

But I thought of someone who just might.

I knew what I had to do.

I told Cara my plan and said I'd be back in a few hours.

I had Paddy Roark's phone number, but after getting no response from Captain Lockett, I decided it might be better to surprise Paddy in person. It's much easier to tell someone no, or not to respond at all, with your phone.

So I decided to surprise him.

I did call ahead to make sure he was working, and sure enough, as walked into Boyle's Grocery Store, he waited there.

The greens and oranges of the store had never been brighter. I'd been to Ireland a few times in my twenties, and walking into Boyle's always brought me back. Under different circumstances, I might have grabbed a Guinness at a local pub afterward.

But this wasn't the time. For obvious reasons.

"Quint, to what do I owe this surprise?" Paddy Roark asked.

"You're becoming less gruff every time I see you, Paddy."

"Don't tell anyone," he said. "Might ruin my rep."

A clerk laughed, and I wondered if she knew the rep that Roark referred to.

Did his fellow employees realize that he was the right-hand man of the biggest bookie in the Bay Area? Or did they just see him as Paddy, the GM of their local Irish grocery store?

I'd guess the latter, since we never, ever talked business in front of other people.

"Let's go back to my office," Roark said, as if on cue.

I followed him along the now familiar course, heading to the back of the store and into one of the offices. Last time, Dennis McCarthy had met us there, but he wasn't waiting when we entered.

"So what is it, Quint? I'm going to guess this isn't a courtesy visit. Something else involving the Bay Area Butcher, if I can be so bold."

"You may. And you're right."

"You know we'll do anything legal to help you catch this asshole. Giving our beautiful area a bad name."

"What if it's less illegal and more frowned upon?"

"What do you have in mind?"

"This killer has a hard-on for me. I still don't know why, but obviously this has something to do with an article I wrote at some point in time. He's attached a listening device to me and entered my apartment complex to leave me a letter. I've got this feeling that he's still out there, watching me. Monitoring me. Closer than I realize."

"Let me guess, you want a tail on you?"

Paddy Roark was a smart guy. The surly exterior may have fooled some people, but not me.

"Yes. If we see a guy who's in a background shot more than once, I'll start to get a little suspicious."

"I know a guy or two who could do a job like that," Paddy said.

I'd assumed he would.

"How would payment work?" I asked.

"Well, I have to talk to the boss man first. But since we are probably a little more flush with cash than you, I imagine Dennis would be rather generous. Maybe we could pay a guy out of our pocket and you could pay for his meals each day. Something like that."

"You're too kind to me."

"Maybe. But having a serial killer on the loose is bad business for anyone. I'm sure Dennis would like to do his part."

"Thanks, Paddy."

"I'm sure you'd love to avenge the loss of your friend. Despite our connections in the police force, I'm not too tight with them usually, but he seemed like a good one. I guess they still exist."

With all that had been going on the last several days, I hadn't thought about Ray as much as I probably should have. Paddy mentioning him was like a stomach punch, prompting immediate and vivid memories of some c our good times together.

"Ray was a very good man. And died way too young."

"Well, let's catch this motherfucker, then."

"That's why I'm here," I said. "What's next?"

"I'll talk to Dennis. Come back tomorrow. Same time."

I looked at my cell phone. It was eleven a.m.

"I'll be here. And thanks for your help, Paddy. You guys are good people I don't care what the general public say about bookies and their right-han men."

Paddy Roark laughed. "There was a time where you might have gotter your arm broken for a comment like that."

"I'm starting to think you're an old softie and the rough exterior is just a front."

Paddy Roark started to stare at me. His eyes were so intense that instinctively looked away.

"Is that what you really think?" he asked.

"No," I admitted.

"Good. And don't you forget it," he said. When I looked at him once more his smile returned.

"I'll see you tomorrow, Paddy. Thanks."

"Take care, Quint."

I arrived back at the apartment and relayed everything that happened to Cara She was on board with being followed and filmed. In fact, she was borderline giddy about it. Not the act of being followed, obviously, but the idea that we could potentially get the Butcher on film.

"But how is it going to work? The videographer isn't going to be here with us, is he?"

She extended her arm, gesturing to the apartment with a flourish like a model on *The Price is Right*.

"We're going to hammer out the details tomorrow. But no, he's not going to stay with us. Don't be silly. My guess is the man will hunker down close to Avalon and I'll text him whenever we leave here. Then he'll start his tail."

"How about doing some things out in public? Walking the trail. Going back to the Lafayette Reservoir. Having a coffee outside at the Starbucks below. I the Butcher is truly following you, the only way to capture him on video is by venturing out."

"You're absolutely correct."

"Thanks."

"There will be hundreds, if not thousands, of people in the background o our lives the next several days. But like I told Paddy, if we see someone appear on the videos more than once, then we'll take interest."

"Exactly," Cara said. "We're going to have a lot of footage to look through.

"If we're going to truly investigate, then this is exactly what we signed up for."

"True," Cara said.

"And one other thing. I hate to say this, but you need to assume the killer is monitoring you as well. That asshole Vitella mentioned you and I'm sure the killer read his column. So he may well take an interest in you."

I hated even considering the possibility and started to wonder how I'd let Cara talk me into agreeing to have her become my right-hand (wo)man.

"I can take care of myself."

"I'll bet Ray, Paul Langley, and the San Jose families thought the same thing."

"I didn't mean it like that. I'll be vigilant. I'll be watchful," she said.

"Okay, I'm sorry. Just a little on edge today."

"Let's be honest, we're going to be on edge every day until this psychopath is caught."

She was right, of course. The little pit in my stomach hadn't really gone away since being told of the Butcher's first letter.

"And at some point, I think we should pay Vitella a visit," I added. "I'd like to know how he found out you were entering Avalon with some of our paperwork."

"I imagine he doesn't give up his sources very easily," Cara said.

"Even if that source is a serial killer?"

My question hung in the air.

"So what can we do the rest of today?" Cara asked, changing the subject.

"Thought you'd never ask," I said. "What do you think about interviewing some neighbors in Tiburon or San Jose?"

"Doing some real investigating, huh? I like it. But I'm sure there are still officers patrolling the San Jose crime scenes. Probably better not to be seen there."

"True," I said.

"We could go interview some of the Langleys' neighbors."

I smiled proudly. "I've created a monster."

"I'll get ready."

Looks like we were heading back to Tiburon.

28.

Bradley Marks looked like an aging former professional surfer. But unless he was Kelly Slater, I'm not sure how he'd afford one of the houses near the Langleys. Multi-million dollar homes each.

He answered the door in board shorts and a tank top, his look replete with bleached blonde, spiked hair. Though probably pushing fifty, he gave off the vibe of a thirty-year-old.

Huge white pillars went skyward toward the second and third stories of his home. The bricks lining the ground around the front door probably had more square footage than my apartment.

"How can I help you?" he asked.

I half expected a "bruh" at the end of his question, but didn't get one.

"We are out here investigating the Langley murders," I said.

"I thought that was you," he said. "Quint, right?"

I hated this part.

"Yup."

"Bradley Marks," he said. "I'm sorry about your cop friend. I watched most of that funeral on T.V. Seemed like a nice guy."

"Thanks. He was," I said.

"And this is?" Marks asked.

"My co-worker Cara," I said.

We'd discussed on the way over how to introduce her and decided co-worker sounded more official than girlfriend.

Marks extended his hand and Cara shook it. He held on for a second too long in my eyes and I immediately regretted not introducing her as my girlfriend. If he'd met Cara at the beach, I could almost guarantee he'd be hitting on her.

I looked at her and nodded, handing off the lead to her.

I wasn't a PI yet, and this wasn't exactly good cop/bad cop, but my instincts had always been solid. I felt Mr. Marks would give Cara more information than me.

"How well did you know the Langleys?" she asked him.

"Been neighbors for about two years," Marks said. "I knew them well enough. Just so terrible what happened."

"It's horrible," Cara said. "In the media this is being portrayed as a random home invasion. Any reason to believe it's someone they knew?"

Bradley Marks thought long and hard, frowning.

"I've got no proof, obviously, but it did seem a little personal, you know? Like, who kills someone's teenage daughter like that?"

"I get your point, but there are maniacs who kill strangers every day," Cara said.

"I guess. I don't know, this just seemed different. Maybe just because I was their neighbor."

"What did you know about the husband's job?"

She briefly glanced my way as if to check if I had any input, but Cara was asking all the right questions, so I kept quiet.

"It was some high-tech dot-com company. Not really my thing. I own a surfboard company, so entirely different."

I wanted to laugh. He was a surfer after all. And it must have been a big time surfboard company to own the house towering over us.

"That's very cool," Cara said. "I've never tried, but it's never too late."

She waxed him up like a surfboard itself.

"You totally should. It would be the ride of your life."

I didn't know if he intended "ride of your life" as a sexual reference or not, but I was growing a little tired of Mr. Marks. Luckily, I trusted my girlfriend implicitly, and she was obviously more focused on questioning him than flirting. I just didn't like the guy's vibe.

"I'll keep you posted," Cara said. "You said you'd only been neighbors for two years?"

"Yeah. I've lived here for ten, but the Langleys moved in a few years back."

"Do you know where they lived before that?"

"Used to live in the South Bay, close to work. But the company opened an office in San Francisco, so Mr. Langley moved up here. Before the South Bay they lived somewhere in the East Bay. Pleasant Hill, I believe."

That got my attention. Pleasant Hill sat adjacent to Walnut Creek. It could mean absolutely nothing, but it intrigued me nonetheless.

Ray had told me the Langleys had moved from Santa Clara to Tiburon, so he hadn't found any East Bay connection. Looks like maybe he hadn't gone back far enough.

Cara glanced over at me, the East Bay reference obviously catching her attention as well.

I decided it was time to speak.

"Do you know why they left the East Bay for the South Bay?" I asked.

"I don't," Marks said.

He'd been significantly more talkative with Cara than with me. I guess I couldn't blame him.

"We appreciate your help, Mr. Marks," Cara said.

"Call me Bradley," he replied with a smile.

No surprise there.

"Okay, Bradley. Are you sure it was Pleasant Hill they lived in? Could it have been Walnut Creek?"

"I see what you're getting at now. The Butcher mentioned Quint's articles and he worked for a Walnut Creek paper. What if I just helped crack the case?"

Bradley Marks laughed. He was way too smug for me. Then he pretended to think hard, which I'm not sure he was capable of.

"I'm pretty sure it was Pleasant Hill. But shit, I don't know. Maybe it was Walnut Creek. I thought that's something you guys would have known."

"Not sure what you mean by 'you guys', but we are not the police, Mr Marks," I said.

"Gotcha."

And no, Mr. Marks didn't ask me to call him Bradley.

"You've been very helpful," Cara said. "Is there anything else you can think of? Did you see any weird people around the neighborhood?"

"See, that makes you guys sound like cops. Because they asked me all those questions. No, I didn't see anybody. But I'm also a pretty good distance from the Langley house. I'm not sure I would have."

"Of course not. I just have to ask."

"I understand, Cara. You're fine."

This guy was good with his double entendres.

"Thanks for your help, Bradley," Cara said. "We'll be in touch if we have any more questions."

"Take care, Cara. Oh that's funny. Care, Cara."

I wanted to tell him not to quit his day job, but he had been helpful, so resisted.

We said our goodbyes and walked back to our car.

"There's two more houses on this block," Cara said. "Do you want to hit them up?"

"Sure," I said.

Neither of the other two homes offered much in the way of new information, but I didn't care. We'd learned enough from Bradley Marks. The knowledge that the Langleys used to live in the East Bay, very close to Walnut Creek, had my full attention.

We went back to my car and started driving to the East Bay. My mother texted me soon after we got on the road.

I looked down at my phone as I drove, which earned me a glare from Cara.

"Sorry," I said. "Here, you can read it to me."

Cara took my phone.

"Peter Vitella mentioned you in another article. You should probably read it."

"Shit," I said.

"Your mother is worried, isn't she?"

"Yeah. Less about Peter Vitella and more about the Butcher. But yeah she's scared."

"Let's catch the guy and set your mom's mind at ease."

"That's the plan," I said.

"And thanks, Quint."

"For what?"

"For not being a jealous boyfriend with surfboard guy. It was obvious he was hitting on me. And I appreciate you not making a big deal out of it."

"You got it. Doesn't mean I wasn't fired up."

"That's human nature. But you didn't act like a jealous boyfriend. And that's sexy."

"Good to hear. I almost interrupted a few times. Glad I didn't."

"We got what we wanted, didn't we?"

"You were great," I said. "And the fact that they lived in the East Bay could potentially be huge. If we can somehow find a connection between the Langleys and any article I wrote..."

"So you don't think those murders were random after all?"

A car almost cut me off and I had to hit the brakes. I spoke slowly, keeping most of my attention on the road.

"It's still likely they were random. But we're absolutely going to investigate the connections now. So let's go with the assumption that the Butcher knew his victims, or at least some of them."

"It's certainly an interesting puzzle piece to add to our collage."

"No doubt about that," I said.

"Should we swing by a store and pick up the *San Francisco Chronicle*?"

"Yeah, I guess so. Is Peter Vitella going to be a pain in my ass until this thing ends?"

"Bradley Marks would bet six surfboards on it," Cara said.

And then we started laughing. I don't know why.

Maybe the absurdity of everything.

Maybe the realization that there wouldn't be much humor in the foreseeable future.

Maybe we just needed a release.

But we laughed as if it was the funniest thing ever said. Which it wasn't, but that didn't matter.

It had hit our funny bone and we rolled with it.

29.

I woke up the following morning and felt like the world was closing in on me.

A new Peter Vitella article in which he again blamed Ray's death on me. A new letter from the Butcher that I'd barely had time to scrutinize. A possible connection between the Butcher and the East Bay.

And finally, I was going to meet Paddy Roark later that morning to set up a tail on my girlfriend and me.

Had I gone crazy?

Cara was still asleep and I didn't wake her up.

I dressed, went downstairs, and bought a coffee. When I arrived back at my apartment, I looked both ways as I locked the door behind me.

This caution would be standard operating procedure until the Butcher was caught.

I took my coffee to the balcony. A few sips later, I started to feel better by looking at the bright side. I wasn't in my office writing some boring article for the *Walnut Creek Times*. What I did these days could potentially save lives.

And with important work comes a lot of stress. Acknowledging the stress worked better than trying to downplay it. So I decided to just embrace it.

Cara walked out on the balcony.

"You looked like you were in your own world," she said.

"Doing my version of meditation."

"The stress getting to you?" she asked.

Cara had always read me like a book.

"Yes," I confirmed.

"You wouldn't be human if you weren't stressed out right now. You've got a lot on your plate."

I didn't like this type of attention, so I tried to deflect it back on my girlfriend.

"So do you, Cara. We're in this together."

"Thanks. I feel safe when you're around."

"Speaking of which, I have to head back to San Francisco in an hour. Would you mind just staying in the apartment until I get back?"

"Quint," she pleaded.

"C'mon, this was part of the deal when you moved in."

"The deal was to stay together when we could. So take me to San Francisco."

She was right.

"Fine, you can come with me. But I can't just bring you in to meet Paddy Roark. It's unfair to them. They're already sticking their necks out for me."

"I'll just ride with you."

"Okay," I said.

"And try to convince you on our way over."

I couldn't help but laugh.

Cara tried to work her magic on the drive over, and while I'm usually a sucker for her charms, I held strong, maintaining that I'd rather she not meet Paddy.

"These guys are now my friends, but they aren't exactly the Cleavers. They've done some bad stuff."

"I'm investigating a serial killer. I can handle a couple of bookies," Cara said.

Maybe I was being a stubborn jerk, but I stuck to my guns.

"I'll be back out in fifteen minutes," I said.

I'd parked a block up from Boyle's Grocery Store. I left the keys with Cara, who glared at me as I got out of the car.

I walked toward Boyle's, already regretting my decision. But I didn't double back.

I entered the grocery store for the second time in twenty-four hours, and once again, I saw Paddy Roark immediately.

He nodded in my direction and started walking toward the back, indicating I should follow him. Which I did.

Once we got to the back, Roark waved me into the first of two offices.

Dennis McCarthy sat there, looking as refined as ever. He was wearing his favorite attire, a Vineyard Vines vest with a long-sleeved shirt underneath. Today, it was a purple vest with a gray shirt. There never seemed to be any creases in the clothes he wore. I didn't know his secret, but he was a pristine dresser.

"Hello, Quint," he said.

"Nice to see you, Dennis. Thanks for accommodating me."

"You're welcome. Before you think you can come to us for anything, however, realize that we are doing this to help catch a serial killer. Not to just blindly help out a friend."

"I understand."

Dennis nodded in my direction and then the chair, suggesting I should sit. Both he and Paddy did a lot of non-verbal communication, and nodding was at the top of the list of favored gestures.

I sat. Roark joined me on my side of the desk as we faced Dennis McCarthy.

"To be honest," I said, "I don't care about the reason, I just care that you're helping."

"And you think this could make a difference?"

"I do. Something tells me this guy is hovering around the investigation in some way. He's always ahead of us."

"Could he be a cop?" Paddy Roark asked.

I thought about it. The letters certainly didn't include many compliments for cops, but he could be disgruntled. Or a former cop.

"Yeah, I guess he could be," I said, mad at myself for not having thought of it earlier.

"Have the cops looked into any of their own? Maybe someone who had a grudge with Ray Kintner?"

"You're asking the wrong guy, unfortunately. I'm kind of on the outside looking in when it comes to the OPD now. I became somewhat friendly with a Captain Lockett, but he's stopped answering my calls."

"We've got some connections in some of these police forces. But it wouldn't be easy telling them that this killer could be one of their own. Not sure how they'd take that."

"Understandable," I said.

"Look at this one," Paddy Roark said, pointing up at one of the two closed-circuit T.V.s they had in the office.

I looked up and sure enough, saw Cara walking down one of the aisles.

"She's beautiful," Dennis said.

I sighed loudly and they both looked at me.

"That's my girlfriend," I said.

"I'm guessing this isn't random," Dennis said.

"She wanted to drive out with me, but I asked her to stay in the car."

"You didn't want us meeting her?"

"I hadn't asked you guys, so I didn't think it would be right."

"She looks tough. I'm sure she can handle it. Plus, I'd like to meet her."

It wasn't a suggestion. It was an order. And considering they were putting their necks out for me, I couldn't just say no.

Plus I didn't think I'd have much luck trying to convince Cara to go back to the car.

I shrugged.

"You guys win. I'll go get her."

I began to stand up, but Paddy Roark put a hand on my shoulder.

"I know you're a regular here now, but I can't have my staff seeing you escort someone to the back of the store. I'll get her."

"Okay," I said, although I didn't love it.

Paddy got up and left the office. Dennis and I continued watching the T.V.s.

Paddy tapped Cara on the shoulder, who appeared surprised. Paddy said something, though, and she smiled. And then started following him back toward us.

Fifteen seconds later, my girlfriend walked into the now cramped office.

"Guys, I'd like you to meet my girlfriend. Cara, this is Dennis McCarthy and Paddy Roark."

Cara smiled and shook their hands. I could tell they were both taken with her. Like everyone else.

"I'm sorry," I said. "I was an asshole."

She looked in the other two men's direction.

"Should I chew him out now or wait till the drive back?"

Dennis and Paddy laughed. I even managed to smile.

"Cara, we are honored to meet you," Dennis said. "Quint has clearly outkicked his coverage."

"You're hilarious. I've only heard that joke five hundred times," I said.

"When you hear something that much, you should accept it's probably true."

"Of course it's true," I said. "I take it as a badge of honor."

"Looks like he's trying to get back into your good graces," Paddy said.

"Well, I'm here now, so maybe I'll let it slide."

Looking around, I realized there were only three chairs in the office. I stood up and offered Cara mine.

"Thanks, babe," she said.

"She said babe. You must be out of the doghouse already," Dennis said.

Everyone smiled. And then Cara spoke.

"Alright, enough of this small talk. Pretend I'm not here and pick up discussing what you were before I got here."

"Actually, Cara, I had just asked Quint if he'd considered that the Butcher might be a cop. Or an ex-cop."

Cara pondered this newfound information.

"It's certainly possible," she said. "It would explain a few things."

"Like what?"

"Like how Quint feels the guy is closer than we realize. A cop would be privy to more information, obviously."

"And Quint has told you what he's here for?"

I jumped in. "Of course. She's not in the dark on anything."

"You just didn't want her to meet us?"

"To get more involved than she needed to be."

"You should be a lot more concerned with her chasing after this maniac."

"That's what I told him," Cara said. "I can handle a couple of old bookies."

For a brief moment, I didn't know how the joke would go over. But then Dennis and Paddy erupted in laughter.

"You are a funny girl, Cara."

"Thanks."

"And now that you know our profession, you can keep that to yourself."

"I will," she said and used her fingers to "zip" her mouth.

That seemed to be the moment that they fell in love with Cara.

"Can we deal with you from now on?"

"Sure. We'll leave Quint out in the car."

More laughs, including my own.

"She's amazing, Quint, but let's get down to business," Dennis said.

"I'm ready," I said.

"We've found a guy. He'll follow you around for four days. If we deem it necessary, we can do it longer, but I think that's a good start."

"Thank you, Dennis. How will this work exactly?"

"I've put our guy up in a hotel over by your apartment complex. Yes, I still know where you live. I'll give you a burner phone to text him. You are only to use it for that. Do you understand?"

He was referring to a time during the Charles Zane case where I'd use my burner phone for something other than he'd planned.

"I understand," I said, thinking the less talking, the better.

"There's no point in sending you the footage each day. Be a waste of time spending hours upon hours viewing it. So I'll have my guy condense it down to something that's watchable. Hopefully only an hour or two."

"That sounds great, Dennis. You've really thought hard about this."

"The guy we have filming you is a tech wizard, so I imagine he'll be able to edit it each night pretty quickly. Make sure you text him when you're staying in for the night, so he can get to work without fear of being called back out."

"Of course," I said.

"So does this start tomorrow?" Cara asked.

"It can. Is that alright with you guys?"

We looked at each other and shrugged.

"Sure," I said. "Why wait?"

Dennis grabbed for a backpack sitting on a shelf in the small room close to him and took out a phone.

"Here you go. The man will contact you tonight."

"Thanks for everything, Dennis. And Paddy." I said.

"When you walk out of your apartment tomorrow morning, he will give you a slight nod. You'll know who he is."

"I appreciate all of this."

"As do I," Cara said.

"You guys are welcome. Cara, we hope to meet you again."

"You will," I said. "Once she has her foot in the door, she's a bulldog."

Cara smiled.

Paddy Roark stood up, meaning the meeting was over.

I exchanged handshakes with the two men and Cara exchanged hugs.

"Be careful," Dennis McCarthy said to us.

"We will," I responded. "Thanks again for your help."

Cara and I returned to my place after stopping at hers. She'd basically moved in, but she had held on to her other place until we figured out whether this was permanent. Since she needed some more clothes, we swung by her house to pick up her stuff.

Back at Avalon, as she rearranged our shared apartment, I started reading back over the Butcher's latest letter, which I hadn't paid enough attention to having been busy with Dennis and Paddy.

I spoke aloud to Cara as she restructured my minuscule walk-in closet. It was going to be all hers by time she finished.

"What does he mean by this poker analogy?" she asked.

"It's something that bridges the gap," I said.

"What does that mean exactly?"

"So in poker, you can have a straight go from ten to the ace. Or from the ace to the five. The ace can be used for high or low. But you can't have a straight that goes something like king, ace, two, three, four. Or queen, king, ace, two, three. So he's saying if you *could* bridge the gap between the two, then you could have a straight. But that's all I know. I'm not sure what exactly it has to do with his name."

"How do your articles end?"

"With my name."

"And how do they begin?"

"Usually with 'Written By,' followed by my name."

"I don't get how his poker analogy fits."

"Neither do I. Well, I get the premise, but I don't get how it's meant to be interpreted."

"Which he's not going to tell us. He enjoys this mindfuck."

"He does. But we're making progress."

"Let's hope a lot more of it happens before his next set of murders."

"Of course."

"Here, can you grab me a *Walnut Creek Times*? Thanks."

Cara had walked out of the closet and came near the assorted papers sitting in the baskets we'd set in the wall. She grabbed one and brought it over.

"These baskets might cost you a pretty penny from your deposit."

"I'll spackle the holes when this is all over."

I grabbed the paper, an edition from 2018, probably ten pages in total, and looked at the top of the front page. And then the back of the last page. Based on what I saw, I tried to figure out any plausible explanation for the Butcher's poker analogy.

It had to mean that something jumped from one thing to the next. Something which we usually didn't acknowledge.

I looked at "Quint Adler." I looked at "Written By." I looked at "The *Walnut Creek Times*."

But nothing stood out.

Maybe this was all some inside joke from the killer and not something I could figure out on my own. Or the creep meant to be intentionally vague.

"Anything?" Cara finally asked.

"No."

I put the paper back in the basket, then jumped onto my bed, where Cara settled next to me with her laptop.

"What are you doing?" I asked.

She tapped some words into the Google search bar.

"Trying to find out if any of the victims in San Jose have connections to the Langleys. Or the East Bay."

I was exhausted and my mind was mush. Seemingly energized by hanging her clothes, Cara continued to work and I tried to get to sleep early.

30.

"Don't forget to text the bookie's guy!"

I was halfway out the door the next morning when Cara reminded me.

"I'm just getting a coffee and coming back up," I said.

"Alright. I think you should tell him anyway. But when we're going to be out in public, you definitely should."

"Why don't you come down with me? I'll text him and we'll have a coffee outside on the street."

"Alright, give me five minutes."

"You look fine," I said.

"I asked for five minutes, not a half hour," Cara said.

"Touché."

I texted Dennis McCarthy's guy, walked downstairs with Cara, ordered coffees, and saved a table sitting out on Treat Boulevard. All the cars sailing by made plenty of loud noise, but the sound was a bit soothing as well.

Cara brought the coffees out a few minutes later and set them down, taking a seat in the process.

As soon as we'd settled in, someone approached us.

The man, in his fifties, wore nondescript blue jeans and a white T-shirt. He had sunglasses and a hat on, making it hard to see his face.

Which I'm sure was the plan.

"This will be the first and last time I'll say hi to you guys," he said.

"Thanks for helping us," I said.

"You're welcome. And now I walk away."

Which is exactly what he did.

"This is so odd," Cara said a few seconds after he left.

"Just imagine him as your own paparazzi cameraman."

"No, thanks. And that's funny coming from the guy who didn't like being approached at the grocery store after all his interviews."

"That's fair," I admitted.

We each took a sip of our coffees, as if doing so could invoke an air of normality.

"You find out anything last night after I went to sleep?" I asked.

"I did."

That surprised me.

"Why didn't you tell me?"

"You were asleep, and then you dragged me down here when I woke up."

"Also fair. What did you find out?"

"As we know, a lot of these can mean nothing."

"I know. We don't have to preface that each time."

"Okay," she said, then cleared her throat. "I found a connection to the East Bay with two of the victims in San Jose."

"What type of connection?"

"They had lived in the Easy Bay before moving to San Jose. Roger and Celia Tiller."

"How were you able to figure that out?" I asked.

"The power of the internet: googling all of the victim's names, and then trying to find places they've previously lived. It's easier than you'd think. Lot of websites have that info."

She was right, which helped our case but made me uneasy overall. It had become way too simple to get information on people these days.

"Did they live in Walnut Creek?" I asked.

"Better," she said.

"How could it be better than that? I wrote for the *Walnut Creek Times*, after all."

"They lived in Pleasant Hill."

And I immediately knew she was right. Surfer guy Bradley Marks said the Langleys had lived in Pleasant Hill as well..

"I'm intrigued," I said.

"That's it?"

"It's great work, Cara, no doubt. But the Bay Area is relatively small. It's not crazy to think that two sets of his victims, out of many, might have both lived in Pleasant Hill at some point. Are you even sure they lived there at the same time?"

"That's what we are going to find out today," Cara said.

"Let me guess. You want to talk with a few of their neighbors?"

"You know it!"

I gave Cara a quick kiss, and as I did the man who was tailing us walked by us for a second time. It was all so odd.

"Great," Cara said sarcastically. "Our paparazzi. Maybe by the end of this we'll have a greatest hits album of us kissing."

"I'd buy it," I said.

Cara smiled.

"Should we go upstairs?" I asked.

"No," she said. "We should be out in public as long as we can. Let's finish our coffees down here and give the guy a chance to record all the people who hover around or walk by us."

"You're more of a natural at this than I am," I said.

"Thanks, Quint."

Even I wasn't sure whether it was a compliment or not, but I let it stand as one.

We stayed outside at Starbucks for a half hour longer. A great many people walked by, but I didn't recognize anyone, except a few of my longtime Avalon neighbors. Not that I expected to. It was a huge long shot that I knew who the Butcher was. Although Paddy suggesting it could be a cop certainly upped those odds. I'd met several in the OPD, after all.

The goal wasn't for me to recognize the Butcher, anyway. It was for the video to find someone who appeared in our vicinity one too many times.

We headed back to my place. Cara and I spent a little more time getting ready for our visit to Pleasant Hill. Sweats were fine for a Starbucks trip, but if we were going to be knocking on doors, we needed to be presentable. By ten a.m., we had become just that.

I texted the man the address we were headed to. But I told him to be subtle, given we might go door-to-door to ask questions.

Pleasant Hill bordered Walnut Creek for several miles. Many of us in Walnut Creek viewed it as a younger brother, not quite as much to do, but not exactly a slouch either.

It was home to Diablo Valley College, one of the better junior colleges in California. If you knew more than that about Pleasant Hill, you were probably a local. It didn't exactly make a huge impression.

Avalon Walnut Creek, although technically located in Walnut Creek (thus the name), connected right to the Pleasant Hill BART station, so it's not like we had to venture far. Pleasant Hill actually lay less than one hundred yards from my apartment.

On Google, Cara brought up the address of the Tillers when they lived in Pleasant Hill, and we headed off that way. We only had to go a few miles.

As I pulled out on the street from the Avalon parking garage, I saw a black Honda Civic pull out a few cars behind me. It followed from a distance, and I wondered if it was our guy. It remained behind us the whole way, keeping a car or two between us, but didn't follow me onto the final street. It had to be him, not wanting to keep the tail too close.

I parked the car. "Okay," I said. "Who should we approach first?"

"Let's try the Tillers' old house." Cara pointed to it. "Then we can hit a few neighbors and see if they remember anything more."

That sounded fine with me. I nodded.

The home was painted a burgundy red you didn't see too often. It looked like a rectangular glass of Cabernet. Judging by the size, it probably had only two bedrooms. Potentially three, but it certainly wasn't extravagant.

Everyone gives the Bay Area shit for their home prices, but I imagined on this block they were actually pretty reasonable.

Our knock was answered before Cara had time to knock a second time.

The woman who answered wore jeans and a casual yellow blouse. She must be smack dab in the middle of her thirties. If I was a betting man, I'd

confidently take 34/35/36 and give someone else every age there is. He
appearance was that uncannily on the grown-up side of young.

"Can I help you?" she said.

Since my acquisition of my investigator's license was still off in the nea
future, Cara thought we could use my "celebrity" to our advantage. She saic
if I introduced myself as Quint, a sizable percentage of the Bay Area woulc
know who I was. Otherwise, they might ask questions like whether we were
affiliated with a police department. Questions we didn't want to answer.

So I took the lead.

"Hi, I'm Quint Adler. We had a few questions about the people who ownec
the house before you. The Tillers."

The woman shook her head. "Quint is standing on my front porch," she
said in a low voice, as if to herself. "So weird." In a louder, friendlier tone, she
told us, "Nice to meet you, I'm Victoria."

I shook her hand, and she held on a little long. It seemed I'd met the female
version of Bradley Marks.

"This is my associate, Cara," I said.

They shook hands. Briefly.

We'd decided to continue with the co-worker/associate angle, making i
sound more official than boyfriend and girlfriend.

"What questions did you have?" Victoria asked, her eyes in my direction
only.

She didn't invite us in, so it looked like the conversation would be taking
place on her doorstep. That was fine with me, even though in my experience
as a reporter, people grew more willing to talk if they invited you inside.

"Do you know why the Tillers moved?" I asked.

"Work. Mr. Tiller got transferred down to San Jose."

"What kind of work was he involved in?"

"Real estate. He was a property manager and his company had bought a
few rental units down in the South Bay. Made it easier if he lived down there
obviously."

"No doubt," I said.

And that's when I realized the mistake we had made.

Victoria wouldn't know if something had happened while the Tillers lived
here. Obviously, she wouldn't have lived here then.

As my mind wandered, Victoria pounced.

"So you are here investigating the Bay Area Butcher?"

We had really no reason to lie. And there was no lie that would truly make
sense anyway.

"We are."

"But I thought all of these murders were totally random. At least, that's
what the media is saying."

"In all likelihood, they are. But we're just trying to see if there was by some
chance any connection we could find between the Tillers and the killer."

"Oh, that rhymes," Victoria said, delighting in her own observation. By the gleam in her eyes, she hoped I'd be impressed, too.

I wanted to turn and run.

Watching Bradley Marks hit on Cara had been preferable to this.

"Which neighbors have lived here the longest?" Cara asked, saying her first words in the entire conversation.

And as usual, she'd found the right question to ask.

"That would be the Dorias. They're both around seventy and raised four kids on this street."

"Which house are they?"

Victoria took a step outside and pointed to a pale brown house about three doors down.

"Is there anything you could tell us that might be helpful, Victoria?" I asked, hoping adding her name at the end might do the trick.

"I don't think so."

I guess not.

Victoria continued. "We met them like two or three times and once the house closed, we moved in, and obviously they moved to the South Bay. So we really barely knew them."

"Sure. I understand," I said. "Well, we'd like to thank you for your time."

"I hope you catch him. We're all scared. Especially with Walnut Creek being all over his letters."

"But this is Pleasant Hill," I said.

"Yeah, but they are contiguous. It's not like bullets stop flying when they pass through city limits."

It was both a funny image and a somewhat perceptive comment. I tended toward the latter.

"Well said. You be safe, Victoria. I think we're going to ask the Dorias a few questions."

Victoria and Dorias rhymed too, but luckily she didn't point it out.

"Okay, thanks for stopping by," she said, like it was something we did twice a week.

"Take care," I said.

We walked three doors down, and once again, our knock on the door was answered almost immediately.

To be honest, the Dorias looked closer to their eighties than their seventies.

I just hoped their memory was intact.

The door had been opened by Mrs. Doria, and within seconds, her husband joined her.

I stuck to our plan.

"My name is Quint…"

"We know who you are," he said.

This was too much.

Was I more well-known than I realized? Maybe my fame just extended locally. Or maybe Peter Vitella had forever screwed my chance to be anonymous.

"We have some questions, if you don't mind."

"Of course. Why don't you guys come inside?"

"Thanks."

The couple escorted us into a pristine home. Everything was immaculate. Even the pictures on the walls were all uniformly hung, with what looked liked exact spacing between each. The walls were white, and I mean lily white. Not a smidge of gray to be seen.

"Your house is beautiful," Cara said.

"Thank you. My husband and I pride ourselves on cleanliness."

I hadn't even mentioned cleanliness, but they obviously equated it to beauty.

They escorted us into a room that had four chairs, two sets of two facing each other, with a glass coffee table sitting between them. It's almost like the room had been decorated just for us. It was perfect for two visitors.

"Can I get you some coffee? By the way, I'm Sandy and my husband's name is Terry."

The husband gave a friendly wave. He seemed nice, but it was obvious that his wife took the lead.

"I'll take a cup," I said. "Black, please."

"I'll have the same," Cara added.

Usually, I would have turned down the offer, but I had an unexplainable feeling that they had something to tell us. So I thought by ordering a coffee we might extend the timeframe and possibly win a better chance to get more information.

"I'll be right back. Honey, can you keep them company?" Sandy said to Terry.

Cara and I sat in the two chairs on one side while Terry sat in one on the other.

"So, how long have you lived here?" Cara asked, initiating the small talk.

"It will be forty-five years in December."

"That's amazing. And by the looks of your pictures, you raised a few children here."

"Four of them. But we've been empty nesters for going on twenty-five years now."

"We just talked to your neighbor, Victoria," I said. "She said you'd been here the longest of anyone on this block."

"By probably fifteen years. The Rasmussens have been here almost thirty. They'd have to be second longest. And after that, it's a bunch of young couples."

"Seems like a nice street to raise your kids."

"It's been almost exclusively families who have lived here. So yeah, it's been great."

Sandy Doria reappeared with our coffees.

"That was quick," Cara said.

"My espresso machine makes them in seconds. Not like the old days of having to heat up water and then waiting five minutes while it steeped."

With her age, I'd thought she was going to mention Sanka.

Cara and I each tried a sip.

"It's great."

"It's excellent."

We spoke almost in unison.

"Well, which one is it? Great or excellent?" Sandy asked.

And we all had a nice laugh.

Followed by a somewhat uncomfortable silence.

"I almost feel like you expected us," I finally said.

"Well, not you two. But I though the police might come by, considering the Tillers used to live three doors down."

"People think these murders are random. And many families were affected," I said. "Where the Tillers used to live is probably not very high on their list of things to investigate."

"Yeah, I get that," she acknowledged. "Just seems more personal to me, I guess. Having known them and all."

"How many years ago did the Tillers move?" I asked.

"I'd say six or seven years."

"That's a long time," Cara interjected. "I'm sure the police feel that if there was any chance the Tillers were targeted, it was based on something more recent. Also, there were ten or so other families affected in San Jose. So the odds the Tillers were the actual target is highly unlikely."

Cara repeated almost verbatim what I had said, citing the police's theories. Sandy Doria picked up on that.

"But you are not buying that?"

"It's still the most likely scenario," I admitted. "But if everyone else is looking at these as just random murders, Cara and I figured it might be better to explore an alternative hypothesis."

"Like what?" Sandy asked.

"Well, that's what we are here for. Was there ever any incident or reason that someone might hate the Tillers?"

"They weren't the most likable people, I'll admit that. And a few beefs arose between them and other families on the block."

"Really," I said, my attention becoming more focused by the second.

"They were just jerks, especially the husband. I hate saying that after they both died. I'm not trying to disparage the dead."

"That goes without saying," I said.

"They were the type of people who would leave vegetables out for Halloween. If their son or daughter stayed at a neighbor's home too long, Mr. Tiller would make a scene and reprimand his children in front of the whole block. He'd physically grab them and carry them down the street as well. Listen, that in and of itself is not child abuse, and I've seen much worse, but it just shows you the type of guy he was. And his wife Celia was a bit of a witch herself."

This was all fascinating information, but it meant absolutely nothing if the Tillers' actions weren't somehow connected to their deaths. Which, despite my rising interest, still appeared unlikely.

Poisoning several families to get at only one true target? Was the Butcher that diabolical?

"How about any issues with someone younger?"

I didn't want to come out and say that I thought the Butcher was likely in his twenties or thirties, so I had to skirt around the idea.

"How young?"

"Maybe someone who might have been in his teens or early twenties back when the Tillers still lived here."

"There were a few of them, too. Mr. Tiller didn't make exceptions for anyone. He pissed everyone off. And yes, some of the older neighborhood kids butted heads with him."

"Anyone you remember specifically?"

"No, he butted heads with a whole bunch of them."

"And here I thought we were getting somewhere," I said.

"Well, that leads us to a question I have for you, Quint."

She emphasized my name and I knew something important was coming.

"Why haven't you asked about the Tillers' old neighbors? I think you may have heard about them—the Langleys."

My mouth hit the proverbial floor.

31.

"So these murders are related?" Cara asked as we got back to our car.

"It's starting to look that way. Well, at least the Tiller murder is related. The other people who died in San Jose might have been collateral damage."

"Maybe he put more fentanyl in the Tillers' cookies. Assuming they were the primary target."

"That's a good point, Cara. After all, they both died. And only one other family had more than one casualty. I'm not sure the police would keep the cookies from each specific house after the murders. But maybe they'd have more toxicity in their corpses than the rest of the deceased. I'll ask Captain Lockett."

"You're going to call him?"

"No, he won't take my calls. We're going to drive to Oakland right now."

We arrived at the 7th Street headquarters.

I'd made the mistake of putting the news on as we drove over. Every other story was something about the Bay Area Butcher. It had truly taken over every segment of life in our beautiful part of the country.

One set of rumors claimed he was a delivery driver and poisoning food. Others thought he worked for the city and planned to contaminate the water supply. To say the Bay Area was on edge didn't do the level of anxiety the proper justice.

Finally, Cara turned the radio off. I couldn't blame her.

I approached the entry to the precinct. Several cops were on duty, and I could tell at least a few recognized me as I arrived at the doors.

"What are you here for?" one of them asked.

"I need to see Captain Lockett."

"He's busy," he responded.

I looked at the other officers to see if I was going to get any help. It didn't appear so.

"This is very important," I said.

"Then call the captain," a different officer replied.

That's when I saw Freddie Fields hovering behind the giant metal detector.

"Freddie!" I yelled.

Seeing me, he reluctantly bypassed the other officers and walked outside to me.

"What is it, Quint?"

"I need to see Captain Lockett."

"He's not going to see you. We're now working with the feds and we've been told that you are no longer part of the investigation."

I shook my head. "This is such bullshit."

"I like you, Quint. I'm just doing my job."

I knew I had to see the captain. This info I'd uncovered was too important not to share.

"Well, if you want to stop more murders, you'll allow me to see him."

That got his attention.

"Do you have something?"

"One of the victims from San Jose used to be a next-door neighbor of the Langleys."

Freddie Fields's jaw hit the proverbial floor just as mine had.

"Jesus," he said.

"Yeah, Jesus. Now can I see the captain?"

Freddie turned around and faced the officers watching the front door. "Officers, let them through."

They acquiesced, and Cara and I followed Freddie into the precinct.

We bypassed the metal detector, just as I used to do with Ray, and headed to the now-familiar elevator around the corner.

"Freddie, you remember Cara."

They had briefly met when Freddie was at my apartment checking for fingerprints.

"Nice to see you again."

They exchanged a quick pleasantry, but I could tell Freddie's mind was elsewhere.

"This better be true, Quint. Could be my ass if not."

"It's true, alright."

We stepped off the elevator and walked around the corner. Captain Lockett saw me before I saw him and approached us with an unhappy expression.

"What the hell is he doing here?" he asked Freddie.

"He found something important."

"You can't just let sleeping dogs lie, can you, Quint?"

"Not when they're killing innocent people," I said.

"Well, fuck. You're here. Let's hear what you got."

"Do you want to hit a conference room?"

"No, we're fine right here."

I could tell he was perturbed about the whole thing.

"Cara, this is Captain Lockett. Captain, my girlfriend."

Their pleasantries barely merited the introduction. Then the captain turned back to me.

"What is it, Quint? You're testing my patience."

"The Tillers were next-door neighbors to the Langleys."

This information hit Lockett like a ton of bricks. He even took a step backward.

"You're fucking kidding me."

"I'm not."

He sighed. "Maybe we should get that conference room."

A few minutes later, I, Cara, Freddie, Captain Lockett, and two other officers occupied said conference room.

"You've got the floor, Quint."

I went over everything, explaining how we'd gone to Bradley Marks' house and he'd mentioned Pleasant Hill. Then, how Cara had found that the Tillers lived in Pleasant Hill several years back. Finally, I got to our meeting Victoria and then walking down to the Dorias.

"And that's when Sandy Doria dropped the bomb on us."

The two other officers nodded when I said that. They wore plain clothes, and I wondered if they might be feds who had let Captain Lockett take the lead.

"You're right there, Quint. It is a bomb. That would be the coincidence to end all coincidences."

"Agreed," I said. "Maybe we've been wrong all along. This wasn't just a psycho killing random, innocent people, but someone getting revenge on people he thinks wronged him."

Cara hadn't said a word, but she spoke up now.

"It might be both. Let's not forget, several other people died in San Jose and a lot of others got very sick. It's not like this guy gives two shits about anyone else being hurt. He'd blow up a building to kill someone he was targeting. At least, that's what I think."

Her words hung in the air. She was right. This didn't suddenly mean the Butcher would limit himself to targeting people related to the Langleys and Tillers. He'd shown he had no problem killing innocent civilians as well.

"True. And well said," Captain Locket said. "Alright, Quint, my phone is available to you again. But the OPD is not the only one working this case now."

And he nodded at the two other men in the room, confirming my suspicions.

"So I can't guarantee we will always be quick in getting back to you."

"I understand," I said. "I'm just trying to help out."

"Of course. We all are."

As he walked with us to the door, he added, "Be sure to call me if any of your articles now stand out more. And I may be calling you if we have some added questions."

"Sounds good," I said.

We said our goodbyes soon thereafter.

32.

Another day passed. We'd accomplished a lot in the last week or so. Much of it thanks to Cara, who had been hugely instrumental. We'd become a team in every sense of the word.

Unfortunately, each passing day brought us twenty-four hours closer to the next killing. Or killings. And as I looked down at my phone that morning, I realized we were only one day from the all too literal deadline. Tomorrow was Friday.

Despite all the great work we were doing, we were still behind the eight ball. And we'd need a huge break in order to catch him before he murdered again.

I'd stayed up until two a.m. going over my articles the night before. Still hadn't found any article that jumped out. Nothing specific to Pleasant Hill. I wasn't going to be that lucky.

I realized that the Butcher could have been mentioned in an article that had nothing to do with either the Langleys or the Tillers. Even if he held a massive grudge against the two families, the article may have involved something completely different.

Even though we'd achieved a lot, I was still at a standstill when it came to whatever clue lay in my articles.

While I was busy reading them for the umpteenth time, Cara looked up at me.

"Let's go out more tomorrow," she said. "Dennis McCarthy's guy hasn't had much to do. A few walks down to the coffee shop and a quick lunch at Hops and Scotch. One trip to Pleasant Hill and maybe he followed us to Oakland."

"I agree. But it's unlikely the Butcher will be out following us tomorrow."

"Yeah, we've been so busy, I almost forgot. Tomorrow is Friday."

"I just hope that whatever happens isn't something catastrophic," I said. "I feel like we're making inroads and may have a chance to catch him before the final killing. But it would take a miracle to catch him before tomorrow."

"You're right," Cara said and shrugged helplessly.

We'd been so caught up in our research and investigation that we'd forgotten how terrible the murders had been. We started after Ray had been killed, so we hadn't experienced a new murder since turning my apartment into a true crime diorama.

Would tomorrow be the day that changed?

Sadly, it likely would be.

33

"Quint! Turn on the news," Cara yelled from the bedroom as I sat on the couch going through old articles.

It was only eight a.m. Although this was the day the Butcher was supposed to strike, I hadn't expected anything so early. My heart rate shot off the charts as I flipped on the T.V.

A young, bespectacled news anchor looked on. I expected something terrible to come from her mouth, but she just talked about how BART was running behind schedule for the next few days.

"You almost gave me a heart attack. I thought you'd seen something online," I shouted back.

Cara appeared from the room. "No, I just thought we should have it on in case something happens."

I let out a sigh of relief, although my chest still felt tight. "His first three sets of murders all took place at night. Not that he couldn't strike early, but I'm not expecting anything at eight in the morning."

And I was right. We didn't hear anything that day. Not at eight a.m. Not at eight p.m. And not by midnight, when we finally decided to try and crash.

It felt like the antithesis of Christmas Eve. Something would be waiting for us the next morning, but it was a surprise we would have done anything to avoid.

The universe, and the Butcher, had different plans.

I woke up at six a.m. and immediately went out to my couch and turned on the T.V.

I'd never bought a T.V. for my bedroom. Some people found it weird, but I explained to them when I fell asleep at night it was usually with my handy laptop next to me.

Of course, that had changed once Cara moved in.

Maybe it was time to buy a T.V. for the bedroom as well.

That inane subject swirled through my mind as the T.V. came roaring to life.

I heard the sound before I saw the newscaster, and what I heard made my heart plummet:

"And authorities are assuming it has to be the work of the Bay Area Butcher."

I pressed pause on the remote and hurried to the bedroom, where I tapped Cara on the shoulder.

"Get up," I said.

She rose and walked out to the couch immediately, without another word needing to be said.

I rewound the remote a few seconds, pressed pause a second time, and the anchor came to life. In her late fifties, she had been a Bay Area fixture for decades. Her voice did not offer a cheerful start to the day.

"And authorities are assuming it has to be the work of the Bay Area Butcher," I heard a second time.

I looked at Cara, who had instinctively grabbed my hand. I tightened my grip around hers and we held each other's gazes for a moment before turning back to the T.V.

"They believe the fire was set just before midnight last night. Walnut Creek authorities have said they first received calls at 11:54, reporting smoke coming from Treeside Manor. Some neighbors arrived before the police and found that the two main doors had been locked from the outside with a U-lock of the kind often used to secure bicycles. All in all, just a horrible scene. The locks on the doors surely added to the high death count, but with it being a retirement home, the lack of mobility of its guests probably contributed as well. We will have more throughout the day here at KRON, but right now the news is that fourteen people have been confirmed dead at the Treeside Manor in Walnut Creek. Beyond tragic. Authorities ask that if anyone saw something suspicious in the area, please call 9-1-1 immediately. That includes people, cars, or any other detail.

"We also have a quote from the Walnut Creek Chief of Police, Millard Lyons: 'We can't be certain this was the work of the Bay Area Butcher, but all signs point to yes.' This has just been an altogether tragic late night and morning. We hope you'll stay with KRON for extended coverage throughout the day."

The anchor's words had slowed, her eyes turning wet and red. Now she bowed her head and took a deep breath to compose herself. I'd watched her reporting for years and had never seen her come so close to losing it.

"We'll be back in a few minutes," she said through a few tears.

I pressed pause on the T.V. Cara gave me a hug and started crying herself.

"Killing defenseless old people in a fire? You can't go any lower."

I nodded. It was a disgusting act. Even for someone as deranged as the Butcher.

"I want him dead with every ounce of my soul. I'd kill him myself if I could," Cara said.

"I feel the same," I said, the first words out of my mouth since we'd sat together to take in the horrible news.

"I'm sick to my stomach."

I leaned in and hugged her again. She'd shown great courage investigating the Butcher with me, but she'd reached her breaking point. I couldn't say that I blamed her.

We intermittently checked the news for the next hour or so. On the one hand, we didn't want to miss anything. But the news was so sad, so sickening, that we couldn't just watch it without a break. It would have driven us crazy.

If any good news could be had, it was that the death toll remained at fourteen. The police and fire department arrived within a few minutes of the first distress call, and were able to save forty-four lives.

A monumental achievement sure to be forgotten as people focused on the lives lost. Understandably so.

I made the mistake of going online. The Bay Area Butcher, as he'd become known across the entire world, led every website imaginable. BBC, TMZ, CNN—even ESPN had an article on the killings. The killer's story had reached biblical proportions and he had taken over the news cycle once again by doing the unthinkable.

At around 9:30 a.m., Cara said to me:

"I don't want to sit around and hear about this all day. It's too tragic. I can't deal with it."

I concurred. My own heart had grown heavier and heavier as information began to come out about the people who had died and reporters interviewed their family members. At the same time, I'd been thinking.

"Want to take a little trip?" I asked. "Something has been bothering me."

"Anything to get me out of here," Cara said. "Where are we headed?"

"The *San Francisco Chronicle* offices."

Cara nodded. She knew there was only one reason to go there.

As we drove up from the Avalon's underground parking garage, we could see three different trucks belonging to local T.V. stations. They camped out either to get a shot of me or to broadcast from my apartment complex, which they'd consider a nice backdrop considering the "rivalry" between myself and the Butcher.

All for some better ratings.

I felt both angry and sad.

Here I was. The guy who knew Ray Kintner. And the possible reason he got killed. They were implicitly saying that I was guilty as well. Not of catastrophic murders like the Butcher, but by broadcasting outside of Avalon Walnut Creek, they were saying a small portion of this was on me.

It incensed me. My knuckles gripped the steering wheel until they turned white. I was doing everything I could to catch this maniac, and yet these T.V. stations saw me as just a tool to improve ratings.

Luckily, the parking garage was dimly lit, and at this time of the morning a lot of traffic passed in and out. None of the media recognized me as I sped by them.

"Is this all because of you?" Cara asked, summing up what I'd been thinking.

"Mostly. I'm sure they'll mention how the Butcher was in this apartment complex to drop off that letter to me. But the main reason they're here is to sell the story of Quint vs. the Butcher."

I felt weird referring to myself in the third person, but it seemed apropos.

"Did you ever think this was going to get so out of control?" Cara asked.

"Never in my wildest dreams. This is utter insanity."

I got on the freeway and pressed down hard on the accelerator. I could feel Cara looking at me side-eyed.

"Calm down, Quint," she said. "The last thing we need is to get into a accident."

I was fired up, maybe more so than I'd ever been in my life. But I lowered my speed. For Cara.

The San Francisco Chronicle began operation in 1865 and had only changed buildings twice in the subsequent 155 years. The current office sat just a few blocks from where it originally began.

Working in the newspaper business for nine years, albeit at a much, much smaller paper than the *Chronicle*, I understood the financial risks they faced. But the *Chronicle* had done a good job and was borderline thriving while so many other papers had either folded or resorted to putting out online versions only.

I parked the car a block from their massive office and put loads of quarters in the meter. I was old enough to remember when a few quarters would get you an hour. Not anymore. The last thing we needed today was a parking ticket, so I kept feeding the meter like it was an old-school slot machine.

Cara had been quiet on the ride over and remained so as we walked toward the huge facade of the building.

"Don't worry, Cara. Peter Vitella may be antagonistic to us, but he's not the real enemy. At least, not the one that matters."

"That's not why I'm quiet, Quint."

She didn't have to elaborate. She was still thinking about the old folks home.

Entering the building, we were greeted by three security guards. I guess I shouldn't have been surprised. Too many had come to see the media as the enemy of the people. Although, I had to admit, they weren't exactly in my good graces at the moment.

Having T.V. trucks camped outside of your apartment complex can do that to you.

"How can I help you?" one security guard asked us. It seemed this position didn't call for a lot of activity. He was pushing three hundred pounds. As were his two co-workers. He didn't really look like he wanted to help, either. His expression said he'd rather be anywhere else. I couldn't blame him. It was a thankless job.

"I'd like to see Peter Vitella."

"You can't just meet with one of the writing staff without having an appointment."

"Well, maybe he'd like to meet with me. Considering I have information on the Bay Area Butcher."

That got his attention, and his two co-workers also looked over in our direction.

"Mario, call upstairs please."

A minute passed and Mario approached with the good news.

"Mr. Vitella will see you now."

"Thanks," I said.

"My co-worker Andre will take you up."

I thanked him again.

We followed Andre, who led us to the elevator a hundred feet away. He escorted us on and pressed the 6th floor button.

Once we arrived there, Andre pointed us toward what appeared to be the front desk. He then went back on the elevator and headed back to the ground floor, seeming relieved to have the excitement over. Meanwhile, I steeled myself for the confrontation I'd come here for.

Peter Vitella approached us before we got to the front desk. I'd never met the man in person, but he wore the derby hat that accompanied his picture for the paper. He was definitely older than the man in said picture. But while he might have been bordering on elderly, I knew his fangs still packed some venom.

"Peter Vitella." He extended his hand. "You must be Quint and Cara. I'm truly honored."

It was an odd introduction. He'd badmouthed us in print and potentially put us in harm's way. And yet there was no acknowledgement of that. It was like he was saying hi to two old friends. And I hated to admit it, but he almost came off as charismatic.

I reminded myself of all the lies he'd spread over the years. The faux charisma probably explained how he got close to people. Before stabbing them in the back.

"Yup, here we are. Do you have a place we could talk?"

"Certainly," he said. "Follow me."

Vitella walked us toward the back of the expansive room. The *San Francisco Chronicle* had to have twenty times the space of the *Walnut Creek*

Times. Maybe more. And that was just on this floor. Not that this came as an surprise. The *San Chronicle* was a world famous newspaper that had bee around for over a century and a half.

I could feel all the eyes turn toward us as we passed. And who could blame them?

Vitella had berated us in print and yet here we were. And on the mornin after the Bay Area Butcher had struck again. It had to be jarring for his co workers.

I heard some whispers that I felt sure were discussing us, but I paid ther no mind. I was here to talk to Vitella and find out how he got his inside information. Namely, how he knew Cara brought files into Avalon Walnu Creek.

Could it have been the Butcher who told him? That was my suspicion.

We bypassed a few smaller offices and found ourselves entering massive one. I knew that Vitella had been with the *Chronicle* for decades, bu it still seemed wrong that a guy who peddled in lies and gossip had one of th most impressive offices at the paper.

Two leather chairs sat opposite a big oak table from another, mor impressive leather chair. It turned out to be the perfect office for three peopl and Vitella gestured for Cara and I to take seats. Which we did.

"So what can I do for you, Quint? Not here to beat me up, I hope."

His smugness showed in his teasing tone.

"I'd probably enjoy it too much and land in jail," I said. "No, we're her because of the true scourge of the Bay Area."

"Ah, the Butcher. What sickening news to wake up to this morning."

"It's unfathomable," I said.

"Truly repellant. Looks like I'll have to keep writing about him. And you."

He said it in a gross, self-satisfied way.

"Almost sounds like you're looking forward to it," I said.

"I'm a writer, like you. Doesn't it feel good to have work?"

"Not because people are dying."

"People die every day."

"Not like this. And they're not just 'people'. These are your innocer neighbors of the Bay Area."

"Semantics," he said.

He was truly as disgusting in person as in print. And now I really did war to kick his ass. But I couldn't. I needed something from him.

"How did you find out that Cara was taking supplies into my apartmer complex?"

"A confidential informant, of course."

Vitella started smiling again, but it was insincere to its core.

"Can you tell us who it is?" I asked.

"You may be able to get information from the police, but I myself will not give it up so easily. If I go around outing my sources, who would I be? You know how important such integrity is to a journalist."

"Fuck off," I said. "Don't even try to equate us. You're a slimeball."

His smile faded.

"I could have you escorted out right now. No one tells me to fuck off."

"I think you're trash, Mr. Vitella. Calling out my girlfriend who never did one thing to anyone."

"She can't speak for herself?"

Cara had been quiet all morning, the murders at the retirement home affecting her deeply. Now she sat straight in the chair, her arms folded, and said steadily, "My opinion of you is the same as Quint's. If not worse."

His shit-eating grin returned as if he found this funny.

"You guys think you are so fucking cool. But you know what, you haven't done shit to catch the Butcher either."

"That's why we're here," Cara said. "And you have no idea about all the work we've done."

Now that she had entered the conversation, she was going to have her voice heard.

"What kind of person would I be if I gave up my sources?" Vitella repeated.

I decided to try a softer path for the asshole in front of us. For the greater good.

"Maybe you could have a part in helping catch this psycho," I said.

It seemed that I'd piqued his interest.

"How is that?"

"Well, if your alleged source was the Butcher himself, maybe the police could trace him through his email. Or did your source call you?"

"Who's to say that it wasn't just one of your neighbors at the apartment complex? Surely it didn't have to be the Butcher."

"Very few of my neighbors know who Cara is. The Butcher certainly would, however. The guy knows everything about me. Or so it seems."

I could see his mind racing. From personal experience I understood that outing sources was a no-no in this profession. But we were talking about the possibility that the Butcher himself had contacted him.

Vitella typed something into his desktop computer. He looked closer at whatever appeared on the screen. And something seemed to register.

"You turned forty last year, didn't you, Quint?"

"Yes."

"During the Charles Zane madness, correct?"

"I ended up in the hospital on my birthday. It's how everything got started. Why?"

That news had become public, so I wasn't exactly shocked that Vitella knew how old I was.

"What was the date?" he asked, ignoring my question.

"June 22nd."

"Jesus fucking Christ," he said.

"What is it?" Cara asked.

"Come here," Vitella said.

We stood up from our red leather chairs and walked around his desk. He moved the monitor in our direction.

"Look at the email address it came from," he said.

We looked. Q62280@gmail.com. Q 6 22 80. Q surely stood for Quint. And the rest spelled out my birthday. June 22nd, 1980.

"Fucking A!" I said. "Do you still think it's just some random neighbor?"

Vitella looked at me with a seriousness that had appeared for the first time.

"No. I don't. But can the police find someone by their email?"

"Probably not," I admitted. "But I still want you to call them right now."

"Your friends at the Oakland Police Department?"

"They are no longer my friends. But you can call them if you'd like. Or the SFPD."

He looked resigned to the fact he had no choice. If he kept protecting his source, he'd be aiding and abetting a felon at this point.

"I'll call both."

It was no use belaboring the point that the man in front of me was an asshole. So I continued to play nice.

"You're doing the right thing."

"I'm sorry about the articles I wrote about you two. I had no idea who I was getting the information from."

I didn't know whether to believe him.

"The Q didn't give you pause?" I asked.

"What's Q and a bunch of numbers supposed to mean to me? It looked like a made-up email. Which is what I'd expect from any source who doesn't want to be outed."

I didn't have the time to continue arguing. I'd gotten what I wanted.

"Make sure you call the police as soon as we leave. Maybe, just maybe, this will lead to something."

"I will. You guys stay safe, knowing the Butcher is out there watching you."

I reached for Cara's hand and turned to go. I was done with Peter Vitella.

"Stop pretending like you care. People die every day, right?"

We walked out of his office before he had a chance to respond.

"We're not going home, are we?" Cara asked once we returned to the car.

"No."

"Off to see Paddy?"

"Yup. It's quite obvious now that he's following us, isn't it? Let's see if the guy we hired has spotted anything suspicious."

"You didn't text him this morning, did you?"

"No. We were just going straight to the *Chronicle*. Didn't think it was necessary."

"I guess," Cara said. "But it couldn't have hurt."

We arrived outside of Boyle's Grocery Store less than fifteen minutes later. It was across town, but San Francisco is very condensed for a big city, so that everything turns out to be pretty close to everything else. It's nothing like Los Angeles, where you could be twenty miles away from your destination but looking at a ninety-minute drive.

I hadn't called ahead and just hoped that we'd find Paddy Roark there. Cara and I made our way into the now familiar grocery store. We walked past the checkers and looked around the aisles.

"Do you want to ask if he's here?" Cara asked.

"If he's here, he'll find us," I said.

And I was right. Less than thirty seconds later, Paddy strolled down the aisle toward us. We exchanged pleasantries.

"I swear, your eyes must be on those closed-circuit T.V.s at all times," I said.

"No, I just smelled trouble walking in."

Cara and I laughed ruefully.

"Can we talk?" I asked.

"Of course. You know the drill."

And we followed him to the back of the store.

We sat down, with Paddy taking the head seat, which was his unless Dennis McCarthy was present. Then Paddy became second-in-command.

"I'm assuming you've heard," Paddy said.

"Sadly, yes. Woke up to it this morning," I said.

Paddy nodded, and something passed between us, both acknowledging that we wouldn't talk any more about what happened at the retirement home.

"You've been a bad boy, Quint," he said instead.

"What did I do?"

"It's what you didn't do."

"Not sure I follow."

"We forgot to call his guy this morning," Cara said.

"Bingo." Paddy nodded. "My guy tells me when he gets a call from you. But nothing this morning. And yet, here you are, out in San Francisco."

"I'm sorry," I said. "We couldn't deal with the news about the old folks' home and I impulsively decided to go talk to Peter Vitella. Not much your guy could have done."

"How'd it go with that asshole?" Paddy asked.

"He'd been in contact with the Butcher about Cara walking into my apartment complex. I wanted to wring Vitella's fucking neck."

"A lot of people would have patted you on the back."

"I thought better of it."

"Smart," Paddy said.

"If I gave you an email address, could any of your guys trace it?"

"I'll ask, but I don't think our guys are that advanced. The cops might be able to get his IP address though."

"Yeah, that's what I figured."

No one said anything for a few seconds. Finally, Cara spoke.

"Has your guy found anyone suspicious tailing us?"

Paddy shook his head. "No. He told me you guys haven't been out all that much. He thought he was going to have tons of footage and many people in the background of your life. But that's not the case."

"It's our own fault," I said. "Today wasn't the only time I forgot to call him. And we've kind of been shelled up in the apartment more than I expected. That's where we've been going over all of our information."

"He said he's got a few hours of footage from the Starbucks you always go to. And he got a little more with you guys walking around a neighborhood one day, but that you were just knocking on doors. There wasn't much to film so he kept his distance."

"Yeah, we saw him follow us that day in his black sedan."

Paddy frowned, his eyebrows furrowing. "He doesn't have a black car."

I looked at Cara and something passed between us. My heart rate accelerated.

"A black sedan followed us from my apartment complex. There's no doubt in my mind. I got on the freeway and then took probably three or four right and left turns after we got on the main roads. The sedan remained behind us through all of them. There's no way it was coincidence."

"What are you saying?"

"I'm saying we were being followed by someone in a black sedan. This wasn't a guy randomly taking the same streets as us. I just figured it was your guy."

"I'll call him right now."

I noticed how Paddy never mentioned his name. Smart.

Paddy picked up a cell phone and dialed a number. He held it to his ear, still wearing a worried expression. All we could hear was his end of the conversation.

"Hey...Do you remember when Quint talked to the people in that neighborhood? ...I need you to look for a black sedan in the background..."

I interrupted, "It must have parked on a side street. Because I didn't see it again once we got to Iron Hill Street."

Paddy continued on his end, "The black sedan was probably parked on a nearby side street, but never got closer. If you were recording, maybe you picked up a license plate... Okay, that's good news. Get back to me as soon as you can."

Paddy hung up the phone and turned to us.

"He says he has a dashcam always recording. He's going to go back through the footage and check for a black sedan. Hopefully we can see whoever was sitting in it, or, at the very least, get a license plate number."

"Thanks a lot, Paddy. This could be the break we're looking for."

"This feels different," Cara said. "Like maybe it's not just another dead end."

"He's got to go through the footage. I'm not sure how long this is going to take."

"Cara and I will head back to the East Bay. But please call me as soon as you know."

"I will. I hope we've got something."

"Me too."

Cara and I thanked Paddy, left Boyle's, and headed back to the East Bay. For the first time, it felt like momentum was on our side.

But that was tempered by the knowledge that fourteen innocent people had been killed in a fire. What a horrible way to die. I tried everything I could to not think about it. But that proved impossible. I was imagining smoke-filled rooms and older people desperately, hopelessly trying to escape via the front doors.

You'd hope they'd have the wherewithal to break the windows of their rooms, but who knows how someone will react when smoke starts filling the area? Especially being awakened in the middle of the night.

Cara hadn't been herself that morning and I felt sure it was because the same things kept running through her head. I decided not to broach the subject, which just would have made it worse.

When we arrived back at Avalon Walnut Creek, the news trucks were still there. They had taken up positions past the parking garage, so I was able to speed inside without being seen.

A small victory in the grand scheme of things, but I'd take it.

34.

Upon returning to my apartment, we threw the news on. We kept the volume low and we weren't actively watching, but our eyes darted to the screen now and then.

It felt like the proverbial train wreck that you couldn't look away from.

Reports of the deceased kept coming in and a few more pictures were shown. It always hit home when you saw the faces of those people who died.

One stood out.

Her name was Ginny Fitzgerald, and she had the biggest smile I'd ever seen. Her hair was gray, and she was quite old, but her picture just gave off the vibe of someone who loved life. A twinkle shone in her eye even though she was in the twilight of her life.

And now she was gone.

I thought again about what I would do to the Butcher if I was locked in a room with him.

That was another thing I tried to push out of my mind. It surely said something about myself as well.

I needed something to occupy my mind.

"You hungry?" I asked Cara.

"Not really."

"Me neither. I'm going to cook anyway."

"That doesn't make a lot of sense."

"I need to do something," I said. "I can't keep watching the news and seeing the faces of the people who died. It's tearing my soul apart."

"I understand completely," she said.

Cara looked down at her phone. "It's one p.m. Why don't you start cooking something low and slow? It will help pass the time, and we can eat it for dinner later tonight."

"That's a good idea, Chef Cara. Any suggestions?"

"We've got that Beef Stew. Why don't you sauté some garlic and onions, sear the meat, and then throw in a few cups each of red wine and beef broth. Add a few carrots and potatoes if you've got them and let it cook for the next several hours."

"Now I'm hungry. That sounds delicious."

"Thanks. It will be perfect around 6:00 or so. Tender as can be."

I walked to the kitchen and took out a cutting board. I started chopping some garlic and onions. It was nice to do a mundane activity that kept my mind occupied.

The day dragged on once the hard part of the cooking was over, each minute more interminable than the last.

At 2:30, I called Paddy.

"Have you heard anything from your guy?" I asked.

"He thinks he found the license plate. He spotted only one black sedan on the recording of the area you drove through. It was occupied by a male, but he could be anywhere from twenty to sixty. My man showed me the picture and all you see is the back of the guy's head, and it's heavily pixelated. Luckily, he was able to focus on and identify the license plate."

"So, do you know who the car belongs to?"

"Not yet. I only got this information twenty minutes ago. I just texted our lone connection at the DMV, but haven't heard back. But I imagine I will soon."

"Thank you, Paddy. If it really was the Butcher following me, this could be the evidence we need."

"Let's hope it was. I'll be in touch when I hear back from our friend at the DMV."

"They're open on Saturday?" Paddy had been exceptionally loyal to me, but I knew he wasn't a saint. I didn't dare ask why he had a connection at the DMV.

"I think so. But they are to me regardless."

I understood what he meant.

"Thanks for everything, Paddy."

"You got it, Quint."

And he hung up the phone.

Cara had been sitting on the edge of our bed, once again studying the collage we'd created. I'd taken the call in the kitchen, but when I looked through the door at her I could tell that she'd heard our conversation.

"Good news?" she asked.

"Not yet, but soon, I think. They found the black sedan and are waiting for someone to run the plate."

"That's great!"

"Yup."

She stood up. "You seem reserved about this. This could be earth-shattering information. And that's not hyperbole."

"I know. It's just hard to celebrate with what happened at the old folks' home," I said.

"I understand. I know I've been a bit off today too."

She emerged from the bedroom and we hugged.

"You've done amazing work, Quint. Don't let this asshole's actions lessen all you've accomplished."

"You are just as big a part of this as I am, Cara," I said. "Don't forget that."

"Thanks."

Fifteen minutes later, Paddy Roark called back.

"Quint, I talked to the woman at the DMV."

The last six weeks had come to this point. All the investigating that Cara and I had done. Meeting Bradley Marks. Victoria. The Dorias. The countless hours spent making the collage. The even more countless hours I'd spent reading everything on the collage. Trying to figure out the Butcher's poker riddle. So much effort and time.

And it had all come to this moment. At least, I hoped so. *Please don't tell me it was some random asshole following me. Peter Vitella's photographer. A member of the paparazzi. A true-crime nut.*

Doubt came over me in a panic. Maybe this wouldn't be the slam dunk I'd hoped for.

"Quint, are you there?"

My mind was such a muddled mess, I hadn't answered Paddy.

"I'm here."

"Are you ready?" he asked.

"Ready as I'll ever be."

"The car is registered to a man named Tyler Anthony Danovich."

I wrote the name down as he said it.

And looked at it for a good ten seconds.

Followed by writing out my name:

Q-U-I-N-T A-D-L-E-R

Could it be???

I thought about the poker riddle. And ran through some other things in my head. Including who I saw on the day the Butcher left a note on my apartment door.

My suspicions were confirmed.

I knew who the Bay Area Butcher was!

35.
THE KILLER

All good things must end. So goes the expression.

So the fact that I'd avoided detection for almost forty-five days, while being one of the most sought-after men in the world, was an accomplishment in and of itself. I chose to look on the bright side. I'd always known my anonymity wouldn't last forever.

Truth be told, I looked forward to the attention. I wanted the world to know they were dealing with a mad genius the likes of which it had rarely seen. If ever.

And that by no means meant I was done killing. Far from it.

My final set of murders would be an all-timer. Like calling your shot in the bottom of the ninth. And then walking off.

Only I'd be sneaking off, never to be found.

I'll get to that, but let's start at the beginning.

I think you deserve that.

I was born Tyler Anthony Danovich in San Bernardino, CA, but my parents moved to Northern California when I was three years old. My father was a salesman in the mold of Willy Loman, and was equally unstable and unhappy with his place in the world. He was also a jerk and verbally abusive to my mother.

Not that I cared or stood up for her. I didn't like that bitch either.

I was an only child, like Quint himself. Although that's probably where our similarities ended. From all I've read, he loved his deceased father and is still close with his mother.

Not me. As you can see, I despised both of my parents.

They tried to love me. In their own, hard-ass, militant way. But I never reciprocated. I was born without the trait of being able to love a fellow human. That was foreign to me. From birth, I was the ultimate narcissist, someone who literally cared about no one else in the world.

Never have, never will.

I knew I was different from an early age and my lack of any compassion or empathy came out in action. It just wasn't in my DNA.

I remember one time when Lucas, a neighborhood kid I'd occasionally hang with, fell off a bike jump and landed on a shard of glass that had been hidden in the nearby dirt. He screamed blood murder with the shard protruding from his leg.

Did I go get his parents or call 9-1-1? No.

I said, "I'll see you tomorrow" and biked home. And if we're being honest, I got a good chuckle out of seeing that glass poking out of poor old Lucas's leg. I wish it had cut deeper.

His parents put an end to that "friendship" soon thereafter.

That became a theme. Adults would realize that something was a bit off with me and separate me from their children. It took a bit longer for my own parents to realize what I was. They saw my behavior as nothing more than childhood immaturity.

My mother contracted breast cancer when I was a freshman in high school and died somewhere during my junior year. I think it happened in the fall, but I honestly don't remember. I attended the funeral and said all the right things, but there wasn't some hole in my heart that would never heal. To me, it was just another death in a world of countless deaths.

Actually, that's not true. It was better than most deaths, since I detested her so.

After the death of the woman he'd abused, my father became a shell of himself. He went full Willy Loman, always lamenting where he was in life. I often wondered if it was due to his wife's death or because he had started to realize his son was the antichrist.

He began looking at me differently, realizing my childhood "peculiarities" were likely something more sinister. When he lost his battle with depression and ate his gun fourteen months after my mother died, it left me alone in this world.

But really, I'd always been.

My father gave a final "fuck you" to me, leaving me nothing in his will, donating his money, and his house, to charity. While I was pissed, I realized why. He saw me as evil. Hey, he wasn't wrong.

As with my mother's death, I said all the right things to people I knew. I was very good at acting normal when I needed to. But all the time, beneath the veneer, I was a growing monster.

When I talked to people and feigned sadness, I was really imagining gnawing their faces off, Hannibal Lecter style.

I was eighteen when my father died, and I enrolled at a local technical school, where I learned how to code. While I didn't get good grades in high school, it wasn't because I was dumb. I was actually acutely intelligent; I just didn't care about school. But coding came easy to me and I advanced quickly, getting a solid paying job upon finishing the program.

My mind, already a sinister place, only got worse once I "lost" my parents. I started imagining wreaking havoc on the world I loathed.

But I didn't want to be some half-wit criminal who killed one person and got locked in a cage for the rest of his life.

So I bided my time. And read. And planned.

When I decided to kill, I would do it right.

I wasn't going to be a one-hit wonder.

A few years passed. I continued to be gainfully employed at my nondescript internet company. I worked as a front end developer, in charge of making your landing pages beautiful and bug free.

I had a few "friends" at work and girls were initially attracted to me. But once they got to know me, they'd inevitably choose to distance themselves.

Maybe it's true about women using a sixth sense that men don't have. Because most guys thought I was pretty normal.

Well, that's not exactly true. But they didn't catch on as quickly as the gals did.

A workplace shooting had crossed my mind a time or two, but those things were often forgotten after a few days on the news.

I wanted to be infamous. Forever. Not just for one news cycle.

My compulsion to kill was only superseded by my goal of not getting caught. So I continued to study my craft.

And I started to think about how it was all going to transpire. Early on I knew I needed to get my message out to the police and the media in some way. Add a little panache.

If a killer commits the occasional murder, the news will report on it, but it will never become a national phenomenon. Not in these times when murders happen every day. But if that killer writes letters, ridicules the police, and even tells them the day he's going to kill?

Now that's good fucking theater!

In my extensive reading on serial killers, I'd found that many tortured or killed animals when they were children. I didn't understand the point. Kill a defenseless dog or cat? Pull the wings off of some butterfly?

That was no game. It left zero chance of losing.

But there is such a chance in killing humans. It's more like a battle of wits. Only instead of failing a debate, the loser dies in my rendition. It's more like a duel in the Burr/Hamilton vein.

In that regard, I'm probably most like the Zodiac Killer, from whom I quote: "It is more fun than killing wild game in the forest because man is the most dangerous animal of all."

If I had a motif, that would probably be it.

I could go out and shoot Bambi, but no one would really care. But if I kill someone's dear old Uncle Harry, you're damn right that will elicit a reaction.

Which is all I want.

I'd never felt much in this world. Other people's suffering is the on
thing that conjures up something like emotion in me.

Approximately two years ago, at the ripe old age of twenty-five, I move
into Avalon Walnut Creek.

There I noticed many pretty girls milling around, and I decided to tr
and shake things up. Start fresh. Or at least, change my name. I was sti
a sadistic son of a bitch. That would never change.

So, at Avalon, and anywhere away from work, I started going by Tac
my initials. Tyler Anthony Danovich.

Tyler certainly hadn't gotten me much in life. Maybe Tad would b
different. At least, that's what I told myself.

Sure, women got scared off because I was a creep, not because c
my name. But I'm a narcissist and, like any true narcissist, that make
me an optimist where I'm concerned. I thought maybe the name chang
would do the trick.

Newsflash: It didn't.

I ran into Quint a few times around the building, but thought nothing c
him either way. A neighbor told me he was a writer for a small, loca
paper, and at some point I read a few of his articles. I wasn't impressec

I'd say hi to him frequently, since we both lived on the fourth floo
As I said, I can act normal and say the right things when necessary. S
I was cordial and I'm sure he thought I was a pleasant human being.

Walking around the halls of a huge apartment complex, I'm a
ordinary as the next guy.

And Quint and I never progressed beyond saying hello in th
hallways, anyway.

One random day, late last summer, I'd settled comfortably in m
apartment at Avalon, reading a biography of Edmund Kemper, the Cc
Ed Killer, when I heard gunshots. It took me a second, but there was n
mistaking what I'd heard.

I headed off in the direction where they'd come from. Some might sa
I'm crazy for following the gunshots, but if you didn't already know
death and carnage fascinate me like nothing else. So it wasn't really
choice. I was under a compulsion.

Going to the source of the sound, I sped past the elevator of th
fourth floor, and then immediately I saw blood on the wall outside th
stairwell next to it. I opened the door to the stairs and was greeted wit
more blood on the floor in front of me.

I walked to the top of the steps and looked down. Someone ha
collapsed at the bottom of the first flight, obviously having been shot.

trail of blood lead down to him and a red pool surrounded his crumpled body.

I leapt, two steps a time, to the bottom of the stairwell. There I recognized the man as Quint. It looked like he'd received gunshot wounds to his upper arm and shoulder, which he'd likely recover from. But he certainly wasn't in good shape and as I stood over him, he flickered in and out of consciousness.

This was the first time I'd ever seen a gunshot victim in front of me, in the flesh and blood, and I have to say, it excited me. The carnage some tiny bullets at a high speed could inflict on a human body proved intoxicating.

But Quint had been cordial with me, so I didn't necessarily wish him harm. To say I cared whether he lived or died would be going too far, but I wasn't actively rooting for his death.

That would come later.

Standing over him, I told him he was going to be alright a few times, not knowing what else to say. I didn't have time to do much else, anyway. In a matter of seconds, a couple other people arrived on the stairwell, and I backed off. A few minutes later, EMTs arrived and I was pushed farther away in the stairwell. Finally, the police arrived, and with curt orders they removed everyone who had gathered.

A week passed and the shooting of Quint showed up all over the news. He was going to live. But I found out he wasn't going to be returning to Avalon. I saw Kayla, who managed the property, and she said his presence was deemed too big a risk since someone had tried to kill him.

Made sense to me. Although I'll admit, I enjoyed the action. A nice change from the boring everyday life of Avalon.

Fast forward a few months. Quint becomes a local hero after taking down Charles Zane in their battle at sea. And then I see him do a few national interviews as well.

That's when I started to turn on him. It built up some major resentment.

This guy wrote shitty-ass articles for a small-town newspaper. And now he's being treated like some sort of hero? Give me a fucking break!

And then, several months ago, he moves back in to Avalon. With what was rumored to be two months rent-free. For what, getting shot? More bullshit.

And then the two things that pushed me over the edge in my disgust for Quint:

First off, Cara. From what I can gather, they were broken up when I first moved in to Avalon, which explains why I'd never laid eyes on her.

I certainly would have remembered. She was one of the most beautiful creatures I'd ever seen. A 10+, if there is such a thing.

And she was hanging out with this average (at best) writer who was probably ten years older than her? My blood boiled.

I preferred him when I thought he was just some pathetic writer. The fact that he had a gorgeous girlfriend, on top of becoming quasi-famous for nothing, was too much for me. My infuriation only increased.

And then the kicker.

Since his return, I'd seen Quint a few times around Avalon, and he told me he had an upcoming article in the *New Yorker*. Keep in mind, I'd never gotten a thank you from him for being the first one at his side. Not a word. And I don't care if he was passed out half the time from the pain. You find something like that out.

Maybe he was waiting to mention me by name in the *New Yorker* article.

But no. All he said was, and I quote: "To the guy who arrived by my side, thanks for telling me I was going to be okay."

Couldn't he have found out who it was? Given me a shout-out?

Instead, the article was just him fellating himself. Talking about taking down Charles Zane and all he had to overcome. Quint. Quint. Quint.

Not one mention of me! About the guy who ran to his side when he was shot!

Fuck, Quint!

I was livid. Enraged. Seething.

If he'd mentioned me in the article, maybe I'd have become a local celebrity as well. Maybe girls would look at me a little differently. Maybe I'd be looked at as courageous.

But none of this happened.

To make matters worse, I'd occasionally run into Quint when we ran errands near Avalon. And inevitably, people would approach him and tell him how great he was. What a hero he was. And other bullshit like that.

I wanted to shoot him in the middle of Trader Joe's. That's how much contempt had built inside of me.

But I knew better.

I told myself for the hundredth time that I was destined for more than the common criminal activity. I was going to be remembered forever. And killing one person in some bullshit grocery store wasn't going to do the trick.

So I decided to bring Quint along for the ride. Incorporating a local "celebrity" could give my killing spree the added juice to take it to another level.

I stopped fantasizing about killing Quint (and being alone with Cara) and started planning. And plotting.

I started making some lists.

I started with people who had wronged me over the years. From the bullies in high school to the adults who allowed it.

I listed ways in which I could kill a great deal of people at once.

I listed ways in which I could escape after my fifth set of murders. This was going to be harder than the killings themselves. How could one of the most wanted men in the world just vanish into thin air?

I'd finally decided that I'd learned and studied all I could. I was ready. I knew the first set of murders had to be both personal and hands-on. To be a great serial killer, you had to get your hands dirty at least once.

So I chose the Langleys.

I'd grown up close to both them and the Tillers.

And hated them for quite different reasons.

The Langleys for the love they had for the world. And the Tillers for the hate they exuded.

Paul Langley was about the most positive man I'd ever met. I abhorred him immediately.

His wife had a permanent smile on her face. But not the kind that looked plastic and fake. That I could have lived with. No, she actually enjoyed being alive. Every day offered some new adventure she just couldn't wait to dive into. I never saw her in a bad mood.

And it ate me alive, knowing I hated people, hated life, was always miserable, and would never have her rosy outlook.

Their daughter Mia was only a few years younger than me. She was the most attractive girl in our section of Pleasant Hill. Making matters worse, she was nice and polite. I wanted a pretty girl to be bitchy so I had reason to hate her. But Mia was the opposite, so I had even more disdain for her.

I understand that might not make any sense.

Let me explain it like this:

I understand people who are miserable. I get that. I am that. What I can't comprehend is going around every day and loving the opportunities that life brings.

That infuriates me to no end.

And it's why I chose the Langleys.

The Tillers were the exact opposite. Roger Tiller was possibly the biggest asshole I'd ever met. He constantly yelled at the neighborhood kids, myself included. He'd embarrass his children by chastising them in front of any and everyone, humiliating himself in the process as well. His wife wasn't much better.

I'd been jealous of the Langleys. And that had driven my hate. But was motivated to kill the Tillers because people like them were wha made the world so dark. They were one reason why I could neve celebrate life like the Langleys did.

I spent some TLC on their cookies, making sure the ones on thei doorstep were laced with a touch more fentanyl than the rest that wen to the people in San Jose.

It seemed to have worked.

RIP.

Haha.

Like I give a shit.

Boy, have the last six weeks been a wild ride.

I can honestly say I've never felt more alive than since I've startee killing. I like being the center of attention. And I love having the powe to end people's lives. I think humanity sucks and I enjoy the misery an chaos that I've created.

The fact that I'll be remembered and talked about forever is the icin on the cake. To me, and this may sum me up better than any psychologist could, it's way better to be remembered as an all-tim villain than to be like Bob from Accounting who worked the same shitt job for forty years and raised 2.5 kids with his fat, unattractive wife.

Am I narcissist? Undoubtedly. Am I a psychopath? Certainly. Do care? Assuredly not.

If I have my choice, I'll go on killing forever.

We'll have to see what the future holds.

36.

"My God," I yelled.

Cara had been watching as I wrote down the name *Tyler Anthony Danovich*. And then the letters of my own name.

"What is it?" she asked.

"Come here."

She sat next to me on the couch.

"Do you remember the poker riddle?" I asked.

"Of course."

I took my pen and drew a huge circle around the T at the end of Quint. I then did the same with the A and the D that started my last name.

"It crosses over from the end of my first name to the beginning of my last. Just like a potential straight that goes King, Ace, Two, etc. And the letters would be in every article I'd ever written."

"I get that part. But who is Tad?" Cara asked, genuinely perplexed.

And then I realized that she had probably never met him.

"He lives in this complex."

"You're kidding me, Quint. The Bay Area Butcher lives here at Avalon?"

"If I'm right about this, then yes. And worse yet, he lives on this floor."

Cara shook her head in disgust.

With my own skin crawling, I stood up.

"I have to go downstairs," I said.

"I'm coming with you."

"You can't."

"You're going to leave me up here with that psychopath close by?"

"I have to ask the manager of Avalon a few questions. If Tad is around and sees us both approach her, he'll know something is up."

"Alright, if you must. But please hurry back."

"I'll be very quick. Obviously, don't answer the door for anyone."

"I won't. I'm scared, Quint. Please hurry back."

"I will."

I grabbed a table.

"What are you doing?" Cara asked.

"You can shove this against the door when I leave."

"Just go. I'll be fine for a few minutes."

"Okay."

I opened the door to my apartment and looked to my left and to my right. saw no one in the hallway. Still, my heart rate remained off the charts.

I locked the door behind me.

I'd seen Tad on the elevator many times over the years, so I decided to take the stairs. I didn't trust myself to act normal if I happened to run into him

When I first saw the initials of Tyler Anthony Danovich, I couldn't help bu think of Tad. The three letters jumped out at me. But could he, someone who seemed so cordial every time I talked to him, be the deranged killer the world was looking for?

I thought back to the day when the Butcher left a note attached to m apartment door. Despite the mania that ensued once the cops arrived, th absolute fear I'd felt at the threat ensured that entire morning was etched int my memory.

In my mind, I recreated my steps when I went to get a coffee, and sure enough, I remembered seeing Tad. I had been approaching the elevator a he was getting off! He would have known I wasn't going to be back for a while Even if I was just going down to get my mail, that would still take five minutes Plenty of time for him to leave the note on my door.

I finished climbing down the stairs and walked into the main office of Avalon Walnut Creek. Kayla, standing behind the desk, looked up at me as entered.

"Can I help you, Quint?"

She had an office and I hated asking to use it, but I couldn't risk havin anyone else hear our conversation.

"Can we use your office?" I asked.

"Sure. This must be very official."

I tried to laugh, hoping to make it sound like no big deal. But faile miserably.

Kayla walked into her office. I followed her and pulled the door shut behin me.

She had a computer on her desk and a nice executive chair behind it. I sa in the nondescript chair that faced her.

"I have to ask a question and I hope you won't tell anyone."

"Well, this is a little odd, but sure. I can keep a secret."

The license plate, the initials, and the fact that I saw him the morning tha note was attached to my door. That should have been enough.

But there was one other thing that bothered me. What article had mentioned him in? I'd never mentioned Tad, Tyler, or certainly Tyler Anthon Davonich by name.

I had a guess, however. And it was what had brought me down to se Kayla.

"Do you remember the day last year when I was shot?"

"How could I forget? The craziest day we ever had at Avalon."

"You told me you were one of the first people who went upstairs, correct'

"That's right."

"Once I was shot and taken to the hospital, that day became a blur. I certainly don't remember much. And once I got out of the hospital, and was persona non grata at Avalon for awhile, I pushed it out of my mind. For obvious reasons. I was almost killed."

"Perfectly understandable. Not sure where you are going with this, though."

I decided to just ask.

"Do you know who were the first few people by my side?"

When I couldn't think of any article mentioning Tad, my mind went to the one I had written for the New Yorker. It was the only time I ever mentioned Avalon Walnut Creek, so it made sense that Tad may have appeared in that one.

And while I hadn't mentioned people by name, I had discussed fellow Avalon residents coming to my aid. Even singling out the person who spoke to me as I sat at the bottom of the stairs, drifting in and out of consciousness.

It had been as good a guess as any. No other article made any sense.

"By the time I got up to the fourth floor, there were probably about five people up there," Kayla said. "We were looking more at you than at each other, but I remember seeing them."

I didn't see any other way than just asking her.

"Was Tad there, by chance?"

She thought about it for a few seconds.

"Yeah, he was, now that I look back at it. I don't know if he was the first one to find you, but he was definitely there."

I wanted to scream. But I had to keep my cool.

"Okay. Thanks, Kayla. One last thing, what was Tad's last name again?"

"Danovich."

"Okay thanks, that's all I wanted to know."

Her eyes narrowed. "Not sure we needed the office for that."

"I just don't want Tad to know I was asking about him. Think I'm going to get him a gift for helping me out."

I had to make something up and that's what I could come up with on the spot.

I stood up and turned to go. It was time to call the police and have them take down this fucking lunatic. I couldn't tell Kayla and risk creating chaos at Avalon. The police would know how to handle it.

"I can try and get you his new address," Kayla said.

"Excuse me?"

"Yeah, I guess you wouldn't know. Tad moved out two days ago."

"Was that expected?"

"Not at all. He said his parents were sick and he had to leave immediately."

My world spun around.

Did he realize we were closing in on him? Had our trip to Iron Hill Street given us away?

I had been forty-five seconds from calling the police. I'd already envisioned a SWAT storming his apartment.

But that wasn't going to happen now.

Tyler Anthony Danovich, a.k.a. Tad, a.k.a. the Bay Area Butcher, had gone on the run.

37.

The previous six weeks had been frenetic to say the least, but nothing prepared me for what came next.

I called the OPD at 3:15 p.m., as soon as I finished talking to Kayla. I told them everything I'd discovered.

Before they arrived, I asked Cara to google Tyler Anthony Danovich and find out where he worked. He did a front-end job at a computer company in Walnut Creek named Caltenics. I called the main line and asked for Tad or Tyler Danovich, with my intention being to hang up if they connected me to him.

"Sorry, Tyler called in sick a few days ago and hasn't returned to work."

Just like I'd suspected.

Within a half-hour, Avalon was inundated with law enforcement of all types. I spotted the OPD, SFPD, Walnut Creek PD, local sheriffs, and many blue and yellow F.B.I. jackets.

For ninety minutes, I fielded questions from any and all of the aforementioned law enforcement. It got tedious as I answered and then re-answered the same questions many times.

But everyone was on edge and trying to get every detail they could about the Butcher. So I understood.

During a quick break, Cara told me she'd seen them going over Tad's apartment with a fine-toothed comb. And no doubt they'd started interviewing everyone who lived on the fourth floor and had interacted with him.

Tad. Or Tyler. Or the Butcher. It was hard to know what to call him.

After a few guys from the F.B.I. told me they had no more questions for the time being, I closed the apartment door and got ready to enjoy a little peace and quiet with Cara.

I went out on my balcony. That was a mistake. Within seconds, I saw someone taking my picture from the street level.

News trucks filled the streets everywhere and obviously their cameramen had arrived as well. Or were they paparazzi from some tabloid?

I wondered how the hell they figured out which apartment I was in. But I knew nothing was truly private these days.

"I should have warned you," Cara said. "They started arriving within an hour of you calling the police."

"How'd they know so early?"

"They probably heard that the police and the F.B.I. were showing up t where 'Quint' lives. And I'm sure word got out that they raided a tenant' apartment."

I sighed.

"Yeah, guess I shouldn't be surprised."

Going back inside, I threw on the news. All three local channels wer broadcasting from out in front of Avalon Walnut Creek.

Within minutes, I saw my face, split-screen with the face of Tyler Anthon Danovich. As if we were two sides of the same coin. I wanted to scream tha he was the homicidal maniac and I was the guy trying to catch him. But wha was the point?

We would forever be linked. His mentioning me by name in the letters ha secured that. And now, with it coming out that we both had lived at Avalon, was unavoidable. It certainly made a great story. For the media, that is. Nc so much for me.

Captioning his picture, phrases declared him the "Suspected Bay Are Butcher" and asked "Is this the Bay Area Butcher?"

It looked like a high school yearbook photo, but it may have been all the could find in such a short time. Tad looked different now. Less innocen Stronger. He was noticeably thicker these days, having been very skinny i the picture they used. His hair had become darker. If this picture was mear to bring him to the public's attention, I wasn't sure it would do the trick. I barel recognized him, as a neighbor who saw him every few weeks.

When I read the caption "Is this the Bay Area Butcher?", I paused to thin *Was* he? Could I be positive he was the killer? Obviously, certainty wa impossible, but there had been just too many coincidences.

His name fit perfectly for the poker riddle the Butcher had taunted me with He saw me get on the elevator the day the Butcher left a letter on my doo He followed us to Iron Hill Street. He moved out of Avalon a few days late And now he wasn't showing up to work?

It had to be him!

But as a news agency, I knew you couldn't risk a massive lawsuit if yo were incorrect. So I understood why they had to phrase it as a question.

I felt sure the police were interviewing relatives, co-workers, and ol friends of his. And most importantly, they must be trying to trace his step since he left Avalon. There would soon be a manhunt of epic proportions. H would become one of the most sought-after men in the U.S. Likely the worlc

We'd seen how many people he had already killed. God knew what he ha planned for his final set of murders.

I changed the channel to try a different news station.

A young Hispanic woman anchored this one. I'd never seen her before They had the same picture of Tad on the screen, though.

"Turn the volume up," Cara asked.

The anchor spoke:

"Here's the information we have so far. Local law enforcement and the F.B.I. have raided the Avalon Walnut Creek apartment towers. Apparently, they are interested in someone named Tyler Anthony Danovich who lived at Avalon until a few days ago. We've heard from sources that these officials are investigating whether he might be the Bay Area Butcher. We do not know why they believe that at this point, and we have no evidence to link him to being the Butcher. So this is all conjecture and at this point he's just a person of interest. Danovich is twenty-seven years old and works as a front line developer for a computer company named Caltenics. They have a few offices across the Bay Area, including one in Walnut Creek. Danovich grew up in the Bay Area and graduated from College Park High School in 2012. It doesn't appear he has a criminal record."

I paused the T.V. on Tad's picture.

His hair was parted too close to the middle and his face held no expression. He looked harmless, and yet there was something just a bit off.

"He looks like a Boy Scout," Cara said. "But there's something about his eyes."

"I agree. Something is off with them. Like they're vacant. Lifeless. Although I saw this guy at least fifty times over the years walking around Avalon, and I never suspected a thing. He was polite and seemed as normal as you or me."

"I imagine psychopaths are pretty good at blending in."

"Probably. It's just odd that I never suspected a thing."

"How could you?"

She was right. I had zero reason to ever suspect the guy.

"You know, he was on the elevator one day when I was bringing up some library books on Ted Bundy and the Zodiac. He saw them."

"And?"

"And he was as normal as could be. I remember him making a joke about me undertaking some light reading."

"You're making my point for me. He was normal when he had to be. There's no way you could have known."

"By the way, he doesn't really look like that picture they're showing."

"In what way?"

"He looks fragile in that picture. Like someone who hadn't grown into his skin. And he's not nearly that skinny any more."

"Is he buff?"

"No, but he's wiry strong. He looks like a pushover in that picture. But that's not the vibe you'd get if you ever met him."

"Hope I never get that honor."

"Of course," I said, instantly regretting I'd mentioned the hypothetical.

"Listen to me, Quint. You're beating yourself up when you should be patting yourself on the back. You have blown this case wide open. This guy is going to have his picture plastered all over the news until the day they catch him. He's living on borrowed time."

"We did do some great work, didn't we?"

"Having the guy tail us was a genius idea. And it led us to him."

I wondered why I wasn't happier. We had done all the dirty work which le to the identification of the Bay Area Butcher. This was massive.

"I'll revel in our accomplishments once he's caught."

"You don't seem confident. The whole world is going to be looking for hin He can't go far."

"What you're saying makes perfect sense. But he's always, always bee a step ahead. It sounds like he moved out the day we went to Iron Hill Stree He must have had a plan. And as I said, he doesn't look like that picture the keep posting. And my guess is that there aren't going to be many othe pictures of him."

"You're probably right. When I found out where he worked, I looked for an accounts on Facebook and on Instagram. Nothing."

"He's been practicing for this. For a long time, I'd guess. There's no othe way he could have gotten this far without being caught. Sadly, I don't thin we've heard the last of him."

"Jeez, Quint. This should be a time of rejoicing."

"Like I said, I'll rejoice when he's caught. Or dead."

"Well, those two things are much more likely because of the work we did

I leaned in and hugged Cara.

"You're right about that. And you've been great. I'm sorry. I just don't thin this is over."

"I understand."

"I'll tell you one thing. I think we're going to learn a lot more about him ver soon. I think he wants the world to know who he is. That's why he's sent a these letters. To make himself famous. And the next letter is going to be doozy. I can guarantee that."

Just then, someone knocked at the door. I got up and looked through th peephole.

It was Miles Lockett. I'd seen him walking around earlier, but we hadn talked yet. I opened the door.

"Hi, Quint."

"Hello, Captain."

"Can I come in?"

"Sure," I said.

Captain Lockett nodded toward Cara and she waved back.

"You can ask me anything in front of her," I said. "She knows everything know."

"Alright. I've been talking to the people who interviewed you. There's on thing they didn't get a good answer to."

"What's that?" I asked.

"You said a car followed you and you suspected it was driven by th Butcher."

"That's right."

"And you got a license plate number?"

"That's right," I said again.

"And how did you find out who owned the car?"

"A friend."

"That's not good enough," Lockett said.

I'd figured this was going to come up, but nobody had questioned me about it too hard.

"A friend who doesn't need to be involved. He knows someone in the DMV and they ran the plates."

Lockett looked at me and sighed. "I'll give you a pass for this. For now."

"What have you found out on Tad?"

"I'll be honest. On my way over here, I had my doubts. A car that followed you. A neighbor that moved out abruptly. Seemed mighty flimsy."

"But..."

"But we've found a few things out. First, Tyler Danovich grew up a block over from both the Langleys and the Tillers. That's a pretty huge coincidence considering those were two families that ended up dead. We currently have officers interviewing people on that block."

"Ask them to interview the Dorias," I said. "An old couple who have lived there forever."

"You know a lot, don't you, Quint?"

"Just trying to help catch this asshole."

"What was he like? I've heard you knew him, at least a little bit."

"I was just talking to Cara about that. He was normal. Cordial. I never, ever would have guessed."

"I wouldn't beat yourself up over that. Neighbors of serial killers always say they were the nicest guys on the block."

"Thanks. What else have you found?"

I looked over at Cara, who had remained silent, but was listening intently.

"He hasn't been to work since he moved out of Avalon a few days ago," the captain said. "We're currently talking to his bosses and trying to find out if any co-workers have communicated with him. He didn't appear to be close to any of the neighbors we've talked to. Let me ask you a question."

"Shoot," I said.

"Did you ever see him with a girlfriend? Or any sort of friend?"

"No, it was always just him."

"I think we're going to discover that he was a loner. It's going to be hard to track him by asking friends."

"How about family?" I asked.

"It appears his parents died within a few years of each other when he was between sixteen and eighteen."

My mouth opened to say something instinctively.

"Don't say it," Captain Lockett said. "He doesn't deserve any sympathy. A lot of people lose parents. They don't turn into murderers."

"You're right," I said. Thinking about my own dad, and Charles Zane.

"Would you like to see the pictures of the people killed at the retirement home? The burned bodies? Or the pictures of the victims in San Jose who asphyxiated to death, fighting to breathe? How about the pictures of the Langleys after they were butchered to death? This guy doesn't deserve an ounce of sympathy from us."

"You didn't even mention Ray."

"I miss him every day."

"So what's next, Captain?"

"We've got his DNA now."

"I thought nobody had found any DNA at the crime scenes."

"They didn't find any that was useful. I just learned that Tyler, or Tad, or whatever the fuck we want to call him, had no criminal record. So we had nothing to run it against But we do now. We're lucky they hadn't started cleaning his apartment just yet."

"That's good news. I'd just like to be absolutely certain."

Lockett managed a slight laugh.

"Could you imagine if we were mistaken?" He pointed to the T.V. "The media would have a lot of apologizing to do."

"You've got a morose sense of humor, Captain."

"In a world where you've got psychopaths like this rolling around, you need it."

"I guess so."

Cara jumped in for the first time.

"I'm sure you've thought of this, Captain, but when he went to Tiburon he would have had to use either the Golden Gate Bridge or the Richmond-San Rafael Bridge. You could probably track him that way now that we know his license plate."

Captain Lockett's eyes widened, impressed.

"Just brilliant, Cara. I'm not saying it wouldn't have come up, but I certainly hadn't thought of it yet. Thank you."

"Anything to help."

"You and Quint have done plenty of that. If we catch the Butcher, you guys deserve a lion's share of the credit."

"When we catch him, you mean," Cara said.

"Of course," he said. "Now, I have more work to do. Quint, don't wander far from your phone. We'll be talking soon, I'm sure."

"I'll be here."

"Do you guys want a police escort?"

I hadn't thought about it. I looked over at Cara.

"I can't imagine he has any intentions of coming near Avalon again," she said.

I agreed.

"I think we're alright, Captain. Thank you, though."

"If you change your mind, just call me. We could have one here within minutes. And it doesn't just have to be here. If you plan on going into SF or somewhere else, we can supply a tail."

"We might take you up on that. Thanks."

"No, thank you, Quint. You two have done amazing work. Now we're going to go catch this motherfucker."

"I'm with you there. Please keep me posted. On anything you can."

"I will. You've done enough to warrant that."

"Thanks. Talk soon, Captain."

"You can count on it."

And with that, Lockett strode out of the apartment and shut the door behind him. I made sure to lock it.

I went back to the couch and sat next to Cara.

"No police escort?" I asked.

"We've gotten this far by ourselves," she said.

"We sure have. I love you."

"I love you, too."

"This isn't over, though. Let's be vigilant. He's still out there and once he sees his name on the news, I'm sure his hate for me will only increase."

"Why does he hate you, though?"

"I don't know. There are so many unanswered questions. It sounds like he was one of the first people who arrived in the stairwell when I was shot last year. But why would that drive you to hate someone?"

"The man's a psychopath. He could have seen you on the elevator and decided you were his rival. Unbeknownst to you."

"True. It's hard to narrow this down logically, when obviously his mind doesn't work like ours."

"This is crazy, isn't it?"

"Our names are likely circulating throughout the whole world right now," I said.

"Yours certainly is. I haven't seen my name mentioned today."

"That's probably for the best."

"No question," Cara said. "I'm going to call my sister. If she and her husband haven't seen your name on the news yet, I'm sure they will soon."

"Alright, I've got a phone call to make myself."

"Your mother?"

"You know it."

Several hours passed. Our phones rang off the hook. Friends. Distant relatives. I got a few calls from employees of *The Walnut Creek Times*, including the owners, Tom and Krissy.

I'd talked to my mother for almost an hour. Part of me thought I should g
over to her place right after we spoke. But there was another voice in m
head, telling me it was better if I kept my distance until this ended.

For now, I was siding with the latter. There was no reason to potentiall
bring her to the Butcher's attention.

The calls finally started slowing down around 8:00 p.m.

The news had as well. There had been nothing fresh to report for a fev
hours.

Which was just fine with me. This had been the longest day of my life.

We'd found out about the fire at Treeside Manor that morning. It felt like
week ago. We'd then made our way to confront Peter Vitella at the Sa
Francisco Chronicle, gone and seen Paddy Roark, and then got the news o
the car.

And then everything that followed. Discovering the Butcher was Tac
Going to see Kayla. Calling the cops. Watching Avalon Walnut Creek bein
overrun by law enforcement. Being interviewed many times. Talking t
Captain Lockett. Reassuring everyone who knew me that Cara and I wer
okay.

Never had more happened over the course of a day.

And I'm including the night I had to fight for my life on Zane's boat in th
middle of the shark-infested ocean.

Just as we thought the news seemed to be slowing down, we heard th
alert for another Breaking News update. We looked toward the T.V. It was th
same young Hispanic woman, who was definitely earning her wage on thi
day. She'd been on for hours.

"More Breaking News into the KPIX desk. Authorities have confirmed tha
Tyler Anthony Danovich is suspected of being the Bay Area Butcher. This i
no longer just conjecture. We've been told that his car has been found jus
north of the Golden Gate Bridge. Items found in the car have all but confirme
he is in fact the Butcher. We have not been told what those items are, bu
we'll let our viewers know as soon as we do. People in Marin are warned t
be extra vigilant, and under no circumstances should you approach th
suspect. He is considered armed and extremely dangerous."

The anchor continued:

"Authorities have also asked that if anyone has a recent picture of M
Danovich, please contact your local police department. All we have is the hig
school yearbook photo that has been making the rounds. And that is eight c
nine years old. Also, anyone who might potentially know Mr. Danovich'
current whereabouts is asked to call your local police departmer
immediately. We here at KPIX would like everyone to be safe out there. An
while we now know who the Butcher is, he's still out there. As they say,
wounded dog is often the most dangerous."

"This woman really likes to put her own spin on things, doesn't she?"
asked.

"Let's give her a break. She's been on the air all damn day."

"That's fair. I feel like I've been on all day myself. My head isn't working all that great anymore."

"Do you want to go to sleep early?"

"I'd love to. Think it'll be possible?"

"Unless they catch him, I can't imagine there will be any new stuff tonight."

"I could use some downtime."

We looked back up at the T.V., where they had moved on to showing more pictures of the people who died in the old folks' home. Who'd been alive less than twenty-four hours ago.

"This is so sad," Cara said. "Can you imagine going out like that?"

"No," I admitted.

"Do you think we'll find out tomorrow that the Butcher had a connection to someone who died in the fire?"

"Wouldn't surprise me a bit. Every other murder has been personal in some way."

"I can't wait until this creep's reign of terror is over."

"Me either. This is insane."

38.

I woke up the next morning to a sharp sound. It came again from the fron room of the apartment. A knock.

Cara sat up next to me, seeming to have heard it first.

"Someone is at the door," she said.

I looked at my watch. It was 8:00 a.m. For what seemed like the first tim in years, I'd been able to sleep in a little bit.

But who was knocking at the front door? The Butcher wouldn't possibl have the balls to show up here, would he?

I got out of bed and threw on some sweatpants over my boxers. It didn seem like much to possibly confront a killer in.

I approached the door and looked through the peephole. And then opene the door.

"Hello, Quint."

"Hi, Captain Lockett. It's a little early, you know."

"Not when there's a serial killer on the loose."

I nodded. "What can I do for you?"

"Let's go get a coffee and talk."

"Alright."

Cara and I were a team in every sense of the word. I headed back to th bedroom to see if she wanted to join, but didn't make it that far.

"You go, Quint. You can update me when you get back."

"I'll lock the door behind me," I said.

I did just that and we started making our way down my hall.

"So you told me yesterday you'd see this guy Tad around the complex' Lockett asked.

"Yup. Quite often, with him being on my floor and all."

"Did you talk much?"

"We always said hello and were definitely cordial. But we never hung ou outside of Avalon."

"A lot of things are coming together. And that's why I wanted to talk to yo But one thing that's bothering me is why he took up such an interest in you.

"It's been occupying space in my brain too," I said.

"Any guesses?"

I pressed the down button on the elevator.

"This guy obviously wants to be known far and wide. Why else write to th police and try to turn this all into the circus it's become?"

The captain nodded and asked, "And what's that have to do with you?"

"For better or worse, I've kind of become a local celebrity in these parts. And certainly within Avalon. Especially after having been shot here."

We arrived at the first floor and started walking through the visitor parking area toward the Starbucks located just outside of the garage.

"So he mentioned you in the letters, knowing that calling you out would bring about more publicity?"

"I think that may well be part of it. He also might have been jealous of my celebrity. Maybe jealous of Cara, I don't know. He's a psychopath and sees me around the complex a lot. Who knows where his mind takes him…" My skin crawled thinking of it.

"That makes some sense."

I opened the door to the Starbucks and let Captain Lockett walk in first.

"Thanks," he said.

I approached the counter and ordered two coffees. We made our way to a corner to talk while we waited for the drinks.

"And you told a few officers yesterday that the article he was mentioned in may have been one in *The New Yorker*?"

"Yeah. I talked to the manager of Avalon and she said Tad was one of the first people there when I was shot. In the article, I referred to someone who told me I was going to be alright as I lay on those stairs. I think I was unknowingly mentioning him."

"Was he pissed he wasn't mentioned by name or something?"

"Could be. But I was in and out of consciousness. I never knew who it was. I didn't intentionally slight him."

"Doesn't matter anyway. The man is a lunatic. He probably felt like he needed a rival and invented one in you."

"That's what Cara said. We can't rationally know why he chose me."

We picked up our coffees and headed outside.

"Do you want to sit?" I asked.

"Too many people milling around. Let's walk and talk."

We walked a good hundred feet without saying anything.

"So what did you find out overnight?" I eventually asked.

"You watch the news this morning?"

"I hate to admit it, but your knock woke me up. Yesterday was such a long day that I slept in longer than I ever do."

"I can't blame you, and I'll be honest, I'm a bit jealous. I'm on about three hours' sleep."

"Sorry."

"Don't be." He took a deep sip of coffee. "So we found his car last night."

"I heard that before I went to sleep. How?"

"The license plate had been plastered all over the news, and some good Samaritan saw it. It was up on a bluff overlooking the Golden Gate Bridge. I was sent there and we worked with the SFPD and the cops from Marin. It's become a theme with the Butcher. Police from different cities, who don't always get along, working for the greater good."

"Nice to hear," I said.

"And we found a few things that all but confirm that he's the Butcher. One, and this is going to hurt, but a map that had been printed out. It was of the area right around Ray's house. Surely he was looking at escape routes. We also found a leaflet for Treeside Manor, the old retirement home where so many people died."

"I had a question about that."

"In a second, Quint. I'll finish up quickly. The map and the leaflet could probably be argued as circumstantial evidence, but the third thing we found cannot be explained away."

Lockett paused, adding to the drama.

"We found some jewelry. And it was obviously a woman's. We expedited the DNA testing on some skin cells from a swab of it, and it came from the Langley daughter. Mia."

I shook my head.

"Just horrible," I said. "I hate thinking about her last minutes on earth."

"It's unimaginable. So I'd suggest trying not to think it."

"That's good advice."

"Tougher to impart in practice."

"Why do you think he left such important evidence in his car?"

"I imagine it was in his apartment and when he found out you were getting close, he just threw everything in his car."

"And then ditched it?"

"Let's assume he's found a place to stay. Do you think he wants that car sitting outside in the driveway?"

"Point taken," I said. "Do we have any idea where he is?"

"No. The car was found on the Marin side of the Golden Gate, but that doesn't mean much. He could have easily walked back over into San Francisco. Or even made his way back to the East Bay. So don't rest easy. We have no idea where he is."

"Well, that's comforting," I said.

Captain Lockett patted me on the back.

"You've done fantastic work, Quint. Ray would be proud."

"Thanks," I said. He'd been right; hearing about the maps that let this creep get away after murdering Ray did hurt. "So what's next?"

"The biggest manhunt this area has ever seen. Really, it's already started. We set up a tip line and we've already got fifty calls. Obviously, some of these are just crackpots looking for attention, but maybe we'll get a real lead as well. He can't stay hidden forever. We're going to find him at some point."

"Let's just hope it's before his final set of murders."

"That goes without saying," Lockett said. "Do you think he'll send another letter?"

"With all my heart. And I think it will be the longest yet. He'll brag about how great he is. How no other serial killer has ever done what he's done. The world knows who he is now, so there will be no holding back."

"Don't you think he'll want to lie low? He's certainly not going to a post office. He may not even risk dropping it in a mailbox."

"Maybe he'll send an email this time. But there's no doubt in my mind we'll be receiving something from him. And I'd guess sooner rather than later. It's terrible to say, but he's the biggest thing in the world right now. He'll want to strike while the iron is hot."

"I wouldn't bet against you. You seem to get a lot right when it comes to this guy," Lockett said.

Then neither of us said anything more for awhile.

"Is there something else?" I asked.

"No, I think that about covers it. Thanks, Quint."

"You're welcome."

We started walking back toward the apartment complex.

Check your email.

At 8:00 p.m. that night, I received the text from Captain Lockett.

Cara was sitting next to me in bed. I showed her.

"Could be the moment of truth," I said.

"The Butcher?" she asked.

"That would be my guess."

I opened up my laptop and went to my email. The most recent one I'd received had been forwarded from Lockett. But it was the email just below that got my attention. And what Lockett had forwarded me was surely just a copy of it anyway.

The subject read: *This is the Butcher speaking…*

His allusion to the Zodiac was obvious.

I didn't even pause to wonder how he'd gotten my email address. As I'd discovered recently, everything could be found these days.

I opened it, sliding the laptop between Cara and me.

Together, we started reading.

Welcome, all. You'll have to excuse me for resorting to sending an email. Figure the less I'm out in public, the better.

I guess I should give myself a proper introduction now that you all know who I am. I'm Tyler Anthony Danovich. Tad. The Bay Area Butcher.

I still hate that nickname I've been burdened with. Makes me sound like some brute who doesn't have a brain. And we all know that's not true. I've lasted this long on sheer ingenuity. Not brute force.

I'm playing a different game than you guys. I hate to use an oft-used analogy but I'm playing chess while you guys are playing checkers. And you may thin I'm currently behind the 8-ball, but you'd be wrong. Everything is going ahea as planned.

You'll see there's a veritable hodgepodge of people CC'd in this email. Th man, the myth, the legend: Quint Adler. The best "cop" in the Bay Area and don't mean that sarcastically. He's done way more than anyone with an actu badge. Congrats, my friend. You found me.

There's also Peter Vitella. A pure scumbag, of course. But he sure came useful when I saw the beautiful Cara walking into our apartment building. Ho did you ever land a woman like that, Quint? Hope you'll let me know. But that for another day.

Then there are cops, local celebrities, news anchors, and even a few athlete on this email. It's a Who's Who of well-known people from the Bay Are Although, let's be honest...I'm currently the most famous person on th thread. And that will likely be the case forever.

Do you think Cynthia Parkey, that trashy-looking news anchor on KTVU, going to be remembered longer than me? I don't think so. How about Regg Ferris, that running back for the 49ers who does nothing but fumble? Not chance.

Welcome to this email though, Cynthia and Reggie.

But I digress.

You are probably reading this in hopes of understanding why I do what I d Why I kill. How much time do you have? I could probably put on m psychiatrist's hat and spend five hours looking inside myself. But it wou surely bore you to death. So I'll give you the Cliff's Notes version.

I don't give a fuck about anything. And certainly not people. I think life is joke. People die every day. And there's certainly not a fucking heaven. I mear what's the point? So if I can become famous while killing people who are destined to die anyway, then why not?

Life is temporary. Infamy is forever. Throw that on my tombstone.

And more than that, I love the chase! Hasn't this been fun? I've never fe more alive. And yes, I get the irony of having to kill to feel alive. But damn this hasn't been exciting, keeping the Bay Area on its toes.

I wish it could go on forever.

Why Quint, you may be asking? Because he's a below-average writer wh everyone grovels over. He's about the hundredth most interesting person our apartment complex, but people treat him like a god. I'd see him at th grocery store and he'd be getting his ass kissed by all these people. It made me want to vomit.

So I decided to bring him into my little game. And sadly, for Quint I mean, that also brought Ray Kintner onto my radar. Sorry about that. But not really.

As you all know by now, I grew up near the Langleys and the Tillers. For different reasons, I hated both of their families. And that's why I chose them. Nothing more, nothing less. But I intentionally made myself out to be some complete and utter psycho in my first letter in hopes that you would think all my murders would be random.

Which seemed to have worked. After all, you haven't caught me yet!

Have you found out my connection to the Treeside Manor yet? I haven't seen anything on the news. Maybe the cops should ask Quint. He's done all the work in finding out about me up to this point.

Maybe I've been selling him short. While he might not be the best writer, he's a much better cop than the rest of you pigs out there.

Sounds like you even needed the public's help in finding my car. Sorry, I couldn't park it outside of my new dwelling. I'm not going to make it that easy on you guys.

Despite this minor hiccup, my fifth and final set of murders will still go ahead as planned. After that, it's clear sailing for me. And you'll never see me again in the Bay Area.

I'll pop up somewhere else in this wretched world and start killing again. And people will talk about how the Bay Area police fucked up and couldn't catch me. The blood of the new victims will forever be on your hands. But that may be years down the road.

As you may have realized, I'm meticulous to a fault. I'm not going to jump the gun on anything. I'm going to prepare and outthink you.

And that's why you will never catch me.

But in keeping with tradition, I'll keep you in the game.

The final set of murders will occur sometime in the next month.

Sorry, nothing more specific. I'm not making it so easy for you guys this time. Even if knowing the date hasn't made you any more effective at stopping me.

Plus, I like the idea of the Bay Area being on edge for the next thirty days.

In fact, I can't fucking wait.

Happy Hunting!

39.
MONDAY

I woke with the news that the police had found the Butcher's connection to the killings at Treeside Manor. And as usual, it was personal. Tad' grandmother lived in Treeside Manor.

She had escaped with her life, but I'm not sure that even mattered to the Butcher. He just enjoyed killing. Fourteen people tragically died, and I think that was a success in his eyes. Sure, he probably wished his grandmothe had been one of the victims, but that wish had just been the impetus. The fac that many would be killed was the real goal.

Everything had gone out of whack. Fourteen elderly people had been killec And any other time, it would be the biggest story in the nation. But since th Butcher's identity was discovered the same day, it took a back seat. Hi potential whereabouts led every newscast. And now, with the release of th new letter to the public, the murders at Treeside Manor became buried. A unbelievable tragedy had been relegated to a supporting role in the bigge drama.

Which was tragic in its own right.

Cara and I spent the rest of the day doing what we'd done so many times Reading articles. Rereading the Butcher's letters. Trying to find anything tha might point us to his current location. Which we knew was a huge long shot

I talked to Captain Lockett, but they hadn't made any discoveries pointin to his whereabouts either. I walked around Avalon and talked to severa neighbors, but they all felt like I had. Tad always acted pleasant enough an we never could have guessed who he truly was. No other tenants had an idea where he might be.

My mother called and we had another long conversation. It kept revertin back to something like this:

"But I really want to see you," she'd say.

"And I want to visit you. But I really think it's best that we don't hang ot until this is over. I'm sorry, Mom."

"I don't like it, but fine."

"I'll make it up to you when this is madness is all over."

She hated it, but I could tell she understood.

There were numerous voicemails or texts from the media, asking if I'd be up for an interview. I didn't answer nor return any of their calls. My email was inundated with the same thing. We could do the interview over the phone, they'd say. Or, better yet, in person.

Fat chance of that.

I didn't respond to the emails either.

"So, what's our plan for tomorrow?" Cara asked as Monday finally wound down.

"I'm not sure. But we're not going to just sit around the apartment like we've done today. We're certainly not getting anything accomplished here."

"Why don't we drive around tomorrow? Head into SF? I'm not saying we're going to run into the Butcher on the streets, but being out and about might get our creative juices flowing. Maybe some ideas we haven't considered yet will come to mind."

"Sounds like a plan. Especially since today has been a total waste."

She shrugged, pointing to the T.V. and then to the collage we'd made on the wall. "We're learning things about the Butcher every time we watch the news. And as usual, we've read his letter dozens of times. Those aren't a waste. Something might click."

"That's fair. I just wish we could be outside."

"Well, we will be tomorrow. Even if we're just going to be two chickens with our heads cut off, driving around randomly."

Despite the gruesome image, I laughed. And hugged Cara. She hugged me back.

"We haven't had enough alone time lately," she said.

"Not the right kind of alone time, anyway."

"It's just hard to think about anything except the Butcher. His killings. His whereabouts. Those are always dominating my thoughts. I'm sorry."

"You don't have to apologize. When this is over, we'll go somewhere together for a few days. Just us. A place on the coast. And we won't leave our bed."

"Sounds perfect. Now let's do all that's humanly possible to catch him before he strikes again."

I hugged her closer.

"We've done more than I ever could have imagined. We just have to finish it."

It sounded good. We were both motivated. And I knew we would do everything we could.

But looking at it honestly, we'd have to get extremely lucky to catch the Butcher.

40.
TUESDAY

"Let's do this," I said.

"I'm ready," Cara said.

"And I'd prefer if we stayed close together today."

"The Butcher's not going to be out in public"

"Humor me. Let's not get too far from each other."

She sighed. "You're right. Sorry, Quint."

"No problem. I know we're both on edge."

She nodded, but already a bit of tension had started growing between us. Going into the belly of the beast could do that.

We headed off toward San Francisco.

As we crossed the Bay Bridge, the forgotten brother to the Golden Gate, but majestic in its own right, Cara turned to me.

"Do you think he'll wait the entire month to kill?" she asked.

"No," I said. "I think he's realized we're getting closer. I don't care where he's hiding, a month is a long time."

"I was thinking the same thing. If he truly wants to escape without getting caught, he'll do it earlier than that."

"Agreed. But he won't just rush into something. We know him better than that," I said.

"About his escape…the only way he's getting out of town is driving, right?"

"It's the most likely," I said as I looked out on the approaching skyline of San Francisco. "He's certainly not going to fly under his own name. And something like a bus or a train seems like a long shot since he'd be surrounded by so many people."

"But you said the pictures they've been using on the news barely resemble him."

"That's true. I've seen two other pictures now and they're just as bad as his yearbook photo. Plus, as part of going into hiding he must have changed his appearance somewhat. Still, I don't see him taking the risk of a bus or a train. And certainly not a flight."

"At least not under his own name," Cara said.

Which gave me pause. Who was to say the Butcher didn't have the resources to create a fake ID to buy bus or plane tickets with? Underestimating him certainly had never worked before.

"Let's hope it doesn't get to the escape phase. Let's catch him before then," I said.

"Amen to that."

We took the first exit off the Bay Bridge and circled back toward the Embarcadero. I found a parking lot and paid them an arm and a leg for two hours. At least, it felt that expensive.

Cara took my hand and we started walking along the world-famous Embarcadero. We strolled past Pier 39, the sea lions, and farther along, Fisherman's Wharf. Along the way we saw great restaurants and views of Alcatraz.

It was a warm day in June and thousands of people milled around, out and about. Usually it would be a glorious time, but a sense of foreboding hung over the scene that I'm sure everyone felt.

"Do you think this place will empty out as the month moves on?" Cara asked.

We had just come up to Pier 39, and now we looked out at the gathered sea lions. They made for a majestic sight. I'd always enjoyed hearing their sounds and watching them dive from the wooden docks into the Bay below.

"You'd think so," I said. "I guess that's part of the genius of saying he'll kill within the next month. People can't just stop what they're doing for that long. Need I mention the pandemic? Now, if a few weeks go by and we get closer to finishing a month, then I think you'd see it start to empty out."

"Not sure I agree. I think we'll see the streets get quieter soon."

"Maybe," I conceded.

"It's possible his goal is to have more sitting ducks throughout the month."

"Sitting ducks?"

"Is it impossible to think of him with an assault rifle taking out people?"

It wasn't impossible, but it sure wasn't a visual I wanted to entertain. Especially in the moment, as we walked around with hundreds of other people in close proximity.

"Anything is possible," I admitted. "After all, he doesn't really have an MO."

I lowered my voice as people walked within earshot of us.

"Exactly. And since he's been building up to the fifth set of murders, I figure it will be something massive. Something that kills more than the cookies laced with fentanyl or the fire at Treeside Manor."

"This could be helpful. Let's talk through the possibilities."

"I've mentioned one. A mass shooting."

"Look, I'm not going to discount anything. But he's talked so much about avoiding capture and killing again down the road. If he tries a mass shooting, there's no way in the world he'll escape. There would be a hundred members of law enforcement on site within minutes."

"I get your point. But it's still scary to think about."

"No question," I said. "And like I said, I'm not ruling anything out. I'm jus‎ expecting something more subtle."

I immediately hated using that word, but it was what came to mind.

"How about you?" she asked. "Have you thought of ways he might kill?"

"Of course. I've probably imagined fifty horrible scenarios. But none hav‎ jumped out as more likely than the others."

We looked back one last time at the sea lions, which had fallen behind u‎ as we walked and talked.

"They are so full of life," Cara said.

"They just lie on those docks all day. When I sit on the couch for an hou‎ you give me shit."

Cara laughed and playfully pushed me. It made for a nice break from ou‎ heavy conversation.

Next our eyes fell on the Golden Gate Bridge, a few miles ahead of us.

It seemed like Cara could tell what I was thinking.

"That would certainly be symbolic, wouldn't it?" she asked.

"Without doubt. It's crossed my mind. But how do you kill on the Golde‎ Gate Bridge without being caught?"

"I don't know."

I took in the sight of the Bay, remembering being aboard Charles Zane'‎ yacht as it sped under the Golden Gate and off into the Pacific. I tried to avoi‎ thinking about what had followed.

"What other sites would be symbolic?" Cara asked.

"Coit Tower. The Transamerica Building. The Bay Bridge. Alcatra‎ Oracle, the Giants' baseball park. Some places right here, like Pier 39 an‎ Fisherman's Wharf. BART."

"Scary. And that's all assuming he chooses San Francisco. Well, I gues‎ BART could be anywhere in the system."

"I do feel like San Francisco is his goal. As you've said, he wants to mak‎ the biggest splash on his last set of murders. And San Francisco i‎ undoubtedly that."

"It's also the only city of the original five that he mentioned in which h‎ hasn't killed," Cara said.

"Great point."

A line of people started boarding one of the boats for an Alcatraz tour.

"There's also a number of possibilities on water," Cara added as w‎ watched them.

"We're both getting somewhere and not getting anywhere at the sam‎ time. Is that possible?" I asked.

"I feel the same way."

A couple walked too close to us and we stopped talking for a moment.

So much movement and noise came from and surrounded the bay that w‎ had been able to keep our undeniably scary conversation to ourselves. B‎

we'd pause from time to time when someone walked too close. No need to cause a panic, or to make anybody suspicious of us.

"Do you want to grab an early lunch?" I asked.

"Thought you'd never ask." She added sarcastically, "This heavy talk has my stomach growling."

"Let's walk up to Fisherman's Wharf and get some fresh seafood."

We had a great lunch at Franciscan Crab Restaurant, with an outdoor table that overlooked the Bay. Given the name, we obliged them with our orders: I had some Dungeness crab melt sliders and Cara ate a crab salad. Both meals were delicious, and we vowed to return when this was all over.

"So, what's next?" Cara asked.

"Let's do something a little more hands on," I said.

"What did you have in mind?"

"Let's go to the Butcher's place of work and see if we can talk to an ex-coworker of his."

"Sounds good."

I didn't feel sure of just how much we'd accomplished by coming to San Francisco, but we'd talked through some of our ideas. Maybe that would be helpful down the road. If nothing else, our sightseeing had been a welcome break from stewing in the apartment.

We headed back toward the East Bay.

From the outside, Caltenics looked more like an apartment complex than a computer company, a two-story building painted gray.

But we saw C-A-L-T-E-N-I-C-S in big, green letters on the sign and knew we were at the right place.

Since we'd eaten early in the city, we arrived at Caltenics by 12:45. Hopefully we might catch some people returning from their own lunch breaks.

Cara decided we should sit on the bench located about fifteen feet from the entrance. With my quote-unquote celebrity status, she thought it was likely at least one of the employees would either recognize me or even approach me.

She was right on both counts.

About ten minutes after we sat down, a woman came over to us.

"Excuse me, are you Quint Adler?"

"I am," I said.

We shook hands and I introduced Cara as well.

"My name is Luann, but you can call me Lu. What are you doing here?"

She was in her early forties, with straight blonde hair and bright eyes. Overall she looked very affable.

"Take a guess," I said, smiling back at her.

"Trying to find out more information on Tyler?" She seemed almost excited.

"You got it. Although to me, he was Tad."

"Yeah, I heard that. He probably put on different fronts to a great many people."

"Well said. Did you know him well?" I asked.

"We worked together for several years, so in that way I did. But we never hung out socially."

"We had similar experiences."

"So how did you think I could help?" Lu said.

I didn't bring up the fact that she had approached me.

"Do you have any idea where he could be?" I asked.

"None at all. The police came by yesterday and asked me the same thing. I'm sorry, but I can't help you there."

"Any tidbits of information might help us, though. Maybe you remember something you hadn't thought to tell the police?"

"Sadly, same answer. Since then I've racked my brain, but nothing."

A few of her fellow Caltenics employees approached the entrance. They looked in our direction and nodded at Lu, but kept walking into the office.

"I have to get back to work," she said. "But it's been nice meeting you two."

"One last thing if you don't mind," Cara said. "Who are the two or three people who were closest to Tyler?"

Cara had made a habit of always asking the perfect question. Now she's done it again.

"I guess there were three of them. All guys, since he kind of creeped the girls out. One was Brendan Cabela, but he doesn't work here anymore. He was fired a few weeks back. And then there's two good friends: Scott Shap and Roy Irving. They were both cordial, I'd even say borderline friendly, with Tyler. They're both very empathetic souls and I think they might have known that Tyler was a little odd. Obviously, they never knew to what level he was off. They just tried to befriend him and make him feel liked around the office."

"Do you have their contact info?" Cara asked.

"Sure, give me a second." She took out her phone. "You ready?" she asked.

Cara took out her phone as well. "Go ahead."

"Alright, you want phone numbers or emails?" Lu asked. "Actually, you could just find their emails on our company website. I'll give you their phone numbers."

"Thank you, Lu."

"You're welcome. And I'm not going behind their back by giving you their numbers. We've all said we'd do anything to help catch Tyler."

I noticed she hadn't referred to him once as the Butcher.

"We appreciate it."

She gave Cara the three numbers.

"Thank you so much, Lu," I said.

She looked at me and then over at Cara.

"You guys are welcome. I sure hope you catch him before his next set of murders. The whole Bay Area is scared as shit."

It was surprising to hear profanity from the polite woman in front of us. But in these times—different times, to say the least—I could certainly understand her choice of words.

"We all are," Cara said. "And let's exchange numbers. You can text me if you think of anything."

They exchanged numbers.

"Got it. Thanks, you guys," Lu said.

"No, thank you," I said.

She waved goodbye and headed into Caltenics.

I called Captain Lockett later that afternoon and asked if we could get the case file on the Butcher.

"That would be highly irregular," he said.

"This whole situation is highly irregular."

"That's certainly true."

"And you've said in the past that I have the instincts of a detective."

"That's also true."

"Look, Captain, we're all on the same team here. All I want is to help catch the Butcher. That's the only reason I'm calling."

"You have helped blow the case open."

As soon as he said that, I knew he was going to share the case files with me.

"I'll give you what I can," Lockett continued. "Some things are meant only for the police."

"I understand. And thanks. Do you want to fax it?" I asked.

"No. Better not to leave a paper trail in case the chief finds out."

"Alright. Do you want me to come to you?"

"No. I'm going to be in the East Bay tonight. I'll text you and you can run downstairs from Avalon and I'll hand it off."

"Thanks, Captain. How are you guys holding up right now?"

"I've never felt more anxiety throughout a police precinct in my entire life."

"I'm sure."

It's all I could think to say.

He sounded tired as he told me, "I'll text you when I'm there this evening, Quint."

"Thanks."

41.
WEDNESDAY

Not that the outside of my apartment complex was conclusive, but noticeably fewer people walked around it on Wednesday than the previous two days.

I couldn't imagine how this would continue if the entire month went by without the Butcher killing. All that tension, building and building. There wouldn't be a soul out in public. It appeared Cara had been right when she'd said the streets would be quieter sooner rather than later.

I'd woken up early as usual and wanted to get out of the apartment, so I went walking along the Iron Horse Trail. It was nice to have it almost entirely to myself, despite the circumstances. I could spend the time thinking.

Captain Lockett had come through and dropped off the file on the Butcher the previous night. Cara and I had each read it, but it was mostly crime scene and autopsy reports, details of the OPD's investigations, and a few psychological profiles.

I learned some things, but nothing brought me closer to where the Butcher could be hiding or what his next kill might be.

Unfortunately, a lot of what I learned was about how the victims suffered at his hands. The autopsy reports had been particularly horrible. Especially those for the Langley family. 'Sadistic' would be an understatement to describe those killings. Luckily for our sakes, Lockett had removed the autopsy photos themselves.

The Butcher had complained about his nickname, pretending he wasn't a savage, but the autopsies told a different story.

He may have been smart, and he had remained a step ahead of the police, but he was still a brute at heart.

What would such a monster have in mind for his final act?

I thought about this over the course of my walk. But as usual, nothing came to mind.

Well, that's not exactly true. Everything came to mind, but nothing more likely than any of the others.

Fuck!

Cara was sitting up in bed when I returned to the apartment.

"I got my first text back from one of the guys," she said. "Roy Irving. He said while he and his friend Scott were nice to Tyler, they really didn't know him that well."

I nodded. "That's not a big surprise."

"But he also said that Brendan Cabela knew him better. I asked if Roy had anything else, even the smallest bit of information that might be useful, and he couldn't think of anything."

"Have we heard back from Brendan yet?"

"No."

"It's still a little early, but we'll try him again in a few hours," I said.

"I feel hamstrung. Like there really isn't anything else to do until the Butcher strikes. It's depressing."

I could have told her I agreed, but that would just take us down the rabbit hole of questioning whether we were accomplishing anything, or the black pit of admitting we hadn't. And we'd done enough of that.

"Hamstrung?" I said instead.

"What? You don't like that word?"

"I can safely say I've never heard you say it."

"I know what you're doing," Cara said.

It was a playful, but knowing statement.

"Oh yeah, what's that?"

"You're trying to make little funny comments to keep my mind off the impending murders."

"Am I wrong in trying to lighten the mood even just a tiny bit?"

"No, I guess not."

"The alternative is much worse."

"We've got to face that fact, Quint. There's a very good chance that there is going to be a catastrophic event sometime in the next month. Likely sooner. And we'll have to live with that for the rest of our lives. That we were unable to catch the Butcher before it was too late."

"I'm not willing to even consider that possibility. There's something in all the paperwork that we have. Or in the letters. Something that can help us catch him. I just know it."

A few hours passed.

"Why don't you text Brendan Cabela again?" I asked Cara.

"Alright."

She bent over her phone, then straightened up.

"Done."

"What did you say?"

"*This is Cara again. Quint and I had a few questions if you wouldn't mind calling or meeting up. Thanks.*"

"Is it showing the message as delivered?"

Cara looked down at her phone. "Yeah, it is. Yesterday's message and today's."

"Weird that he won't text back," I said.

"Is it, though? If I had been friendly with a serial killer, I wouldn't be in a rush to talk about it."

"That's fair. But wouldn't you be in a rush to catch him?"

"Of course. It's likely he doesn't know anything that would help. And it' possible he's already talked to the police and doesn't feel the need to talk t two civilians. Which is all we really are."

Despite having started the arduous process of becoming a privat detective, Cara was right. I wasn't one yet.

"All you've said is true. And yet, this guy is one of our few possible leads Can you find out his address? Let's go to his place."

"I could probably find it, but are you sure we should just show u unannounced?"

"Cara, I'm willing to do almost anything to try and catch the Butche Showing up unannounced at a prospective lead's house doesn't come clos to crossing that line."

"Okay. I'll try and find it."

And several minutes later, she did. Meanwhile, I'd accomplished nothing

"Looks like Cabela is a pretty uncommon last name. Only one Brenda Cabela in the Bay Area that I could find. He's thirty-two and lives in Sa Francisco."

"Hmmm," I said. "He lives in the city."

"Quint, that means absolutely nothing. What do you think, the Butcher ha convinced his former co-worker to now become a co-conspirator in murder?

It did sound silly. And yet, the fact that he lived in San Francisco ha piqued my interest. I still had a feeling that was the most likely city to b targeted.

"Plus, we should have expected that he lived in the city," Cara said.

"Why is that?"

"When Lu gave us the phone numbers, his was the only one with a 41 area code. San Francisco, as you well know. The other two were 925 are codes. The East Bay."

"That's good detective work, Cara. What's the address?"

"1584 Union Street. That's the Marina, right?"

"Could be Russian Hill. Hard to say exactly where on Union one become the other."

"Are we headed that way?" Cara asked.

"You know it."

We both showered and changed. The city itself was often twenty or thirt degrees colder than Walnut Creek, so we both wore jeans. She threw on green fleece sweatshirt and I wore a long-sleeved Lake Tahoe T-shirt I'd ha for over ten years.

Hopefully our dressing casually would improve the chances of Brenda Cabela talking to us. A uniformed police officer or someone dressed in a su might scare him off. At least, that was my thought process as we headed o toward San Francisco.

Halfway there, we received a depressing message.

"Brendan just texted me," Cara said.

"What did he say?"

"*I've already talked to the police and I'd rather not do any more interviews. I'm sorry.*"

"Damn," I said.

"We aren't giving up that easy, are we?" Cara said.

I smiled.

"Of course not! We're still going to his place."

"Good!"

42.
THE KILLER

My fastidiousness should be quite obvious by now.

And it continued to manifest itself as I planned my getaway from Avalon Towers. I had known Quint and Cara were getting close and tha I needed a backup. An alternative place to stay. If they discovered wh I was, my name would be plastered on every news station and medi outlet imaginable, making a hotel or Airbnb out of the question.

So I had come up with another one in my long line of brilliant ideas And it involved my lone friend at Caltenics, Brendan Cabela.

Although even saying that was a stretch. We were friendly, no friends.

Two weeks before Quint and Cara discovered who I was, I had alread started to plot. I just had an overall sense they were getting closer t me. Call it intuition, or better yet, call it genius. Discovery wasn imminent, but that didn't mean I shouldn't start thinking. Living a Avalon was getting too risky.

Many possibilities had flooded my sordid mind. But one stood out.

I knew my co-worker Brendan Cabela lived alone in San Francisco He had no girlfriend either. The apartment had been a hand-me-dow from his parents, who had long ago passed on. Unlike my father, wh gave his house to charity rather than giving it to yours truly. Fuck tha asshole!

With no parents, no girlfriend, and living alone, Brendan was perfed for what I had in mind.

He also performed at children's birthdays, usually dressing up a Sesame Street characters. He'd made the mistake of telling everyone a Caltenics that one day and took a good ribbing. I had stocked tha information away, then and there. Whether it would it become usefu going forward depended on how everything played out.

Who would suspect Big Bird was about to kill people? I have to say the idea grew on me as the days moved on.

However, if my plan was to succeed, I couldn't have Brendan workin at Caltenics. If the police found out that a co-worker of a serial kille was missing work, they'd probably be alarmed. And likely stop by hi place. And I couldn't have that happen.

So I got him fired.

In the break room, Caltenics had a small jar that contained petty cash. It didn't hold much, something like a hundred or two hundred dollars. We'd been told it was there for any purpose we collectively needed it for, but mainly it was used to get more K-Cups for the Keurig Coffee Maker we had in the office. Whenever we ran out, employees were encouraged to buy more, take the money from petty cash, and leave a receipt with the K-Cups they had purchased.

Simple enough.

A day after hatching my plan, while no one was looking, I grabbed the jar of petty cash from the cupboard above the Keurig.

Later that day, when Brendan left his cubicle to get a coffee of his own, I put the jar in the bottom of his desk, hiding it behind a few other things.

As if the gods smiled down on me, we ran out of K-Cups later that day.

Virginia Gary, the oldest woman working at Caltenics, and a dinosaur for the coding industry, happened to be the one to put the last one in the Keurig.

"Where's the petty cash?" she said to someone near her. "I can get some more on my lunch break."

My cubicle lay a good forty feet away, but I heard Virginia's loud voice clearly, and a sly smile crept across my face. Within a few minutes, several employees were looking in the cabinets around the break room to see if they could find the jar. To no avail, obviously.

That mystery became the talk of Caltenics for the rest of the day.

Who took the petty cash? Why? How could someone stoop that low?

That night, I grabbed the pre-paid burner phone I'd recently purchased and texted Lee Bavaro, the manager of the Walnut Creek Caltenics branch. He'd never be able to trace the phone so I wasn't worried. I just concentrated on trying to sound like a genuinely concerned employee in my anonymous message.

I hate to snitch on a coworker, but I saw Brendan Cabela steal the petty cash earlier today. He threw it in his desk. I was too shocked to say anything, because I like Brendan. But I saw it clear as day. I hope you don't mind that I texted this from a friend's phone. I don't want to be known as a rat.

The next morning, as I arrived at work, they were escorting Brendan off the premises. They must have waited until he came in and went through his desk, finding the jar of petty cash just where I'd left it.

He was professing his innocence while two security guards led him from Caltenics. And I watched him go, laughing on the inside.

Lee Bavaro, the man who fell hook, line, and sinker for my text, notified us later that day that Brendan's employment at Caltenics had been terminated.

Phase One of my plan had worked to perfection.

I kept in touch with Brendan after his firing. Not that I cared what had happened to him, but I did plan on eventually showing up at his apartment in San Francisco. And it would have seemed odd to do that if we hadn't been talking in the meantime.

Trust me, I'd thought out every aspect of what was to come.

He'd repeatedly tell me that he hadn't stolen the petty cash and I had to keep playing along. I hated hearing him whine, but I needed him. So I listened.

And then everything changed. I followed Quint and Cara to Iron Hill Street and saw them talking to my former neighbors. They would surely find out that the Langleys and the Tillers lived a few houses from each other. And then he might realize that a man named Tyler Anthony Danovich grew up a block over.

Quint was getting too close.

It was time for Phase Two.

I immediately went back to my apartment at Avalon. I put my clothes and anything else I could stuff into my car.

Everything I couldn't fit, or didn't want, I threw down the garbage chute on the fourth floor. I wiped down all the walls to my apartment, despite knowing it was pointless. I didn't have the time or resources to rid the entire apartment of my DNA.

Quint and Cara might still be a week or more from finding out I was the Butcher, but I saw no reason to tempt fate. The longer I waited, the more I risked having the police show up at Avalon before I could get out, leading to me spending the rest of my life in a cage. No, thanks.

However, I did have my fourth set of murders planned in two days' time, so it wasn't an easy decision. I mulled it over.

In the end, I concluded that staying at Avalon was just too big a risk. It was time to move on.

My original plan had been to keep paying rent at Avalon, so nothing seemed amiss, but I thought of something better. If I told them I was moving out, they'd come and clean the place to prepare it for a new renter, hopefully erasing any evidence or DNA I'd left behind.

Sure, it seemed inevitable that at some point they'd put the clues together and realize I was the Butcher, but why serve it up to them on a silver platter? I liked the idea of my apartment being cleaned completely. Make them work harder to find my DNA.

I called Kayla at the front desk and told her some bullshit story about my parents being sick and that I had to move out immediately. I told her that even though I'd already paid for the next month, they could start cleaning the apartment right away and renting it out as soon as possible. I wouldn't be back. I must have sounded so thoughtful.

Next I called Brendan. I told him that I wanted to come by his place and talk to him. He wasn't suspicious in the least; in fact, he seemed genuinely excited to see me. He was a lonely guy, especially after losing his job, and probably appreciated someone reaching out.

I had one more stop to make. I went by my bank and took out an astronomical sum of cash. In the process I received a few suspicious stares from the bank's employees, but it was my money and there was nothing they could do about it. I made up a bullshit story about entering some big poker tournaments, not that it mattered.

It's not like I was a wanted fugitive. At least not yet.

Certainly when my name was released to the world, they'd tell their friends that I'd come by their bank and withdrawn $20,000 cash from my checking account. What a great story that would make for them when it was too late to stop me.

I drove into San Francisco that night. On my way over the Bay Bridge, I saw a huge cruise ship docked down by the Embarcadero.

Would that not be the perfect getaway? You're surrounded by people on a bus or a train. And driving out of state would just keep me on the perpetual run in the United States.

But a cruise ship, with my own room, that dropped me off somewhere in South America? Now that could work!

I arrived at Brendan's place at nine o'clock that night, once it had gotten dark. I'd picked a time late enough to make it tough for anyone to see me enter his apartment, but not so late as arouse Brendan's suspicions.

I took a backpack from my car and loaded it with some of the stuff I'd tossed in the back seat—my laptop, a few days' worth of clothing, the fentanyl I still had left over from my cookie killings, and my cash.

He opened the door, we said a brief hello, and I walked on in. The less time standing outside of his apartment, the better. He didn't ask why I was carrying a backpack and didn't seem fazed by my entering his apartment so quickly. It appeared he was just happy to have the company.

Brendan stood an inch or two shorter than me and slightly skinnier. But we had similarly colored brown hair, and as we exchanged pleasantries, I did think I could pass for him if necessary. He looked pretty young for his age, which was important since I was a good five years younger.

His place was a two-story flat, more a townhouse than an apartment. He obviously hadn't done much since taking it over from his parents. It gave off a feeling of being not just old but museum-like, with antiques seemingly anywhere. There was ceramic clowns, Tiffany lamps, and even animal-footed ottomans. The most prominent colors were pale green and dark brown. No one would have guessed that a guy in his thirties lived there.

Brendan played the gracious host, seeming to enjoy showing me around the place. I bet I could have talked him into just letting me live there for awhile. But that would have led to too many complications. And once they showed my face on television, which I knew was coming at some point, he'd assuredly call the police.

No, Brendan couldn't be around. I needed his townhouse, but I didn't need him.

I struck gold early on in our conversation.

"Are you still entertaining kids at parties?" I asked.

"I sure am. It's helped keep me distracted after that bullshit at Caltenics. The kids put a smile on my face."

"I've always respected you for doing that. When's your next one?"

"Next Thursday," Brendan said. "They want me to be Elmo."

"Very cool. Who's throwing the party?" I asked, knowing if I could find out the name, I could probably find out where and when.

"Some woman named Vanessa. She's got a daughter turning six."

I had to get more information.

"Vanessa Charles, by chance? I know a Vanessa in the city with a young daughter."

He responded just the way I hoped he would.

"No, this woman's last name is Mathers."

"Gotcha. It would have been funny if I knew the woman."

Brendan smiled, but it was an awkward smile. I was way too good at getting information, but his expression made me worry I'd aroused his suspicions.

It was definitely time for me to have the townhouse to myself.

Thirty minutes later, I had my chance. We'd engaged in some more small talk, mostly about Caltenics. He asked who I thought had really stolen the money. It was so pathetic.

He offered to make us some drinks and walked into the kitchen. Looking around the room, I saw a paperweight that resembled a very large snow globe. Or a small bowling ball. I grabbed it, settling the weight in my palm.

A few seconds later, I followed Brendan into the kitchen. I did a brief check of my surroundings, making sure no neighbor might be looking in. The blinds were shut and that made now as good a time as any.

He'd heard me enter, but he didn't turn around.

"I'm really glad you stopped in, Tyler. It's been a tough few weeks for me since I was fired. I miss my work friends."

He poured what looked like vodka into two large glasses.

"It's good seeing you as well," I said, inching closer.

"How is everything else? Any new girls in your life? I know you didn't get along with that many at Caltenics."

And then I struck. I lifted the paperweight over my head and brought it crashing onto the back of Brendan's skull.

He let out a terrible shriek and fell down to one knee. He was severely injured, but I hadn't put him out of commission yet.

I raised the paperweight once again and brought it crashing down a second time.

This blow was even more brutal, and he went from his knees to flat on the floor. Two huge gashes showed on the back of his head, blood sticking to his hair, but he was still alive, and thus, a threat to me.

He muttered six final words: "But...I...was...nice...to...you."

Then I brought down the paperweight a third time. And I didn't hear any more from him. I followed with a fourth, fifth, and sixth strike to the back of his skull, but at that point I was just showing off.

Brendan was dead.

I walked through both floors of the townhouse and shut every blind. I found a downstairs bathtub in which I could keep Brendan's body. Every piece of it.

The apartment only had to last me until the final set of killings. Which, with this news about the children's party, might well be next Thursday.

Going outside and disposing of the body somewhere, even just throwing it in the garbage, was too risky.

I'd chop up his body, throw the parts in the bathtub, and add Clorox or some other household supplies to diminish the smell that would surely arise.

I looked around the kitchen drawers, in which found some extremely sharp knives. In particular, a few serrated ones I thought might do the trick. With no hacksaw, I wasn't going to be slicing the body into fifteen parts, but if I could just cut it down to three or four, I could carry the parts down to the bathtub without the noise and work of dragging a whole body.

The body parts wouldn't be the only mess. I'd be cleaning a lot of blood off the kitchen floor as well.

As I took off his clothes, I found a cellphone in his jeans.

An idea popped into my head.

I took his right thumb and placed it on the phone screen. It came to life, with the thumbprint serving as his password.

I scrolled through his contacts and found Vanessa Mathers. Her number was there. More importantly, their text conversation showed the address and time for next Thursday.

I'd hit the jackpot.

His Elmo outfit had to be somewhere in the townhouse. This couldn't have worked out any better.

I certainly would need Brendan's cellphone.

I could probably change its security system from his thumbprint to numerical code.

But just to be safe, I started by cutting off his thumb.

Phase Two of my plan had worked to perfection as well.

Two days later, I left Brendan's townhouse for the first time.

I drove back to Walnut Creek and carried out my fourth set of murders. At the Treeside Manor. My joke of a grandmother lived there, which seemed as good a reason as any to pick it. But she'd just be the cherry on top. The killing of any innocent people made up the delicious ice cream sundae for me.

I'd surveilled the place when I still lived in Walnut Creek. With the two U-locks I'd used to barricade in the doors, and the fact that Treeside Manor's elderly occupants couldn't be too strong or quick on their feet anyway, I knew the loss of human life would be considerable.

Not to state the obvious, but I'd always been a terrible person. And I had become much worse once I started killing. It whetted my appetite. Now, death consumed me. I wanted to kill more and more.

I'd entered my most manic stage yet.

The next morning I woke up and watched reports of the carnage at Treeside Manor flooding the news. I gloated, loving the attention brought to me—albeit not the true recognition of calling me out by name.

But to my shock, that changed later that day.

It was probably around two p.m. when I first heard my name mentioned on the local news. I spun to look at the T.V. and saw my old high school yearbook photo staring back at me.

They had finally found out who I was!

It had to be because of Quint. *Well done, my friend. Maybe you truly are the adversary I was looking for.*

Just as I soaked in the idea of being forever infamous, just like I'd always wanted, I realized I had to get rid of my car. It was parked a block away from Brendan's apartment.

Driving it any distance meant taking a huge risk, but surely there would be an APB on my car soon. If one wasn't out already. I had to move it. The risk of having it found so close to Brendan's outweighed the risk of taking it somewhere else.

I also realized they might try to ping my phone, so I powered it down. Luckily, I hadn't needed to use it since taking over the townhouse. Plus, I had a pre-paid burner and now Brendan's phone as well.

I borrowed a hoodie from Brendan (he wouldn't be missing it), covering my face before I exited the townhouse and walked to my car.

I drove over the Golden Gate Bridge. It'd possibly throw them off the scent of San Francisco if my car was indeed found.

A sight-seeing bluff just north of the bridge faced back toward the Golden Gate. I parked my car. Other cars surrounded mine, and I thought it might get lost in the shuffle. There was incriminating evidence in the car itself, but I couldn't carry everything back to Brendan's, so I just left it all.

The Golden Gate Bridge loomed large as I looked out from the bluff, and I took a few seconds to take in its splendor. Yes, I can take beauty in things. It's humans I despise.

I walked in the bridge's direction.

Obviously, I couldn't take an Uber and leave a trace. I'd considered calling a yellow taxi, but there would still be a record of someone being picked up near where my car might be found. I couldn't chance that either.

I decided I had no other choice, so I walked back over the Golden Gate and into the city.

I wasn't nearly as scared as I probably should have been. But the high school yearbook photo looked nothing like my current self and I figured it was a thousand to one I'd be recognized.

Still, I kept my hoodie on as I walked the several miles to Brendan's apartment. I didn't close the drawstrings and make it obvious, but I did make it tough for someone to see my face clearly.

When I arrived back safely, I knew I couldn't risk going out again. Although I didn't have many pictures out in cyberspace, there were a few, and they'd surely be on the news soon.

So I'd have to stay in.

I set up a delivery from Safeway to provide me with food for the next week or so, Thursday being six days away. I'd already gone through what little Brendan had left in the refrigerator.

There was a slight smell coming from his corpse in the bathroom. Nothing egregious yet, but some more Clorox would help limit the odor. So I added that to my Safeway order. It was a common, everyday product and nothing that would arouse suspicion.

And for good measure, in the notes section, I said that I was an invalid, and asked that they please leave my groceries at the front door. No need to meet with the delivery guy.

Obviously, I used Brendan's credit card and not my own.

My mind flashed back to when I drove over the Bay Bridge and saw the cruise ship. It really was the perfect getaway. Get on a cruise under the name of Brendan Cabela. I had found his passport in his room. I also had his driver's license and his credit cards.

While we didn't look identical, it's not like I was trying to get into a bar at nineteen years old. Once they saw the passport, I should be home free.

I used my burner phone (I worried about them tracing the IP address on my laptop) and started searching for cruises leaving out of San Francisco or the Bay Area. But none would be departing for two weeks.

Even though taking over Brendan's townhouse had been a rousing success, that was far too long to wait. He'd already started receiving a few texts from friends, and I had needed to make excuses so they wouldn't get suspicious.

I had to get out of the Bay Area either next Thursday or Friday.

No, it had to be Thursday.

They would find out that Brendan Cabela was originally scheduled for the kids' birthday party.

I started to realize for the first time that I hadn't been as meticulous for this final set of killings. After leaving Avalon, I'd been flying by the seat of my pants. And it just might get me caught. For the first time, I was scared.

And a cruise ship? What the fuck had I been thinking! They'd be sending someone aboard to arrest me as soon as they'd found out the room was booked on Brendan Cabela's credit card.

My mania had gotten worse. I wasn't thinking right.

I tried to settle down.

I could change the plans for my final set of murders.

No, it was too perfect. That would remain.

I thought more.

A flight to Europe was out of the question. They'd be waiting for me when I landed.

But I figured I could make it to Mexico. I'd spent time in Mexico City, but that was over a four-hour flight from San Francisco. Too big a risk. Tijuana lay only an hour and a half away. I'd fly there.

And once I got to Tijuana, I'd give Brendan's credit card to a poor Mexican. Tell him it was a gift. Let the FBI, or the Federales, follow the card around Tijuana while I headed off to some other part of Mexico. Paying with cash, of course.

I checked Brendan's phone again. The party was at two p.m. on Thursday. I'd confirmed with Vanessa Mathers, the woman throwing the party, that I'd be there. She had no reason to be alarmed. And she'd told me there might be as many as twenty or thirty kids present at the party. Perfect.

I began looking at flights to Mexico. With the amount of cash I had withdrawn, I could live there for a year under the radar. Maybe longer.

A flight left at 5:00 p.m. on Thursday night for Tijuana. The timing couldn't be better. People say you're supposed to be three hours early for an international flight, but that's rarely truly necessary. If I arrived at the airport by 3:30, I had no doubt I'd catch the flight.

And it seemed unlikely the police would find the connection with Brendan Cabela that soon. So they'd be out looking for Tyler Anthony Danovich.

All I had to do was land in Mexico and it would be easy to do the rest. Go undercover. Go underground.

I purchased the flight on Brendan's credit card and thought my getaway plan just might work.

But in my mind, I could still hear a voice of doubt that hadn't been there before. I wasn't as confident as I had been with the other murders. Once I'd moved out of Avalon, plans had changed. And I hadn't had time to be as thorough as I had in the past.

I needed to recharge my brain and stop thinking of the worst. I lay down for a nap.

I spent that night thinking about Quint. The asshole had found me. I'd been so busy all day, I hadn't had time to consider how he'd done it. And it had to be him. The police were always a step behind. But not Quint.

It must have started when he found out that I'd grown up near the Tillers and Langleys.

Could he have seen me tailing him to Iron Hill Street? I thought I'd been cautious, but you never know.

And would that be enough for him to suspect me?

Maybe that and my name did the trick. Maybe he saw how T-A-D fit so perfectly at the end of Quint and beginning of Adler. My poker analogy might have finally hit home. And could I really be mad? It was I who instigated our little game after all.

I guess it didn't make a difference in the end. They had discovered who I was. And that's all that mattered.

Things had changed now.

And for the first time, I had to play a little defense.

The next day, Sunday, I wrote another letter to Quint, the police, and th media. I even added a few local celebrities to my mailing list. I couldn' risk leaving the townhouse, so I emailed it. I couldn't wait to see th attention another message to the media would bring me. I had to b rising up the list of most famous serial killers in history. It brought huge fucking smile to my face, I can tell you!

It was a welcome change after the paranoia which had filled me th day before.

I told them I'd kill sometime in the next month.

I certainly couldn't tell them I was killing before the week was ou The city would be even more infiltrated by police than it already wa But by saying the murders could occur anytime in the next thirty day I spread out the potential timeframe and made it tougher on the cops.

My manic state passed as nothing much happened the rest c Sunday nor Monday. I spent most of my time watching the T.V. an browsing the internet, soaking in the attention from all over the world. took the occasional trip to the bathtub to pour more Clorox o Brendan's corpse. It smelled worse by the day, but I didn't think the odc would have made it to any neighbors yet.

My confidence was slowly coming back.

And then, on Tuesday, out of the blue, Brendan's phone received a tex from none other than Cara. I ignored it, knowing nothing good coul come of responding.

Wednesday came and I received another text. I was only one day from the killings that would cement my infamy forever, and I wanted to ignor it.

But thought better of it.

I realized I couldn't risk them showing up unannounced. So I texte back, pretending to be Brendan and telling them I'd already talked to th police and didn't want to deal with anyone else.

It didn't work.

Thirty minutes later, I heard a knock on the front door of th townhouse. From a room upstairs, I opened the blinds a half inch an looked down on the front step.

To my initial dismay, but then my growing excitement, there stoo Quint and Cara.

I quietly tip-toed down the stairs.

43.

We made our way into the city and parked two blocks down from Brendan Cabela's apartment. I'd never known it to be easy to find parking in San Francisco, and this day was no different.

"Let's hope he answers," Cara said.

"The woman, Lu, told us he'd been fired from Caltenics. So it's unlikely he's already found a new job. He'll be home," I said.

I was thinking positively, but I really had no idea.

Cabela lived in a pleasant area of San Francisco, with two-story townhouses intermingled with local businesses. We strolled past two residences and then a laundry service. Three more townhouses and then a hole in the wall restaurant. May not sound like it, but it was charming.

We approached the apartment.

"It's 1584 Union Street, right?"

Cara looked down at her phone.

"Yup."

So I rang the doorbell. But no one answered. I rang it again a minute later. Still no response.

"Did we come all the way out here for nothing?" I asked rhetorically.

I rang the doorbell a third time and could feel my frustration rising. The impending murders had made me easily irritable. Who could blame me?

"Try calling him," I said to Cara.

"Yeah?"

"Worth a try."

I tried to look in the townhouse windows, but the blinds were shut. At the bottom they left a small, half-inch space to look in, but that wasn't going to help. I wasn't sure what I expected anyway. Brendan Cabela, sitting on a couch, ignoring us?

"No answer," Cara said.

"Shit."

"How about sending one more text? I'm not worried about bothering the guy at this point. Say we're outside his apartment and can wait here if he's out and about."

"Alright."

And then I heard a faint noise from inside.

Or at least thought I did.

"Did you hear that?" I asked Cara.

"No. What?"

"I'm pretty sure I heard some movement behind the door."

"Are you sure?"

I put my index finger to my lips, hoping we'd hear something else. We waited a good thirty seconds. But nothing more came.

I knocked loudly on the door.

"I heard you in there, Brendan," I said. "Come out and talk to us. All we' doing is trying to catch a killer. Maybe you can help us."

"I hope you're not losing your mind, Quint. I didn't hear anything."

"It was a small movement. Very quiet. Like he was right on the other sic of the door," I told her. Then I turned back to the door and yelled, "Yeah, know you can hear me."

Maybe Brendan wasn't there and I was shouting at thin air. But maybe h was and I'd elicit a reaction.

"Just give us two minutes of your time," I said.

Two people walking on the sidewalk looked in our direction.

"This is crazy, Quint. You look like you're talking to yourself."

I sighed.

"I'll stop. But I know I heard something."

"Yeah, well, I didn't."

"That asshole is in there."

"Say he is. What do you want to do? The guy has already talked to th cops. Knock the door down?"

Unfortunately, Cara had a point.

"Fine. Let's go."

And we headed back toward our car.

"What's next?" Cara asked as we sat behind the dashboard, unsure of wh; to do.

I thought long and hard. There was one Hail Mary I hadn't yet tried.

"Maybe I can poke the bear," I said.

"What did you have in mind?"

"I'm going to email the Butcher. Tell him that if he really wants to make th a fair fight, I need some more clues."

"And you think he'll respond?"

"He loves all the attention he's getting. But I think he's missing out on on thing."

"And what's that?"

"Talking to me personally. Telling me that he is winning. That he's bett than me."

"What about the letters and the email?"

"Those are too impersonal. A bunch of other people are reading them. H wants to let me, and only me, know that he's got the upper hand. To rub it in

Cara frowned. "Let's hope you're right. We're running out of time."

When we got back to Avalon, I started composing an email.

I addressed it to both the Butcher's work email that Cara found and the Q6221980@gmail he'd used to email Peter Vitella.

"Can I read it?" Cara asked.

"Of course," I said.

She looked over my shoulder and read:

Hello, Tad. This is Quint. Since I probably won't be seeing you in the Avalon elevator anytime soon, I figured I'd send you this email.

Let's get this out of the way first: I think you're a piece of human scum and I'd love to have a few minutes to tear your fucking head off.

Now that I've said my piece, I'll get to why I've really written this.

Do you know why Muhammad Ali and Joe Frazier were badasses? Because they fought fair fights. They didn't put brass knuckles in their gloves.

But that's what you've done. And so it's not a fair fight. It's amazing that I've got as close to you as I have. I'm the one who is actually winning. You've had a 25-mile lead in a marathon and I'm right on your heels.

I think in your heart you truly want to win a fair fight, and if you do, you've got to give me something else. A fighting chance is all I want. And knowing it's going to happen within the next month hardly makes for an even playing field. Not even close.

Give me a city. Or a specific date. Or how you are going to kill people.

You'd still have all the edge in the world. But at least I could say I was given a shot. That's all I want.

You may win, but don't let it be because you made this game unwinnable for your opponent. Namely, me.

All I want is a shot.

Quint.

"You were far too nice," Cara said. "Even with the human scum line."

"That was intentional. I have to play mostly nice if he's going to take the bait."

"And you made it sound like a sporting contest," Cara said.

"That was also intentional. To make it like a competition. He feels that he's lost the game of life to me. He hates that I've become a pseudo-celebrity, that I'm well-liked, that I have you. Maybe this will conjure up those competitive feelings. And he'll feel like if he wins this last battle on an even playing field, he'll surpass me in some way."

"It seems like you know him way better than you may have realized."

"I didn't know Tad, but I think I know the Butcher. If that makes any sense."

"A little," Cara said.

It was time to be completely honest.

"There's something else," I said.

"What?"

"I think he'd love nothing more than to kill me before he finishes. I'm giving him the chance to bring me closer."

"I wish you hadn't told me that. Although, I can't say I'm all that surprised."

"I figured you should know. We'll see what happens, but there's a chance I may head out on my own at some point."

"How many times have you said we're a team?" Cara asked.

"We are. But I love you. And if I think it's too dangerous, I'm not taking you with me. I'm sorry."

"Let's see if we even get to that point. He's probably not going to respond to your email."

"We'll see," I said.

And the next morning we got our answer.

44.
THURSDAY

At 10:52 a.m., I got an email alert on my phone.

Quint. My nemesis. So you found out who I was and that makes you Sherlock Holmes? Absolutely not! You're not my equal in this game. Or in this fight. Not even close! How many times have I seen you at Avalon since this all started? If you really had some sixth sense, or any sense at all, you'd have realized something was wrong with me. But you never did, and so you'd go on schmoozing with me, not knowing you were in the presence of evil! Unadulterated evil. You have no idea what I want to do to every person I see. Rip them limb from limb if I could. But I'm also smart and restrained. It's a Daily Double you rarely see in serial killers. They are usually just brutal and dumb. A lot of low IQs in the history of serial killers. But not here. Not with me.

And maybe because I know you've got zero chance of catching me, I will take you up on your offer to keep you in the game. But it's going to come at a price. Cara, and also your mother, are now fair game. I don't know exactly where your mother lives, but I'm sure I can find out. That will be swell. As will be making some sweet time for Cara. Show her what a real man is.

I'm sure you'd like to rip me limb from limb right about now. See, we aren't that different, Quint.

I don't have time for a pen pal, so this will be our only back and forth. We're in the ninth inning, Quint, and you are way behind. I'll leave you with my clues:

(1) The cause of death will be the same as one from my first four sets of killings. In case you need reminding: Stabbing/bludgeoning. Poisoning. Gunshot wound. Fire/smoke inhalation.

(2) Although this will be my most memorable set of killings, it will be on a much smaller scale than some of the others.

(3) And while I shouldn't give you any more hints, I'll leave you with a final one. It will take place in San Francisco. I will complete my plans with the fifth and final city that I mentioned in my first letter.

That is all, Quint. I bid you adieu. I'd do the same for your mother or Cara, but I may be seeing them one more time.

You were a better adversary than the police. But not enough in the end, I'm afraid.

I called Captain Lockett as I read the last lines of the email.

"Hello, Quint."

"Captain, could you send a police car to my mother's house right now? The Butcher just threatened her."

"You've talked to him?"

"Yes. Where are you right now?"

"At the headquarters on 7th Street."

"I'm coming to you. Can you send a car to my mom's right now, though?"

"Sure. What's the address?"

"116 Adams Place. San Ramon. Please send them immediately. Thank you."

"I will. See you soon. Looks like we have some talking to do."

I hung up the phone and turned toward Cara, who had read the Butcher's message with me.

"Are you okay?" I asked.

"Yeah."

It was a tepid response, and I knew the email had shaken her up.

"You're going to be with me and you're going to be safe. I promise."

"But you said we might separate at some point."

"Only to keep you away from the Butcher."

"I don't care. I want to stay with you. And see this out."

Cara had a stubborn streak that I'd always loved. I didn't enjoy it at the very moment, but she was right. She'd been with me on this the entire time. She deserved to see it out to its conclusion.

"Alright. We're attached at the hip until this ends."

"Good."

"Let's pack our bags really quick. We're going to get a hotel in San Francisco."

"Okay."

"And we have to stop in Oakland first to see Captain Lockett."

"I heard. I'll be ready in a few minutes."

We got dressed and packed in record time, arriving in less than thirty minutes.

As I drove, I asked Cara to screenshot the Butcher's email and text it to Captain Lockett.

We saw him as soon as we approached the entrance to the headquarters. I couldn't help but be reminded of Ray, who'd waited for me there a few times when this whole crazy case was getting started. It seemed like a year ago, even though it had only been a matter of weeks.

We exchanged brief pleasantries.

"Let's talk as we walk," Lockett said.

He was all business, and who could blame him?

"Sure."

"Thanks for the text of his email. Ninth inning, huh? Sounds like time may be of the utmost of importance."

"Looking that way. Who knows exactly what he means by the ninth inning. Is that today? Tomorrow? Sometime next week?"

"Did you send any response to his email?"

"No, we came straight out here. And he said he was only corresponding once," I said. "I guess I still probably should have."

"Once we're done here, send him a message. See if you can get one more response. It's worth a try."

"Will do."

"It's like with a hostage negotiator. Keep him on the line as long as you can."

"Gotcha."

Lockett pressed the elevator button for the third floor.

"Did you send a police car to my mother's?" I asked.

"Yes."

"Thank you. Should I tell her?"

"It's a plainclothes officer in an undercover car. Your call, but she probably won't even notice he's there."

"Alright, I won't tell her." I closed my eyes and sighed. "This fucking sucks."

"I'm sorry he dragged your mother into it, Quint. But it's a million to one he'll ever show up there. Especially after alerting you to the fact."

"Thanks. And I know you're right, but can we please keep that officer there until this is over?"

"The only time that officer will leave is when another one takes his place."

"I appreciate it, Captain."

We arrived on the third floor. I turned to Cara.

"Are you okay?" I asked.

"I'm fine. I feel safer about your mother now."

"Yeah, so do I."

I saw the Chief of Police, Alfred Ronson, approaching us. We'd both said some regrettable things the first few times we'd met.

He shook my hand and this time, to my surprise, acted almost cordial.

"Thank you for all you've done, Quint. And you must be Cara. I'm the Chief of Police."

"Nice to meet you," Cara said.

After they shook hands, Chief Ronson turned back to me.

"We didn't get off to a great start. And I could probably chastise you for getting a bit too involved in this case. But I don't care about any of that. None. All I want is to catch this psychopath before he kills again."

"I'm with you 100%, Chief. That's all I want too."

"Good. Let's get it done. Now follow me."

Lockett, Cara, and I followed Ronson to a conference room. It was th
same one as we'd been in the day I found out about the Butcher's first lette

About ten members of law enforcement agencies had gathered in th
room, including an F.B.I. agent and someone wearing a SFPD uniform. Th
had truly become a melting pot, with agencies overlapping, all in hopes
catching the Butcher in time.

"Please sit," Chief Ronson said.

Each of us took a seat around the long table.

"This is going to be a very open discussion. We'd like to welcome Qui
and Cara, who just got an email from the Butcher within this past hour. I'
printed out copies."

He went around the table and handed one to each person gathere
including Cara and me.

"Let's start with your thoughts, Quint. What do you make of it?"

I stood up.

"First off, he says that we're in the ninth inning. So I don't think he plar
on waiting the full month. I hate to say it, but my guess would be in the ne
day or two. Second, he said that he's going to kill in one of the same ways h
already has. I don't want to eliminate anything, but I doubt it's going to be t
knife. He wants to go out with something unforgettable, and stabbings seer
unlikely. Plus, he's always said he despises the nickname the Bay Are
Butcher, so I don't see him ending with a knife.

"I also think a fire is unlikely. Just call it a gut feeling. So my guess wou
either be a firearm or another poisoning. If he had more fentanyl, that wou
certainly be possible. So that's the one I fear the most.

"He also said this will be his most memorable set of killings, but smaller
scale. My mind went to him targeting someone important. The mayor. Or th
CEO of a social media company. I haven't decided exactly what he means t
that, but those are my first ideas.

"And the last thing. I believe him when he says he will be killing in Sa
Francisco. Not that he deserves any credit on anything, but he's been prett
honest with us. I guess because it's more fun for him. So, not to step on you
toes, but I'd allocate most of my officers to the city."

I sat back down, my heart pounding. I hadn't realized I was going to ta
that long. But I had a lot to get off my chest.

"That's quite a summation, Quint," Chief Ronson said. "Especially sinc
you received this email only recently."

"I've been thinking about this guy all day every day for several weeks now

"I believe you have. Does anyone else have something to say?"

I heard a familiar voice. Freddie Fields.

"I hate considering the possibility, but if he is able to complete his killing
we have to think about how best to catch him afterward. Do we shut down th
bridges and bring the city to a standstill? Can we even do that?"

"I've been talking to the mayors of both Oakland and San Francisco," Captain Lockett said. "We're not going to shut down the bridges entirely, but if the Butcher strikes we will put officers at each bridge to check every car as they enter or leave the city. We'll be checking IDs and, obviously, be very wary of men in their twenties. Officers will be stationed at the south edge of town as well. So it's not just the Golden Gate and Bay bridges. I'd be confident of catching him if he tried to drive out of the city."

"Thank you, Captain," Chief Ronson said. "That's good work. I'm appreciating all the cooperation between multiple agencies."

He nodded to some of the non-OPD officers at the table.

"Anything else?" he asked.

"Do we have a lot of people at Oracle, the San Francisco Giants ballpark?" an officer asked.

"We do. They have night games today and Friday, and then afternoon games this weekend. We've talked to them about suspending the games, but it isn't going to happen."

"What if him saying the ninth inning was a reference to the Giants?" Cara asked, drawing all eyes to her.

Several of the officers in the room nodded.

"It's something to think about, Cara. It certainly hadn't crossed my mind yet," Ronson said.

"I'll talk to the SFPD," Captain Lockett said. "I'll see if we can send more officers to Oracle Park. We've never had as many Bay Area and Federal law enforcement working on one case, and yet I still feel we're going to be understaffed at certain places. It's inevitable with so many potential targets throughout San Francisco."

"We are going to catch him," Chief Ronson said. "I just got a text from the Chief of the SFPD and I have to call him back. Most likely we'll be sending a bunch of you out to SF, so stand by. Sorry this was so quick, but we are adjourned."

Everyone started to rise and Chief Ronson headed out of the conference room.

Cara and I hung around. I held her hand and turned toward Captain Lockett.

"Hey, Captain. You're still in touch with the SFPD yourself, right?

"Several times a day.

"Can you ask them something for me?"

"Sure. What is it, Quint?"

"Find out who talked to Brendan Cabela and what he said? We went by his place in San Francisco and he didn't answer. But I swear I heard him moving around inside. Just want to make sure he's not hiding anything."

What Lockett said next shocked me to my core.

"Who is Brendan Cabela?"

"He used to work with the Butcher. He was fired recently, but was apparently somewhat close to him."

"I really don't remember seeing his name mentioned," Lockett said, frowning.

Cara and I exchanged a glance. She didn't need to say anything. We both knew what the other one was thinking.

"Is it possible you could have missed it?" I asked.

"It's possible. There is a lot going on, of course. But I've been reading the SFPD's daily briefings and I don't remember anything mentioning a Brendan Cabela."

"He said he talked to the police and he lives in SF, so I just assumed it would have been someone from the SFPD who interviewed him."

"Give me one second."

Captain Lockett took out his phone and walked to the other end of the conference room. Still gripping Cara's hand, I watched Lockett hold a rapid conversation in a low voice. He came back thirty seconds later with a mystified look.

"The SFPD has not interviewed him. I'm not even sure he's on their radar. And he said he'd talked to the police?"

"Yup. That's what he told us. It's possible he just doesn't want to talk to anyone about his friendship with the Butcher and so he made up an excuse. But this seems a bit odd."

"Can you head out to San Francisco right now?" Lockett asked.

"Yeah, we were planning on getting a hotel out there," I said.

"That can wait. Give me Brendan's address and I'll meet you there."

Cara quickly scrolled through her phone and read off the address we'd been at yesterday. "It's 1584 Union Street."

"It's the SFPD's jurisdiction, so I can't promise anything, but I wouldn't mind another set of eyes who have already been there. Plus, as I've said many times, you guys have been a step ahead of everyone else. I like the idea of having you guys close."

"Thanks," I said. "We'll meet you there."

45.

We arrived outside out of Brendan Cabela's townhouse for the second day in a row. It was approaching 1:00 p.m.

But we weren't the first ones there.

Five SFPD officers had already arrived. A few of them stood at the front door while one knocked.

Once we got within about fifty feet, another officer stopped us from getting any closer. Captain Lockett saw us and walked over.

"It's okay, they're with me." He escorted us away from the officers. "We have to let them do their stuff. Even though we're working together, I have no jurisdiction over here."

"I understand," I said.

"Will they raid the house if he doesn't answer?" Cara asked.

"I'm not sure. There would have to be a reason," Lockett said.

An idea had been percolating on our drive over, but I wasn't sure if I should voice it. I decided this wasn't the time to hold anything back.

"Captain, what if the Butcher knew he had to move out of Avalon and had a backup plan? Somewhere else he knew of to go?"

"Are you saying what I think you're saying?"

"It may not be likely, but it's certainly not impossible. How attentive has the Butcher been to every detail? I don't think he just moved out of Avalon and started living on the street."

"Give me a second."

We watched as Captain Lockett approached the SFPD officers. At 6'5", he was an intimidating presence, but he held himself as deferentially as possible. As he'd said, this was their jurisdiction.

And if he was telling them what I thought he was, he'd better tread lightly.

He returned to us a minute later.

"I think I talked them into it," he said.

"Into what exactly?"

"Going into the house."

A few minutes later, we heard a member of the SFPD yelling.

"Mr. Cabela, this is your last chance. We are coming in."

Thirty impossibly tense seconds passed. And then they broke down the door. It involved some sort of ram-like instrument that I couldn't make out from our distance.

The next few minutes took forever. It was probably the most nervous I have been since this whole thing had started. I couldn't say exactly why, but I knew something wasn't right.

An SFPD officer came outside and approached one of his fellow officers standing out by us. He spoke in a whisper, trying to keep us from hearing, but we stood too close not to.

"Miller, call the coroner."

Our jaws dropped.

"Officer," Captain Lockett said.

"Yes."

"I'm Captain Miles Lockett with the OPD. I'm going to assume Brenda Cabela is deceased?"

"Hard to tell who it is. The body is in five parts."

Cara turned away.

It was just another shock in what had been six weeks full of them. But this one really hit home, considering we'd been knocking on that door less than twenty-four hours ago.

"Do you think it was the Butcher that you heard inside?" Cara asked me quietly.

"Probably," I admitted.

The other officers heard us.

Captain Lockett pointed at me. "This is Quint. He…"

"I know who he is," the SFPD officer said.

"Well, Quint and Cara have been highly instrumental in identifying the Butcher. In fact, they were outside this residence yesterday, trying to talk to Brendan Cabela. They've been a step ahead of us at the OPD, I have to admit it. And I'd like to ask for a favor."

"What is it?"

The officer didn't look like he was the type to grant many favors.

"Before the coroner gets here, can they do a quick five-minute walkthrough of the place? They seem to know more about the Butcher than anyone. Something might jump out. They will put on shoe covers, stay out of your way, and not get close to the body. I don't even have to come in. But please, I'm begging you, give them a few minutes."

It was a monumental ask by Captain Lockett. And it meant more to me than he'd ever know.

I saw the officer mulling it over.

Lockett spoke again. "If what we're really trying to do is catch the Butcher, you'll grant me this favor."

The officer motioned in our direction. "Alright, you've got five minutes. I'll give you some shoe covers. Stay out of the officers' way and don't get near the body."

"Thank you, officer," I said. "I don't need to see the body."

In fact, I didn't want to.

"Alright, let's do this quick. When the coroner gets here, you guys are out."
"That's fine. Thank you for allowing this."

Cara and I took off our shoes and put on a plastic covering over our socks. We also wore the masks and gloves they gave us.

On entering the townhouse, we were immediately struck by the smell. It was foul in a way I'd never experienced before. It had to be the dead body.

But Cara and I couldn't concentrate on that. We only had five minutes to gather any information.

An officer tailed us, but he allowed us basically to roam free.

You entered the townhouse in what was almost like a middle level, but it was too small to even call it that. You either went down a set of stairs to the bottom floor or walked up the five or six steps to the top floor.

The bottom level of the apartment held what looked to be two bedrooms and a bathroom. I couldn't tell for sure. Officers' voices rose from down there, and I assumed it was where they had found the body.

"Can't let you down there," the officer said.

So we walked up the tiny set of stairs to the top level.

The living room took up the majority of the space. It held a few couches and a T.V., and through the door I saw a kitchen space.

The townhouse seemed stale. It didn't feel lived in, although obviously it had been. Figurines sat on several small tables scattered throughout the room. They looked to be clowns. Too many ottomans littered the room. Lamps as well.

A bathroom was on the left of the living room and two closets to the right. I made my way to the closets.

"Are these alright to open?" I asked the officer.

"Yeah, I guess so," he replied.

I opened the first one. It was filled with five or six trench coats. I know San Francisco could get cold, but it seemed like a bit much. I slid the coats to the far left of the rack to see if anything had been hidden behind them. There hadn't been.

I shut the door and moved on to the next closet.

I was startled when I opened it. Not that it was anything too crazy, I just wasn't expecting what I saw. Hanging on the rack were several full-length Sesame Street costumes.

Big Bird. Snuffleupagus. Bert and Ernie. And a few I didn't recognize.

"Weird," I said.

"This guy must really love Halloween," Cara remarked, standing beside me.

"Not anymore," the officer said.

It was a completely unnecessary thing to say, and I didn't give him the satisfaction of answering.

"Seems a bit odd to have that many Sesame Street outfits," I said.

"Yeah," Cara said. "But does it mean anything?"

"Probably not," I admitted.

Since the kitchen door lay close to the closets, I headed its way.

I looked in, but it wasn't what I saw. I smelled something.

"Do you smell that?" I said to Cara.

The officer interjected.

"I do," he said. "Brownies?"

"I think you're right."

"It's definitely brownies," Cara said.

I turned to the officer. "Can we open the oven?"

"I'll do it," he said. "It's still a bit warm."

Just then, the officer who had permitted us to enter the house made hi way up the stairs.

"The coroner is here. I'm sorry you didn't get your full five minutes, but have to ask you to exit the townhouse."

We started to leave.

The officer who'd opened the oven spoke up, "Officer Vernon, I think th killer may have just left."

"What are you talking about?"

"Come here." He led Officer Vernon into the kitchen. He opened the ove door.

"Jesus Fucking Christ," Vernon said. "We might have just missed him. I put out an APB right now."

We were quickly escorted downstairs and out of the townhouse.

Lockett walked over.

"What happened?"

"He may have just left," I said. "The oven was still warm. It smelled like h was baking brownies."

"What an odd thing to be doing," Lockett said.

And then it hit me.

"Maybe not," I said.

"What do you mean?"

"He killed a bunch of people with poisoned cookies. Would brownies b that different?"

Officer Lockett clearly wanted to say something, but he couldn't g anything out.

Within minutes, at least thirty police officers had gathered outside of Brenda Cabela's place. We were pushed well back as they installed yellow tar around the townhouse.

Not long after, the first member of the media arrived. I knew if I hur around, I was going to get mobbed.

I could already see the questions coming.

"Quint, what are you doing around another crime scene? Are you following the Butcher? Does this have something to do with him?"

"I think it's time to go," I told Cara.

"Agreed. But where should we go?"

Assuming the Butcher had just left Cabela's apartment, it seemed foolish for us to go check into a hotel. Things might be coming to a head sooner rather than later.

I looked at Captain Lockett and secretly hoped he might ask us to join him. But as generous as he had been with his access, I knew this would be a bridge too far.

He seemed to have read my mind.

"Quint, I have to go. I'm going to be canvassing this area for the Butcher. They've got this crime scene under control. My phone is on for you at all times. If you think of anything, please, please call. We've got officers all over the city. If you have any suspicions, I'll send some of them wherever you want."

"Thanks, Captain. I'll be in touch."

We watched as Lockett got in his police car and sped off.

"Let's walk toward our car before the media makes out who I am," I said to Cara.

We headed past the townhouse, keeping our faces averted from the cameras.

It had to have been the Butcher who'd made the noise from inside yesterday. Why hadn't I called the police right then?

Obviously, I'd had no reason to suspect anything yet. But maybe I should have been more suspicious.

Cara snapped me out of my thoughts.

"Stop daydreaming! The next few minutes are of massive importance. If he recently left that townhouse, he may be heading out for his final set of murders right now."

"You're right. But what can we do?"

"You know his face better than anyone. I think we should drive around ourselves. Maybe we'll find a needle in a haystack and see him. His car has been found. Unless he stole Cabela's, he could be out there on foot."

"That's a good point," I said.

"Thanks."

We arrived at the car.

"I'll drive," I said. I handed her my phone. "Scroll to Captain Lockett. Text him and ask him if he can find out if Cabela's car has been stolen. And if so, what make and model?"

"I will."

We climbed in the car and shut the doors. Cara pulled out her phone. I did a three-point turn, not wanting to head in the direction of the townhouse, which was now swarming with media and police.

My mind went over our brief time in Cabela's townhouse. Something clicked.

After driving only a few blocks, I abruptly pulled over.

"What is it?" Cara asked.

"Do you remember the two closets?"

"Of course. What about them?"

"Think back," I said. "What did that first closet look like?"

"I don't know. A bunch of trench coats next to each other."

"And you'd say they were about equidistant apart, right?"

"Yeah. It was pretty uniform, I guess. Hadn't really thought about it."

"How about the second closet?" I asked.

"I don't know."

Time was important, so I had to push her in the right direction.

"Was it as clean?" I asked.

"No, it was more disheveled. Some were scrunched together. It was anything but uniform."

"Exactly!"

"Are you saying what you think I'm saying?"

"I think the Butcher grabbed one of the Sesame Street costumes."

"My God!" Cara exclaimed.

"You have his co-worker Lu's phone number. Call her right now."

She did and handed me the phone. I put it on speaker so Cara could hear the conversation.

"Hello?" a woman's voice said.

"Is this Lu?"

"Yes, it is."

"Lu, this is Quint. I'm sitting with Cara. Can you answer a few questions?"

"Sure," she said, but sounded nervous.

It was unlikely Cabela's death had already made the news, but you never know. Of course, just the fact that her ex-coworker turned out to be a killer on the loose could be reason enough to make her worried.

"This may sound weird, but did Brendan Cabela like dressing up?"

"Huh? What do you mean?"

"In like, children's outfits. Sesame Street stuff. Big Bird. Bert and Ernie, etc."

"Oh, that. Yeah, Brendan is still a kid at heart. Probably because he isn't the most popular adult. Anyway, he sometimes performs at children's birthday parties as Sesame Street characters. He'd occasionally tell us at Caltenics about it."

I looked at Cara. A pit opened up in my stomach. Her expression told me she felt the same.

"You have no idea if he had a party coming up, do you?"

"No, how could I? I haven't talked to him since he got fired."

"We never asked you. Why was he fired?"

47.

"Would someone really have a children's party with the Butcher out there?" Cara asked.

We drove in circles around a five or six-block radius of Cabela's townhouse.

"Sure," I said. "Remember, the news is reporting that he might not strike for a month. You think every kid's birthday for the next month will go uncelebrated? No chance. Plus, what would be safer than a birthday for a kid? Especially if it's occurring during the day. Every one of the Butcher's killings happened at night."

"I guess that's all true. And we don't even know if Brendan Cabela had a gig today. It could just be that the Butcher took the outfit. Maybe he's planning on hitting up a carnival. Or a local park."

"You're right, it could be anything. But with the way he said 'smaller in scale' in his email, I feel like he planned this out and didn't just make some knee jerk decision to go to a park and hand out brownies."

"So what do we do?"

"I've got to call Captain Lockett and tell him to be on the lookout for an Elmo costume."

"This is insane," Cara said.

"There's no doubt about that."

Lockett said he'd put out an APB for someone in an Elmo costume. He also informed me that Cabela's car was indeed missing. It was a 2011 green Lexus and he gave us the license plate.

I relayed the information to Cara.

"Let's drive farther away from the townhouse," she said. "It's been almost a half-hour and I don't see him hanging around this area if he's got a car."

"I'll do that, but I need you to do something."

An idea had just come to me.

"Sure, what?"

"Google Brendan Cabela. See if you can find out if he got his work through a kid's birthday catering company. Or whatever you might call that type of business."

As Cara typed on her phone, I tried to prevent my mind from painting gruesome pictures. But that proved impossible.

What if the Butcher was currently arriving at a birthday party armed with fentanyl-laced brownies? It would be the ultimate catastrophe. My head flooded with images of children lying in a house or around a backyard. Not moving. Toys and party decorations scattered uselessly around them. Presents that would never be unwrapped, maybe bloodstained. As helpless as the elderly people who had died at Treeside Manor, but with so much life ahead of them.

I couldn't imagine a worse scene.

"Fuck!" I yelled a bit too loudly. The swear echoed in the car.

Cara jumped in her seat. "What?"

"I keep imagining a bunch of dead kids."

"Don't say that, Quint."

"You think I want to?"

It was rhetorical and she didn't respond.

"Anything on Cabela?" I asked.

"No, his LinkedIn profile only has his former job at Caltenics."

I took a left turn onto Lombard Street. It was busy, and my eyes found it difficult to look at every car that passed. The chance of seeing the 2011 green Lexus had to be a thousand to one. Still, I tried.

"How about this?" I said. "Find a company in San Francisco that deals with children's party planning. If they don't employ a Brendan Cabela, ask them for other companies that do the same thing."

Cara looked me and nodded in agreement. "I like where this is headed."

She looked down at her phone, thumbs moving rapidly in her Google search.

"Found one called A-1 party planning."

She dialed their number and someone answered quickly. I heard Cara's side of the conversation, and it was obvious early on that Cabela did not work for them.

"No luck," she said. "But they told me to call Private Party Planning."

I looked to my right and saw a Lexus. But it was gray and a much more recent model than 2011.

A minute later, Cara told me Private Party Planning was a dead end.

"Did they mention another one?"

"Yeah, I'm calling them right now."

Once again, I could tell within ten seconds by Cara's reaction. No luck.

She was about to hang up the phone when I thought of something.

"Ask the agent if any companies specialize in Sesame Street characters," I said.

She nodded and asked the question I'd put forward.

I saw her nod again and then she said, "Thank you."

"We get something?" I asked as soon as she hung up.

"The dispatcher wasn't positive, but she thinks a place called For the Kids does a lot of Sesame Street characters."

Cara searched on the internet and found the number.

I pulled in next to an old school motel on Lombard. I had to hear this.

"Put it on speaker," I said.

Cara did and we heard the number dialing.

"Hello, you've reached For the Kids," a woman's voice said.

Cara had the phone in her hand, so she spoke.

"Do you have someone named Brendan Cabela who works for you?"

"The name rings a bell. Let me check. Are you trying to book him for an event?"

"No, I'm actually trying to find out if he works today."

"Are you a family member?"

The voice seemed guarded, not wanting to give out info. I nudged Cara and nodded.

"Yes, I'm his sister. And there's been a family emergency."

"Did you try calling him?"

"He's not answering. That's why I want to find out where he's working today."

"Alright, give me a few seconds. I'll put you on hold."

"Oh my God," Cara said. "What if he is on the schedule?"

"Listen to me, Cara. If we get an address, I'm going to drive like a bat out of hell to get there. I want you to call 9-1-1 and tell them the address. Then call Captain Lockett and do the same. With all the cops on patrol in the city today, hopefully they can get there first."

A voice came back on the phone.

"So Brendan is working for us today. In fact, he should be getting there any moment. He starts at 2:00 p.m. for a woman named Vanessa Mathers."

My heart sank. We were going to be too late. The horrible visions in my brain were going to come true.

"What's the address?" Cara asked.

"571 Presidio Boulevard."

We were four blocks from the Presidio!

I pulled off from the curb and veered into Lombard traffic, narrowly missing getting rear-ended. The car I'd pulled in front of honked and flipped me off.

"Is she still on the line?" I asked Cara.

"Yes."

"Can you hear me?" I yelled.

"Yes, what's going on?" she said.

Obviously our questions and reactions had rattled her.

"I need you to call the owner of the house on Presidio Boulevard and tell them that the Bay Area Butcher is coming as Elmo."

"What?" she screamed. "What kind of—"

"This is not a joke. Call them right now!" I yelled.

I switched lanes quickly after seeing approaching traffic.

"Now!" I repeated. "Okay, hang up the phone, Cara. Call 9-1-1!"

I continued accelerating toward the Presidio.

Cara dialed. With my focus on the road, all I could hear was her end.

"We know where the Bay Area Butcher is. 571 Presidio Boulevard. We jus know. No, this isn't somebody seeking attention."

The light in front of us turned red. I would have driven around the car i front of us and gone through it, but a car on my right had boxed us on.

C'mon light! Turn green!

"For the last time, the Bay Area Butcher is at 571 Presidio Boulevard, Cara said. "Dressed as Elmo. This is not a joke!"

The light turned green and I started honking my horn when the car in fror of us didn't move. Finally he did, and I hit the gas and accelerated into th right lane and back into the left after passing him.

"Hang up on 9-1-1! Call Lockett!"

"It's busy!" she said.

"Cara, I need you to GPS 571 Presidio Boulevard. I'm a block from th Presidio itself, but I don't know exactly where Presidio Boulevard is."

"Okay," Cara said.

She had been great so far, under extreme duress.

We heard the familiar voice:

"Stay on Lombard Street for .3 miles and then take a slight right on Presidi Boulevard."

She tried calling Lockett again. Still busy.

"When we get there, Quint, I want you to leave me. I'll keep calling Locke and 9-1-1. Run as fast as you can into the house. Every second matters."

We'd talked about not leaving each other's side, but she was right. Ever second did matter. Assuming we weren't already too late.

"I love you," I said.

I wasn't sure if I said it because of her unselfish decision or if I feared might never get a chance to say it again.

But it felt right.

We approached the beginning of the Presidio.

"In .two miles, take a slight right on Presidio Boulevard, and then you destination will be on your right."

I was doing sixty miles per hour in what was probably a thirty-five or twenty-five zone. Maybe a cop would see me and follow our car to i destination. That would be a good thing.

Or, better yet, they might already be there.

But after the botched call to 9-1-1 and Lockett's phone being busy, I ha my doubts.

I had to slow down as we approached Presidio Boulevard or we wou have gotten into an accident. I took the slight right and began looking at hous numbers.

"You have arrived at your destination."

As soon as the GPS said it, I saw the address. 571 Presidio Boulevard.

And in front of it sat a green Lexus.

I'd never been more terrified in my life.

48.
THE KILLER

Fifteen minutes before I was to show up at the birthday party, I pulled my car to the side of the road.
And had a moment of clarity.

I wasn't going to be flying to Mexico in a few hours. I wasn't going to be reappearing in five years and killing again.

It was over.

The cops had surely found Brendan's body. If I tried to catch a flight under his name, they would know.

And every other escape route would likewise be cut off. I had no doubt.

So if this was to be my final day on earth, I was going to be as savage as I could. I'd punctuate the dreariness. The homicide detectives who first arrived on the scene at Vanessa Mather's home would be talking about it for decades.

The brownies would do their own damage. The knives would do the rest.

I was parked in the Presidio, a few blocks from where the party was to take place. I'd chosen a vacant area and felt sure I'd be safe until the festivities started.

I grabbed the Ziplock bag of brownies. They were only half-baked, but what the fuck did I care? They'd work fine.

I pulled out the Elmo suit from my backpack. I looked and then felt around, but found only one small pocket in the costume. Certainly not big enough to hide one of the two huge knives I had brought with me.

I wore jeans, so there would be no keeping the knives there either.

The Elmo suit was long-sleeved, obviously, and it gave me an idea.

I grabbed some of the duct tape that I always kept in my backpack. Then the knives. I looked outside of the car, making sure a random jogger wasn't running by.

No one in sight.

I set one of the knives against my forearm and taped around both the handle and the tip of the blade. I then moved my arm around to make to make sure I wouldn't be stabbing myself. But the knife lay flush up

against my arm and I could move it fluidly. I strapped the second blad
to my other arm in the same way.

With knives taped to my arms, I couldn't risk stepping out of the ca
to change. So I did it inside. I took my jeans off and slid the Elmo su
over my legs. Next I put my arms through the arm holes, carefully pullin
the sleeves over the knives.

I looked at myself in the mirror, knowing I might well be sayin
goodbye. But what a goodbye it would be. I smiled, then I took the fac
of Elmo and slid it over the top of my head.

I looked at my new face in the mirror.

And I loved what I saw.

A Sesame Street character killing a bunch of kids. What fantasti
irony.

Maybe part of my legacy would be making children and parent
everywhere terrified of a PBS character.

I started up the car and headed off for 571 Presidio Boulevard.

I arrived less than three minutes later, at 2:01.

No point in delaying any longer. Time to get down to business.

I stepped out of the car, grabbing the Ziplock bags.

And I made my way toward the front door.

The woman who answered my knock was in her forties, and cute in
country-club-blonde type of way.

"Hi, I'm Vanessa. You must be Brendan."

This was the time—maybe the last time—to turn on the "normal" se
which I had mastered over the years.

"I am. Nice to meet you."

She extended her hand.

I made sure to only grab the tips of her fingers. If she someho
extended her grip past my wrist, she might touch the knives hidin
under the arms of Elmo's costume.

"So you like to stay in character?" she asked.

"I figured we might as well just start up right away," I said. "Sinc
you're paying by the hour and all. Plus I don't want to traumatize yo
child, you know, by them seeing a headless Elmo or something."

She laughed.

"Sounds good. The kids are out back. I'll walk you through. And m
daughter is Lily. I think she's the only one in yellow."

"Great. I brought some treats for the kids too," I said.

"How thoughtful."

We entered the house. It was bigger than most in San Francisc
which held mostly townhouses like Brendan's. It must have been a

advantage of living in the Presidio, where there was much more open space than in the city itself.

Another woman, close in age to Vanessa, approached.

"I'm Lynn. Thanks so much for doing this for the kids. They are going to love you."

Stay normal, I told myself.

"You're welcome," I said.

"Do you want me to grab the treats and set them down?"

Stay normal! Think of something that makes sense.

"No, I've got it. Sometimes I like to take them with me and pretend to eat one. When the kids realize I can't because I've got a mouth that doesn't open, they always laugh."

"Ahh, that's cute."

Jackpot! I would have been a great normal person.

The two women walked with me through another room. I hoped they were the only chaperones. I could easily dispose of both of them with the knives.

We entered a playroom of various colorful, noisy kids' toys everywhere. Two huge glass doors at the end of it opened out on to a big lawn.

And out there, probably twenty-five little children were looking my way.

Elmo is here, you soon-to-be-dead fuckers.

Vanessa opened the sliding glass door for me.

"Elmo is here," she yelled.

The kids started screaming in unison.

And as several made their way toward me, I realized a potential problem. If they grabbed at my wrists or forearms, they'd likely touch one of the knives.

I quickly put a Ziplock bag over each forearm.

The kids jumped up and down around me. I looked over at Vanessa, who didn't look impressed. I couldn't risk this ending early.

In the closest voice I could approximate, I started talking like Elmo.

"Elmo loves you all!"

The kids went even more nuts.

"Elmo loves this green stuff! Is this called grass?"

The kids loved my voice.

Meanwhile, I couldn't wait to start feeding them the brownies.

I saw a young child dressed in yellow and remembered what Vanessa had said about her daughter Lily.

"Are you the birthday girl?"

She smiled.

"I'm six," she said.

I looked over at Vanessa, who now smiled along. Lynn, the woman who'd asked to carry the brownies, stood on her left. One other woman had been outside, and she watched the kids running around me from the other side of the lawn.

With two knives I thought I could take care of three women.

"I'm six," Lily repeated.

At that moment, I heard a phone ring. It was definitely a house phone.

I looked over at Vanessa, who was having too good of a time watching the kids. She didn't head towards the house.

But it scared me.

And my manic side kicked in. Again.

Is someone calling to warn her? Have I been found out? If they're calling her, can the police be far behind?

I couldn't take the chance.

It was time!

"Elmo brought everyone some dessert. Does everyone want a little brownie?"

The kids screamed the loudest they had yet.

"They are really good. You kids are going to love them."

More screaming.

"So let's all start a single file line and I'll give you each your treat. You know what a single file line is, right?"

"I do! I do! Me! I want to be first!"

I heard all their voices shrieking with excitement. And knew they would soon be silenced.

They started forming a single file line. Or as close to one as a bunch of six-year-olds could.

Lily found her way to the front of the line.

"It's the birthday girl in front! Come get your present from Elmo!"

She stepped forward.

49.

I hopped out of my car.

"Keep trying Lockett! And call 9-1-1 again!" I said to Cara as I ran away.

She had given me permission to go ahead without her. And it was the right decision.

I sprinted to the front door and rang the doorbell. I knocked as loud as I could. But there was no response.

I began to yell.

"Is anyone here? Please answer! It's a matter of life and death!"

Still nothing.

I couldn't waste any more time at the front door.

I ran to the left side of the house, but all I saw was a narrow little alleyway that didn't look like it led anywhere.

The images of dead children sprang back into my mind. I couldn't shake them.

I sprinted past the front door and to the right side of the house.

And this time I heard voices. Kids' voices.

I considered yelling, but I didn't know if the Butcher had a gun or a knife. If at all possible, I wanted to keep the element of surprise on my side.

I moved quickly along the side of the house, heading toward the kids' voices.

I heard someone say, "You know what a single file line is, right?"

It sounded like an adult trying to talk like a baby. I knew why.

I moved closer. The kids' voices got louder.

A gate opened in the wall a few feet in front of me. I was tall enough to just barely look over it.

Elmo, a.k.a. the Butcher, stood in the middle of the lawn. His back to me.

Approximately twenty kids and a few adults surrounded him.

I slid the gate open, trying to be quiet. Once I started running, I was going to be going full speed at the Butcher. I just hoped that none of the kids would scream too early and give him time to react.

I tried to wait until I had slid the gate fully open, but I heard the voice say, "It's the birthday girl in front. Come get your present from Elmo."

Looking closer, I saw a Ziplock bag by his side.

He took something out of it.

I couldn't wait any longer.

I pushed the gate open and started sprinting toward the Bay Area Butcher.

50.

A parent screamed as I set off in the direction of the man dressed as Elmo.

They probably assumed I was a crazy man headed for their kids. For all knew, they feared, in that split second, that I was the Butcher himself.

But the real Butcher didn't turn around right away. And I might have ha the kids' voices to thank. Surrounded by their excited shrieking, he probabl didn't hear the grown woman's alarm.

I heard another scream from one of the parents.

Finally, a few feet before I was going to blindside the Butcher, he starte to turn around.

It actually worked to my advantage.

By time he faced me, my feet had already left the ground. I catapulte through the air. I met him chest to chest and we went flying a good five fee The Ziplock bags flew across the lawn, away from us. I landed on top of hir and started throwing haymakers at his face.

If, by some miracle, it wasn't the Butcher, I'd surely be going to jail. I woul have taken that in a heartbeat.

I punched him two more times, using leverage to keep on top of him. I wa winding up to punch him again when something hit me over the head.

It didn't hurt that badly, but it cost me the split second that the Butche needed.

He rolled off of me and I saw him reaching for something underneath hi costume. It glinted as he brought it out. A knife. He lunged at me with it. managed to slide my body back and avoid his wild swing. As he pulled th knife back, it fell out of his hands.

I slid over and grabbed it off the ground. But as I did, he produced anothe knife.

We each rose to our feet.

The children had all gathered together around one of the adults. I walke to put myself between them and the Butcher.

The other two women were nearer the house. One of them held th remnants of the flowerpot that she'd hit me with. But now it had hopefull become clear that I was protecting the children. I'm sure they had no ide what to think.

"Call the police!" I yelled to them.

They both ran inside. I believed there was still an adult behind me, but didn't dare turn around.

The Butcher and I remained in a standoff. He was now ten feet from me. Not close enough. It's not like he had a gun and could just shoot me. We each had a knife.

His Elmo outfit looked off-centered, the eye-holes not where they should be.

He sighed and pulled off his mask. Like I knew it would be, underneath was the face of the man I knew as Tad.

"Good to see you, Quint."

"It's not too late to turn yourself in."

"That will never happen."

He stared at me, seemingly deciding whether to rush me or not. I was deathly afraid of him running to the front with Cara being out there. But obviously, I couldn't leave the kids.

So, in case he went toward the front of the house and I had to follow him, there was something I had to do.

"Can the woman back there hear me?" I said without turning around and giving the Butcher a chance to rush me.

"Yes," a woman's voice said.

"Those brownies are poisoned. Do not let the kids touch or eat them. Do you understand?"

"Yes."

As she answered, the Butcher ran toward the gate I'd entered from.

I ran after him, but he definitely had a head start.

Please, Cara, still be in the car!

51.

I was right behind the Butcher as I approached the gate, but he slammed back at me, which cost me a split second opening it.

I started sprinting past the side of the house.

"Cara! Get inside the car," I yelled as loud as I possibly could. "Get in the car, Cara!"

I was only ten feet behind the Butcher, but once he turned the corner, there would be a few seconds where I couldn't do anything.

"Cara! Get inside the car!" I yelled again.

The Butcher rounded the house. I was going to be two seconds late, and they were the longest two seconds of my life.

Please, please, please, don't let me see Cara out in the open.

But I did.

She had obviously heard me, and was headed back to the car, but she was a good ten feet from getting there. The Butcher moved quickly toward her. She wouldn't have time to get the door open and climb in.

Our eyes quickly met and there was an intense fear in her eyes.

I shouted the only idea that came to mind.

"Cara! Dive underneath the car!"

She did as I said.

And the Butcher realized if he got on his knees to go after her, I would be on him in no time and stab him in the back.

He turned around to face me.

"Another standstill, huh, Quint? You've been a good adversary."

And then the sound of police sirens filled the air.

The Butcher ran toward the green Lexus.

"Cara, you can get out from underneath there."

She did.

"In or out?" I asked.

The Butcher had started his car up and headed away from us, not wasting time on turning his car around.

"In," Cara said.

She threw me the keys and we both got in.

I peeled off the curb and pressed the pedal down as far as it could go.

"Where do you think he's going?" Cara asked.

"If I had to guess, I'd say the Golden Gate Bridge."

"You could do a lot of damage with a knife and everyone walking around

"If I have the chance, I won't let him get there."

We took another turn and that was when I saw his car, about one hundred feet ahead of us. I was already going as fast as I could, but maybe he'd slow down on the turns and I could catch up.

If he had been driving a 2020 Lexus, I'd have no chance. But I could compete with a 2011 model.

As he took a sharp right turn ahead, I saw brake lights flash on the Lexus.

"Hold on tight," I told Cara.

I had to slow down a tiny bit, but I took that turn as fast as I possibly could. As we made it back on the straightaway, I had cut the distance between us by more than half.

Another turn was coming up, and then we'd be on the final road that led to Highway 101.

I realized something.

"His car is more of a deadly weapon then that knife would ever be," I said to Cara.

"You're right. Jesus."

My mind was made up. If I had a chance to T-bone him, I'd have to do it.

I had no doubt that if he saw a group of pedestrians, he'd try to take them out.

We approached the final turn. Once again, I saw break lights coming from the Lexus.

It gave us a fighting chance.

I took this turn even faster than the previous one.

We were now on Lincoln Boulevard, which would take us right to Highway 101 and then the Golden Gate Bridge. I couldn't let him get there.

We had pulled even with him.

It was a two-lane road, and that presented me with two choices. I could veer into potential oncoming traffic and try to push him from the side. Or I could just try to hit his bumper and send him off stride.

Truth be told, if Cara hadn't been with me, I probably would have gone with the former. But I didn't want to risk heading into oncoming traffic with her in the car.

So I started bumping the Lexus from behind. I did it once, twice, three times. But he stayed on course. And I realized we would be at the bridge in less than a minute.

I'd tried the safer way. With no luck.

"I'm going in the other lane," I told Cara.

"If you've got to do it, do it! Just get him off the road."

I looked ahead on the other side of the two-lane road. No car was coming. I accelerated and drew parallel with the Lexus.

I saw the Butcher look over in my direction.

And as he did, I swerved my car into his. The paint on the two cars hit. The noise was awful. But I'd initiated the collision and that gave me the upper hand. I looked over and could tell he was losing control.

But as I looked over at him struggling with the wheel, I lost some concentration, and hit the curb on the other side of the road. It was now me who had lost control and I went over the edge. Luckily, it was just a ten foot ravine and our car settled at the bottom without anything being broken. It was too steep to drive back up, however.

Cara and I hurried out of the car.

"Do you want to come with me?" I asked.

I looked at her and could tell just how exhausted she was. Her forehead had a small scrape, likely from when we went down the ravine. But I didn't think her exhaustion was all physical. Everything had likely finally caught up to her.

She shook her head. "I wouldn't be any help. You go. Get him arrested or kill him. And then come back to me."

"I will," I said.

And I ran up the hill.

I looked ahead of me. On the right side of the road, with smoke coming from the engine, was the Lexus. And twenty feet ahead of that, headed toward the Golden Gate Bridge, was the Bay Area Butcher.

52.

Like I had been in the cars, I was behind on foot and had to catch up.

As with everything I'd done over the last half hour, I moved as fast as I possibly could. Before you knew it, I was forty feet behind him. Thirty feet. Twenty feet.

It worked to my benefit that he still had his Elmo outfit on. Heavy and bulky, it must have been hard to run in.

The air filled with the sounds of police sirens. And not one or two. But many. And they were getting louder and closer by the second.

The Butcher had to know it was ending.

We had made it to the last little bluff before the Golden Gate Bridge.

He was only ten feet in front of me. Down at his side, he still carried his knife. I couldn't let him get to the bridge first.

My lungs burned with each breath. I was running on fumes.

As we passed the final bluff, I could now fully see the spectacular view in front of us. The first bright red arch of the bridge went skyward directly above us. A few hundred feet down, the uncompromising Pacific Ocean.

I was trying with all my might to catch up to the Butcher, but the surroundings were impossible to ignore.

He hit the start of the bridge with a five-foot advantage. The closest people to us were a family of four, posing and taking pictures, about twenty feet from us.

I realized the Butcher was going to reach them first.

"Turn around," I yelled. "The man in the Elmo costume has a knife."

The father heard me and quickly turned around.

He saw the onrushing madman with a knife and had time to do only one thing. He pushed his wife and two young children behind him.

The Butcher stabbed him in his right flank. The man crumpled and his family screamed.

The Butcher removed the knife and was about to stab him again. When I tackled him. I sent him flying down the walkway on the bridge, and we rolled over each other a few times.

But unlike at the kids' party, the Butcher ended up on top.

And I saw him raise his knife above his head and send it down toward me.

The sirens of the cop cars were getting louder and closer. It seemed like they were the last noises I was ever going to hear. The police were too late. The Butcher was going to kill me.

As the blade got closer, I didn't have time to move my whole body. So just moved my head.

I heard the blade hit the concrete where my face had just been. Someho my desperate move had succeeded. And the follow through of his wild swin had taken the Butcher off to the side of me.

I quickly rose to my feet.

The cars on the bridge had come to a standstill. A few people had gotte out of their vehicles to see what was going on.

The Butcher looked down the pedestrian walkway, eyeing some othe families who stood frozen, terrified, only a few dozen feet away.

He ran in their direction. And although he had the weapon, and I ha nothing, I followed him.

I'd proven to be faster again and he realized he wasn't going to get ther first. The Butcher turned around.

"What do I care about them?" he said. "Let's end this with you."

He lunged at me with the knife, but I managed to lean back and avoid it.

"Where are the cops?" I heard a woman yell.

"I can see them approaching the bridge," someone else yelled.

A few good Samaritans had exited their cars and were headed toward u no doubt intending to help me. But I didn't want to put them in harm's way.

This was mine to end.

The Butcher lunged at me again, leading with his knife.

I moved my body backward to avoid it. Once he missed, and m momentum stopped going backwards, I charged forward as quickly as I coul

Swinging and missing threw him off his stride, giving me the advantage.

I knew he'd raise the knife again, but I could block it with my forearm.

I bum-rushed him as fast as I could.

He swung the knife as I'd expected, but I blocked it with just the cost of flesh wound on my forearm.

My momentum continued to carry us, as I pushed him with me, four fe until we were flush up against the only rail that the Golden Gate Bridge ha to offer.

After that, it was 220 feet down to an almost certain death.

I'd heard that they had started building suicide nets, but I had no idea they had completed them under the spot where I grappled with the Butcher. didn't want to find out.

I pushed him up against the rail.

My goal was to push him over. Attempting to show mercy might get m killed.

But he was smart and realized this. He sent his body lower so he wouldr go over the side. Instead, his back hit the base of the rail.

With my left hand, I had a grip on his right wrist, which held the knife. couldn't release that. My right arm held his left shoulder. I tried to push hi higher so I could topple him over the railing. But he continued to hold his base low, not allowing me to.

"Somebody help him!" I heard someone say.

"Which one?" a person responded.

I couldn't concern myself with them. I had to finish this myself.

And I realized the one way I could get the Butcher to raise his center of gravity.

I kept my grasp on the wrist that held his knife.

And for a split second, I lowered my right hand.

And with as much force as I could muster, I brought it back up in the form of an uppercut.

I connected with the bottom of his chin and it lifted his body just enough. I immediately took my left hand off the knife and joined it with my right hand to push him in the chest.

He knew he was going over. I saw it in his eyes. As if in slow motion, he went sideways over the Golden Gate Bridge.

His only chance was to drop the knife and reach out for the railing. Which was what he did. He got ahold of the railing, but the momentum shot his feet and torso over. He now held on to the rail with his body dangling below him.

It was all but over, and the look in his eyes confirmed that. I looked down below him and couldn't see any netting to stop his fall.

Up on the bridge, several cops made their way toward us.

But I wanted to ask him something before they got there.

"Why?" I asked. "Why all this unnecessary killing?"

I had to lean over the railing to see his face where it hung three feet below the Golden Gate Bridge.

"Is there anything I could say that would satisfy you?" he asked.

"No," I admitted.

I saw his grip beginning to loosen on the rail. Now his expression showed genuine fear. Good. After all the pain he'd inflicted, I was happy to see it.

"I'm going to be infamous. Forever," the Butcher said.

"You're going to be known as a coward. I'm going to tell the stories of how you were afraid to go at those kids when I stood between you and them with a knife. Whenever you were confronted with someone who was your equal, you ran. You could only kill those who weren't suspecting it. You are a coward. And I'll make sure every history book says so."

He looked disgusted. It wasn't the time, but I took some satisfaction from it.

His left hand loosened some more. He was going down soon.

"Quint, step aside."

I was pretty sure it was the voice of Captain Lockett. But I refused to turn around. I wanted to see this through to the end.

The Butcher's left hand slipped off the railing. He tried to hold on with just his right hand, but that was a losing battle.

And he knew it.

A few seconds later, his right hand gave way.

His eyes remained fixed on mine as he started falling through the air.

I'm glad the last person he ever saw was me. And he knew that I'd gotten the best of him.

I saw his body hit the water two hundred feet below.

And I knew it was all over.

53.

It had been Captain Lockett behind me.

He and nine other officers faced me once I turned around.

No one said anything for a long time. It was as if we were all absorbing the drama that had just unfolded.

"Where were you guys?" I finally asked.

"We all converged on the house in the Presidio. And I guess you had just left. Once we heard about something going on at the bridge, we all headed this way. But cars on the bridge stopped and it created a huge traffic backup."

I walked away from the railing.

Lockett came up and hugged me. I hugged him back.

"I wish Ray were here," I said.

"Me too, Quint. Me too."

He looked down at my forearm.

"Are you okay?"

"Just a defensive wound. A few stitches and I'll be fine."

"You're a hero, Quint."

"Do me a favor. Send the Coast Guard down there right now. Fish out that body. I just want to be certain."

"Of course."

I looked out at all the people assembled on the Golden Gate Bridge. I heard a few say my name. Others were taking pictures. A few looked shellshocked. It was safe to say that none of them would ever forget what they had just seen.

And then, out of the corner of my eye, I saw Cara running toward me. A few of the cops stopped her at the edge of the crowd.

"Let her through, please," I said.

She made her way to me and we hugged for what seemed like forever.

"I love you," she said.

"I love you, too."

"Is he dead?"

I nodded. And she hugged me closer.

"I'll tell you all about it later," I said.

"I don't care," she said. "I'm just glad you're here with me."

And then she noticed my forearm.

"Captain Lockett, can you get Quint to a hospital?"

"Of course."

Lockett looked at the police officers assembled on the bridge. Even more of them had arrived.

"Guys, I'm going to drive Quint to the hospital. An ambulance isn't needed."

A few nodded.

"Bring him over to the SFPD headquarters once he's stitched up," one said.

"I will," Lockett responded.

"You don't want to stay?" I asked.

"They've got it covered. Plus, I'll learn a lot more from you than I will by staying here. Follow me, guys," Lockett said.

I turned to Cara.

"Remember when I said we'd be going on a brief vacation along the coast?"

"Yeah."

"And we weren't going to get out of bed."

"I remember."

"Well, we will be doing that very soon."

She smiled and leaned in and kissed me.

Captain Lockett turned around.

"My car is down here to the left. Are you ready?"

"Ready as I'll ever be," I said.

And we walked off the Golden Gate Bridge.

Lockett drove us to the nearest hospital, where they inserted several stitches on my arm. They didn't seem too concerned.

Cara sat next to me the entire time.

I realized the irony of finding myself back in a hospital, being stitched up again. It was how the whole Charles Zane case had begun more than a year ago. And now the nightmare of the Bay Area Butcher was ending with a few stitches.

At one point, I made the mistake of listening to the television from the neighboring room. I was being called a hero by some news anchor. It's the last thing I wanted to hear. Hopefully I'd learned something from the aftermath of the Charles Zane case. I was done being a media whore.

I knew the case would rent space in my head in the weeks and months ahead, but I wasn't going to contribute to the hoopla or the hysteria. I'd deal with it on a personal basis, not through the media.

I needed some time out of the public eye. And boy if that wasn't the understatement of the decade.

The hospital released me. Cara and I walked out, and the sun was still shining. It didn't seem right with all that had occurred that day.

"How are we getting home?" I asked, knowing my car was still at the bottom of a ravine.

Captain Lockett appeared.

"From me," he said.

"You been here the whole time?"

"They got you stitched up in forty-five minutes and believe you me, I had plenty of phone calls to occupy my time. You should see the reaction this is getting."

"No, thanks," I said.

"It's the lead story around the world. And you are front and center."

"I'm turning off my T.V. and my cell phone starting tomorrow."

"I can't say I blame you," Lockett said. "You're going to be famous."

"I don't want it and I'm already tired of talking about it," I said. "Now, can you take us home?"

"Yes. But I do have to take you to the SFPD first. They've got a question or two."

"I figured."

The interviews with law enforcement were going to be impossible to avoid, but that didn't mean I had to be happy about it.

"And the Coast Guard found that fish, Quint. You don't have to worry about him ever again."

"Thanks, Captain."

I looked at my girlfriend. "We did it, Cara. It's over. And don't say I did it. We were a team."

Tears came to Cara's eyes at the same time a smile spread across her face. That was enough for me. We'd have plenty of time to talk about all we'd accomplished.

"Can I borrow your phone?" I asked.

She handed it over.

And I dialed a number.

"Hi, Cara. Did Quint finish his stitches?" a familiar voice said.

"Ah, so she did call you. I should have known."

I heard my mother start crying on the other end. The waterworks were definitely on display.

"My baby. I'm glad you're okay," she said.

I started to tear up as well.

"I'm fine, Mom. Listen, we can talk all about this later. What do you think about cooking a late dinner tonight? Cara and I would be coming over."

"Of course. What time?"

I looked at Lockett. "What time is it?"

"A little after four."

"Can I be in the East Bay by seven or so? I'll be around the next few days to answer more questions if need be."

"Sure, I'll get you there by seven."

I turned back to the phone. And realized I was going to need a shower Maybe more than I'd ever needed one.

"Mom, we'll be there by eight."

"What do you want to eat?"

"Surprise me. And Mom, we never took Glenda Kintner to dinner. We are doing that soon."

"I'd love to," she said. "In fact, I hope I'll be seeing a lot of you in the near future."

"You've got me till next weekend."

"What's next weekend?"

"I'm taking Cara on a trip. And we are not going to leave the bed for three days."

Cara and Captain Lockett laughed behind me.

"Quint, this is your mother! I don't want to hear that."

"Bye, Mom. See you at eight."

I hung up the phone and kissed Cara. And we kept kissing.

"Get a room, you two," Captain Lockett said.

"Stop pretending that cops have senses of humor," I said.

"I'll give you guys a minute. I'm parked straight ahead."

And Lockett walked in that direction.

Cara turned to me. She looked serious.

"You saved those kids' lives, Quint. If it weren't for you, they'd all be dead

"I told you. We saved their lives, Cara. It was a team effort."

"You're being generous, but thanks."

"It's true," I said.

"Do you think we can take a few months off from crime lords and serial killers?"

She smiled again. I was happy to see we were going in a lighter direction

"I don't know. They seem so attracted to me."

"That's not the right word. They are drawn to you. Out of curiosity. I'm the one who is attracted to you."

"Tell me more," I said.

"No one, and I mean no one, is more attracted to you than me."

"We are going to wear that bed out," I said.

"You're damn right we are!"

I put my arm around her shoulder and we walked toward Captain Lockett' car.

"I love you, Cara."

"I love you, Quint."

There was nothing more to say.

THE END

A note to my readers:
Thanks so much for reading my novel! You're a rock star!

I hope you enjoyed going on this adventure with Quint.

I'm going to assume you have read the first book of this series,
<u>Revenge at Sea</u>! If not, what are you waiting for?

My other novels include the two-part series, <u>The Puppeteer</u> and <u>The Patsy</u>, featuring the charming, relentless duo of Frankie and Evie.
Both books are political thrillers sure to get your pulse jumping.

And not be forgotten, a personal favorite of mine, the standalone
novel, <u>The Bartender</u>. It's a multi-narrative thriller in the vein of *Gone Girl*. Only much better :)

Finally, I'd be honored if you <u>followed me on Amazon</u>.

Thanks for everything. It's readers like you who make this all
worthwhile.

Sincerely,
Brian O'Sullivan

Made in the USA
Las Vegas, NV
22 June 2023

73729861R00134